CROSSING VINES

Chicana & Chicano Visions of the Américas

Chicana & Chicano Visions of the Américas

Crossing Vines

A NOVEL

Rigoberto González

UNIVERSITY OF OKLAHOMA PRESS • NORMAN

ALSO BY RIGOBERTO GONZÁLEZ

So Often the Pitcher Goes to Water until It Breaks
(Urbana, Ill., 1999)

Soledad Sigh-sighs
(San Francisco, 2003)

LIBRARY OF CONGRESS CATALOGING-IN-PUBLICATION DATA

González, Rigoberto.
Crossing vines: a novel / Rigoberto González.
          p. cm. — (Chicana & Chicano visions of the Américas ; v. 2)
     ISBN 0–8061–3528–x (cloth : alk. paper)
1. Mexican American agricultural laborers—Fiction.
2. Viticulture—Fiction
3. California—Fiction.   I. Title. II. Series.
PS3557.O4695 C7 2003
813'.54—dc21   2002075019

Crossing Vines: A Novel is Volume 2 in the
Chicana & Chicano Visions of the Américas series.

The paper in this book meets the guidelines for permanence and durability
of the Committee on Production Guidelines for Book Longevity of the
Council on Library Resources. ∞

1 2 3 4 5 6 7 8 9 10

Dedicado a los uveros del Valle de Coachella, California.
Dedicado a mi apá y a mi abuela María.

ACKNOWLEDGMENTS

A thousand thanks and much gratitude to the early champions of this book: Jewell Parker Rhodes, Alberto Ríos, Manuel de Jesús Hernández-Gutiérrez, Theresa Delgadillo, Rudolfo Anaya (for that residency at La Casita, Jemez Springs, New Mexico), Lauro Flores, Christine Yuodelis-Flores, Eric-Christopher García, and Susan Straight. Gracias Mahsa Hojjati por ofrecerme un hogar en Cuernavaca en el cual pude concentrarme y trabajar. Gracias Texaco Alex, my research consultant and compadre in labor and grief. I must also acknowledge the John Simon Guggenheim Memorial Foundation for the generous gift that allowed me to travel to México and complete this novel. Life and writing would not have been the same without the unflinching support of colleagues Richard Yáñez and Francisco Aragón—mil gracias. Finalmente, quisiera reconocer a la obra que inspiró este libro: ...*y no se lo tragó la tierra* del maestro Tomás Rivera.

PART ONE

Fuego

TELL ME STORIES

Doña Ramona   3:05 a.m.

"I once heard talk about a woman . . ." Doña Ramona leaned forward on the reclining chair to speak into the small tape recorder in her hand. She paused to hear the tape running. Leonardo had coached her on how to record and how to stop and replay the miniature tape to listen to her own voice talk back. She had taught herself to press the buttons in the dark, memorizing the locations of the function keys through touch. Since the housing project was susceptible to blackouts, she had learned to do a number of things while partly blinded, guided only by the mercy of moonlight. She had learned to recognize, for example, the number keys on the telephone. Using the index and ring fingers, she could call doña Gertrudis to ask if the lights were out on her side of the projects as well.

I once heard talk about a woman. The machine repeated the phrase with a staticky sound. Doña Ramona pressed the stop button to reorganize her thoughts.

The first times she spoke into the recorder she had felt embarrassed. She spoke too softly, afraid that her husband could overhear her talking to this little black box, and when Leonardo replayed the tape he chided her for her shyness.

"I've heard you on the phone, Ma," he said to her as he rewound the tape. "You speak so loudly I wonder why you bother using the receiver when you can scream the conversation across the projects all the way from the couch."

With practice she learned to work the tape recorder, just as she had mastered the microwave, the remote controls, and the bank's card machine. A panel with buttons didn't intimidate her the way it scared off the other women. After an automated security gate had been installed at the housing project, for months none of her friends ventured out alone, afraid that they'd fumble the security code and lock themselves out. Not doña Ramona; she found any excuse to drive out and back, proudly pressing the buttons, knowing that any woman who looked out her kitchen window and through the spaces between the lemon trees would recognize the brown Chevy and its skillful occupant.

She walked into the kitchen and searched in the dark for the coffeemaker. For a few seconds she considered trying to work two machines at once, but then she put the tape recorder down to feel along the wall for the light switch.

Her kitchen was small but armed with all the modern technology. Leonardo had introduced the first gadget: the warm, humming microwave. After that electrical appliances became her obsession. Doña Ramona became fascinated with the efficiency of food processors and self-cleaning toaster ovens and cookers. Any device that plugged into the wall excited her. But in truth it was the machine noise she desired. The chaos of machines like the electric can opener and the vacuum cleaner soothed her because they broke the silence of the apartment or the monotony of television whose sound was tempered at any level. Her half-deaf husband didn't complain too much; besides, the inside of the house was her domain, which is why the frequent noise-seizing blackouts irritated her—that and the housing office rejecting her yearly petition to allow for the installation of a dishwasher. The women neighbors criticized her for being lazy, doing things the easy, gringo push-button way. But she knew they envied her for stepping into a world they still knew very little about, and feared.

She set the coffeemaker for five cups and then moved back to the living room. With the swamp cooler long since shut off, the room was silent and she was able to listen to the coffee drip. When the stillness of the night made her restless she used the earphones attached to the radio on the nightstand, but sometimes even that wasn't enough to calm her into sleep. She needed to be up and about, like a firefly.

Three remote control panels were lined up neatly on the armrest: the TV's, the VCR's, and the stereo's. All human noisemakers also kept to their places: she in the living room, Manuel fast asleep in their bedroom, and Leonardo, on visits from the college in Los Angeles, in his old room. After the fight the evening before, it was she who was annoyed into insomnia, so she took up the tape recorder, the quietest machine she could operate before dawn. Besides, this was Leonardo's college project and it would please him to know she was taking it seriously. God knew she could do very little else for her son, the future professor.

"What do I say to it?" She remembered asking him after he had made the strange request. Leonardo had shoved the recorder against her face and she drew away from it with suspicion.

5

CROSSING
VINES

"Anything you want." Leonardo's skin glowed with an unblemished smoothness because he never had to work in the sun. "You can tell me about your childhood in México. Or about the first time you crossed over to the United States. About your friends, your lovers."

"Leonardo!"

"Or tell me stories."

Stories. Not fairy tales, not legends, Leonardo made it clear. People stories.

"You mean, like chisme?"

Leonardo laughed. "Why not? But stories about people you know. Like the ones you tell me all the time."

She had lost track of how many entries she had made since Leonardo's arrival two weeks ago. He came to take things from the family album, to make photocopies of birth certificates, church records, old postcards and letters. He even took her palm prints by pressing her blistered hands into a dish with blue paint. Now he wanted to take the stories she had been telling him all along. Now he wanted to pay attention, but through the little black box. As usual, documents held the only truths, the only valid facts. No matter. Leonardo got his reward, and she got hers: listening to her own voice embedded in the static had the effect of someone else talking to her. Hearing the stories through a different voice made them sound so fresh and new.

With the coffee ready, she poured herself a cup before sitting back down on the recliner. She drew a lengthy breath and pressed the record button.

"I once heard talk about a woman . . ." doña Ramona said, and she began to relax with the warm cup in her hand "... who became very lonely after her husband's death. Her name was Cleotilde and she had dedicated her life solely to her family. Her children were married and far away. Alone in that house, her husband's absence became too painful for her. A neighbor suggested she sell the house, the furnishings, and then use the money to move closer to one of her children, but Cleotilde could not bear to part with the house or the rooms still flourishing with the memories of her deceased husband. Still, she thought it a good idea to rid herself of a few things here and there, if only to lessen the burden on the old floors. And with her house located along a main avenue her front lawn was quite visible. She held a yard sale."

Doña Ramona paused to take a drink from the steaming cup. The coffee was black and bitter. She stopped the tape, rewound it, replayed the last few sentences, and then pressed the record button once again.

"On the first Sunday of the yard sale many people showed up but very few purchased anything because Cleotilde had put out useless things: things broken, out of fashion, or worn out. Things no longer beautiful. No one stayed for long since the yard was littered with junk. In fact, many visitors left with resentment at having stopped for nothing. Embarrassed, Cleotilde felt compelled to bring out a few items in decent condition, and that changed everything. People browsed longer, some even joked as they bargained with her, and many, to Cleotilde's joy, politely chatted with her before driving off with their purchases. The following Sunday she brought out even better items for sale. Some people bought, others didn't, but there were people present at every hour. Entire families on the way home from church stopped by. Her front yard was a commotion of *Look at this!* and *How much for this, Cleotilde?* Cleotilde walked around like a proud hen, hands on her hips. With such success she began to hold her yard sale on both Saturday *and* Sunday. To keep up with the demand, as soon as one item sold she reached into the house and pulled out another. Weekend after weekend, Cleotilde's sale. In a month everyone seemed to know her by name. Strangers approached her with the warmth of trust and familiarity. How could they not? Hers was the house of the perfect bargain. Anything could be bought at Cleotilde's: complete sets of silverware, clean sheets, mattresses and bed frames, curtains attached to their rods, flashlights with batteries included, photo albums with old family pictures on every page.

"Yes, slowly Cleotilde had emptied every room of her house into the yard until the lawn became barren of merchandise. Cars stopped pulling over, and the house became invisible again. And Cleotilde, poor, poor Cleotilde, went back to being what she had always been: an old woman all alone in the world."

Doña Ramona pressed the stop button and rewound the tape. Just then don Manuel walked out of the bedroom, carrying his homemade chamber pot—a plastic Clorox container sliced at the top with the handle left intact for easy carrying. His hair was flat on the left side of his head. And with his left eye drooping, permanently damaged after a stroke, his face had the effect of having been smashed in.

"Are you talking to that chingada machine again? You're going to use up what little voice you have," he said right before his mouth stretched out into a yawn.

"If it's for Leonardo I don't care," she responded, suddenly aware that she had just recovered from a sore throat.

"It's a waste of time that's what it is. Idle talk is a waste of time," he said with no conviction in his voice.

"It's too early to be up, Manuel," doña Ramona said. "Go back to bed, I'll wake you up in a while."

"What?"

Doña Ramona spoke up. "Go back to bed, Manuel. It's still early!"

"I'm too anxious," he said, emptying the urine into the toilet, then flushing. "I'm worried about the hours we'll get at work today."

"Hopefully more than yesterday," doña Ramona muttered.

"And don't forget to take the camera!" Leonardo called out from his room.

"What? What the hell is he screaming about?" don Manuel asked. His skinny legs appeared even thinner under the wide bottoms of his boxer shorts. The white bathroom door caught his shadow.

"To-to-to take pictures out in the field," doña Ramona said with hesitation. "You know, for his project."

"Project?" don Manuel sneered. "Wasting our time is what he's doing. Chingado project. The foreman's going to think we're playing around instead of working."

"He's not going to think anything," doña Ramona snapped back. "You stay out of it, Manuel, he's not asking *you* to take the pictures." She took another sip of the coffee; her hands trembled.

Don Manuel walked back to the bedroom as he scratched the flat side of his head. He paused at the entrance and farted.

"Cochino!" Leonardo yelled out.

"I saved it just for you," don Manuel said as he walked into his room, chuckling.

"For the love of God," doña Ramona cried out. "A woman can't get some peace until she's dead and buried."

In that instant the house became silent, as if she had cursed the world into a dark paralysis. Slightly unsettled, doña Ramona leaned her head back, bringing up the squeaky foot rest on the recliner. The shadow against the wall kept up with her. Her legs were dry, the skin cracked into a map of white lines. That reminded her of another woman, her own mother, who had died without having known the pleasure of a chair like this, and who had warned her daughter to expect nothing but the solitude that was her lot in life, no matter that she lived *up there* in el norte. Who would have thought way back then and way back there that the old stories would keep her bones from aching? Pressing down on the play button, she focused on the grainy voice. *I once heard talk about a woman . . .* She already knew this story, but it was a good one. And she was always willing to listen to a good fill-up-the-dead-air story that spun like a spirit in the room and breathed out the words along with her.

Moon Music

Don Nico   3:45 a.m.

The moon beamed, fat and bright as a tostón. Don Nico leaned back, forcing the folding chair to grate its metal legs against the elevated deck. Tostones did not exist anymore, only in coin collections. He suspected the U.S. had something to do with its disappearance because people were bringing tostones across the border by the bagful. For a while, Laundromats and arcades in the Caliente Valley had been witness to the invasion. The tostón, that fifty-centavo piece, was the same size as the quarter. But now that war was over. Motecuzoma Xocoyotzin, the face on the coin, finally enjoyed his rest.

The weather was cool, typical for the June desert just before dawn. The sky had cleared away the stars. Coyotes would soon stop prowling and return to their hideouts in the brush, leaving behind only tracks in the mud and scat packed with date seeds. Pifas blamed the coyotes for his vanishing jerky. That or el chupacabras, he joked. Don Nico knew better. As soon as he heard Pifas snoring off to sleep, don Nico snuck out to the back and triggered the chicken wire traps under the clothesline. The cured meat was out of reach, but not the traps; he didn't want to take another crippled cat to the salts across the highway to die slowly of dehydration—or from el chupacabras. The jerky was no great loss. Whoever came to take it did so sparingly.

Staying awake through most of the night was a habit don Nico kept from his days as a watchman at the funeral parlor in Monterrey. He had been a watchman for a brewery, a hotel, a bus station, and lastly for the funeral parlor where he heard the empty coffins crack because they were anxious to be peopled. A few hours of sleep were all he needed. San Pedro de Alcántara, the patron saint of watchmen, had slept no more than two hours each night for thirty years. At sixty-five, an old man like don Nico could put in a hard day's labor in the grape fields and be ready to work the next day with little rest. In the meantime he waited. He watched. He listened.

Across the dirt road sat a broken-down trailer. Inside, a flickering light. Don Nico recognized a votive candle even with his failing eyesight. With Pifas snoring in the background, he imagined it was Pifas threatening to put the flame out, so he chuckled. Then his smile grew sullen because thinking about Pifas was like thinking about Eloisa, his look-alike sister. A few days ago Eloisa had been waiting for them on that same chair don Nico now occupied. Despite her size she was able to balance herself on its hind legs with the back of the chair set against the wall. She smoked a cigarette and she waved her left foot in the air, teasing a kitten with the shoelace. She still wore her work clothes and a dusty bandanna around her hair. Bruises on her face; more trouble with Tenorio, her husband. Pifas walked directly to the door, bringing up his bony shoulders as he struggled with the key.

"I'm going to get my Winchester and put a hole in that sonofabitch. Maybe I'll shoot off his good arm."

Eloisa calmly brought the chair back down and bent over to tie her shoelace. "Good afternoon, don Nico," she said, lifting her head up, the cigarette between her lips. "Long day today, wasn't it?"

Don Nico stomped on the wooden boards to dust off his work boots. The kitten ran back under the building.

"Nine hours today, with the threat of getting called back to repack," he said. Eloisa shook her head. "We can't complain nowadays," he added, "what with how slow the season's been."

"Oh, I'm sure Pifas can. You know how he gets if he doesn't have his beer by three in the afternoon," Eloisa laughed. She put out her cigarette and followed don Nico inside.

The apartment was only one room, so don Nico was used to private matters unfolding publicly. He threw his straw hat over the mattress in his corner of the room then sat in one of the two chairs at the table. Eloisa washed her hands in the small sink and turned on the gas stove that ticked when the flame rose. Pifas fumbled theatrically with the items in the broom closet, among them the old Winchester he bought cheap off the owner of an auto body shop.

Pifas tried to cock the rifle, having forgotten in his excitement that it was still missing the gunlock hammer, so instead he angled it up in the air, aiming at himself to inspect the barrel.

"Good Lord, put that down before you poke your eye out," Eloisa said. "Don Nico, I can't find the rice again." Don Nico pointed at a cardboard box above the refrigerator. Eloisa swatted at Pifas. "Put that thing away before you break something!" she commanded.

Pifas glared, reluctantly storing the rifle, but not before striking the floor two times with the heavy butt. "Once I get it fixed I'm going to shoot him," he declared.

"Once you get it fixed I'm going to shoot Tenorio myself," Eloisa said. She pulled out three beers from the refrigerator, opening hers first. The skillet smoked on the stove.

"I'll take care of him all right," Pifas said. "Then I'll take care of those goddamn coyotes. I'll even go after that pinche chupacabras."

Don Nico was embarrassed for Pifas, who concentrated on the beer's pull-tab instead of looking up when he spoke. The wrinkles on his sunburned face made him look older than his forty years.

Eloisa refused to serve them until after they had showered, scolding them for neglecting the up-keep of the single room. She folded the sheets and the clothing that lay scattered on the floor while he and Pifas scooped up the fried pork and rice. They kept quiet, listening to Eloisa's mutterings until she turned on the transistor radio on top of the empty milk crate.

"I heard talk that the grape will last only a few more weeks," Pifas said too softly.

"That's what people say," don Nico replied.

"Crop's not too good after all that cold in the winter."

"I heard talk about a strike if they make us work piecework again," don Nico said.

"I hope we do!" said Pifas. His eyes lit up, but only for a second.

The conversation ended there. Neither of them spoke until Eloisa left without saying good-bye because it was understood she was only there to give the effect of distance from her husband, to go back to him as soon as she convinced herself all was forgiven. As soon as she stepped out the door, the radio went dead momentarily as if she had taken the sound with her. Don Nico and Pifas looked at each other just as the announcer spoke again. Pifas pronounced, "I hate it when she comes." Don Nico knew it wasn't true.

They didn't talk about Eloisa because there was no time and no energy. They got back from the fields by noon, by three, sometimes by six, sometimes by midnight when their crew was sent to the warehouse to repack a shipment that hadn't passed inspection. They got home, showered, ate, rested. Squeezing in a domestic dispute was like stuffing both feet into the same shoe.

Don Nico didn't need a clock to know that he had an hour before going back inside to wake Pifas. A light went on in the trailer across the dirt road. He told time by the woman's activities: she got up to fix work lunch at four; by four-thirty the rest of the trailer was lit—the other workers got up; by five, she came out to warm up the old van parked beside the trailer. At that point don Nico went in to nudge Pifas and prepare work lunch while Pifas slowly rolled off the mattress. But until then don Nico waited, watched, and listened. The woman sometimes sang, a faint song that managed to reach him because it was the only sound at that hour.

Was it an old man's senility that made him believe he was in love? After all these years the feeling danced in front of him like a cruel joke. As a watchman he had learned to be so patient with dawn and daylight that the idea of time running out was foreign to him. There was always time. All he had to do was wait, watch, and listen. Eloisa sometimes sang when she came on a weekend to make flour tortillas. She sometimes brought her youngest children with her; don Nico kept them entertained with card tricks. They called him Abuelito. But he preferred the weekends Eloisa came by herself. Without the noisy children, Eloisa hummed in harmony as she kneaded the dough. She might even break out into song when she brought down the rolling pin across the wooden board. On those occasions don Nico sat outside, on that same folding chair, closed his eyes and listened as he did at that moment, making believe that his woman had come to bless his ears with music.

Don Nico took out his handkerchief from his back pocket and breathed in slowly and deeply. The fresh morning air filtered through the scents collected in the cloth was painful and pleasurable.

WITH THE UGLIER PEOPLE

Hernán   4:20 a.m.

Hernán shivered. He slipped a flannel shirt on, knowing that by eight in the morning his body wouldn't be able to breathe through the cloth. But it was either that or come home with his arms all scratched from the twigs on the grapevines. The shirt felt heavy, so did the socks, even the medal around his neck. A neighbor friend of his mother's had gone on a pilgrimage to la Villa in Mexico City and had purchased dozens of San Ignacio de Loyola medals for all her friends back in California. His mother made him wear his all the time though he suspected she only wore hers when doña Chepina came over.

His mother's face had become ugly to him because hers was the first face that stared down at him at dawn. *Get up now, mijo.*

Lately he had been training himself to wake up as soon as she opened the bedroom door so that he could stir in bed and let her know he was already awake. On more frustrating mornings he'd jerk his body up in reflex to the door opening, all to avoid hearing that annoying phrase. *Get up now, mijo,* spoken with an apologetic tone that pierced the nerves in his ears. He hadn't given her a chance to say it today, but the victory was short-lived because he let the words slip out of his own lips, mimicking his mother's voice with such precision that it made him cringe after all.

Ernesto and tío Severo were already in the living room, waiting. Their laughter made him nervous. It was too bold and comfortable for this early in the morning. Hernán could barely utter a word without draining energy from his body. He'd rather be asleep again—unconscious of the long day ahead.

Hernán walked to the bathroom across the hall. And though he tried to keep from looking toward Ernesto and tío Severo, his head turned on its own to catch a glimpse of them having coffee with his father at the kitchen table. As soon as he shut the bathroom door he turned the faucet on full force, splashing cold water on his face to wake up. And make noise. Ernesto and tío Severo were his mother's brothers. They lived with Mamá Patricia on the other side of town and stopped to pick him up each morning because his parents didn't work the grape, they cleaned hotel rooms. The hotel manager didn't hire fourteen-year-olds for the summer the way grape companies did.

Ernesto was only seven years older than Hernán, which was why he insisted Hernán call him by his first name, as if they were cousins, not uncle and nephew. He also demanded they use English, though no one else in the family understood the language very well. Ernesto spoke it with a heavy accent, unlike his nephew, which made him resentful and hostile.

As the three men spoke over coffee, Hernán's ear captured Ernesto's voice the clearest.

Canary's playing at Los Arcos next Friday.

Hernán pictured Ernesto's posture: knees spread out wide to suggest length, one hand across the leg, back straight and rigid to give the illusion of tallness.

I don't know how! That cabrón can't even play Las Mañanitas... Los Arcos will go broke with that kind of talent. . . . The whole band stinks! Remember that time in El Paraíso? They had to send for their instruments two days later just to avoid a lynching . . .

Ernesto's laugh was not a laugh—it was a cackle, thick with self-confidence and pretense.

Hernán watched the water droplets run down his face in the mirror. He imagined that's what he looked like in the fields when he sweated, except that his face was flushed, his eyes bloodshot—so unlike Ernesto whose dark skin only glared.

"Come on, stupid," Ernesto called out frequently at work. "Why don't you move? Move those rocks in your pants!"

Hernán was forced to speed up, prodded like a pack mule, the heavy box of grapes in his hands.

"I think we should leave this little girl at home with his Mami. What do you think, Severo?"

Tío Severo never responded. He tolerated the show of harassment, which made Hernán hate tío Severo even more than he despised Ernesto.

Hernán felt a knot caught in his throat. He gagged on the tap water.

"Hernán, are you okay?" His mother knocked on the bathroom door after he started coughing. "I'm packing sandwiches today. Do you want a slice of avocado in them? How about a chile?"

"Go away," Hernán muttered. "Whatever!" he answered, his heart beating fast.

"Your tíos tell me how hard you've been working. And this week you get your first paycheck." She moved away from the door to address the others. "He told me he's buying new clothes with all the money he makes. You know how these boys are nowadays with their strange tastes in clothing, my goodness."

"You fucking sow. You cunt," Hernán muttered, already imagining how Ernesto would turn that piece of information against him in the fields. He reluctantly exited the bathroom to sit on the living room sofa. He put on his shoes then leaned back to rest for a few more minutes, arms folded and eyes shut, waiting for tío Severo to say, *It's time.* Tío Severo didn't just say the words; he threatened Hernán with them.

"Are the grapes any better this week?" Hernán's father spoke.

"The cargoes are still falling because of the sugar levels," tío Severo responded. "It's going to be our turn to repack the next time that happens. It's going to be Hernán's second time at the warehouse."

"He's ready for it this time," Ernesto interjected.

Hernán pictured the three men looking at him. He didn't want to think about the warehouse, about the human chain that unloaded and reloaded the cargo. He had bruised the entire length of his arms because he didn't know how to catch the boxes tossed to him. The palms of his hands remained swollen for days, splintered because he also didn't know how to toss. He knew Ernesto had followed him to make sure they stood next to each other in the chain. Ernesto threw the boxes incorrectly on purpose.

Today was Wednesday. Hernán had been to work only eight days, four weeks fewer than all the other pickers because school had still been in session. This was the eighth day he waited for tío Severo to speak, to get up from the side of the table where he always sat to drink his morning coffee and say those menacing words: *It's time.*

When Ernesto spoke, Hernán envisioned the thin mustache stretching like elastic, highlighting that grin of perfect teeth. Ernesto was the only one with straight teeth. But he was too short. And too skinny. And he had never had a girlfriend. He spent his evenings with other losers like Lalú, that Colombian his father called Lulú because he was small and effeminate.

On weekends Hernán went to Mamá Patricia's to play with her fortune-telling games, to unwrap the Bazooka Joes and catch up with the horoscopes, which he translated into Spanish for her. When Mamá Patricia became engrossed with the astrological charts, he snuck into Ernesto's room, which was off-limits. Among the elaborate collection of pornography and muscle magazines he discovered weight-gaining powders, skin creams, a hair-waxing kit, and a brittle newsprint article that had yellowed with age. The article declared: GROW AS MUCH AS TWO INCHES IN HEIGHT IN ONLY SIX WEEKS! There was a vertical column of drawings depicting feet and legs at various stages of stretching exercises. Directions were included on how to create an accurate height measure against the wall. Hernán had found the place where Ernesto kept track of his progress. Dozens of marks overlapped at the same spot; he could sense the frustration in the way the ink had been engraved into the wall repeatedly. Whenever Ernesto was at his cruelest Hernán thought back to those marks, which his own height would catch up to and eventually surpass.

"It's time," tío Severo said finally. Hernán's heart skipped a beat as he reached for his baseball cap and bandanna.

"You be careful," Hernán heard his mother say as usual. He learned to walk out swiftly, before she had time to bless him or kiss him or do anything that might make his body buckle. At the moment of leaving the house he was on the verge of crying, his throat swollen. How many times had he fantasized that his mother changed her mind about letting him go into the heat of the fields. He imagined her rushing out into the parking lot before they drove away, her eyes gushing with tears, to have her son returned to her.

Stop! Don't go! she would plead to tío Severo behind the wheel. *Give him back to me!* Even Ernesto's eyes would soften and he would help Hernán out, guide him back to his mother. But this would never happen. His mother was a stupid, fat sow who didn't know any better than to wave good-bye from the door, sending her only son off to work with the two men he hated most.

Hernán climbed on the back of tío Severo's red pickup truck and lay down across the cold, corrugated metal. The morning was exceedingly cold, which meant the day was going to be exceedingly hot. Just before the truck pulled out Hernán signaled tío Severo to wait.

Tío Severo stuck his head out the side window and asked in alarm: "What happened? Did you forget your clippers?"

"Where's the blanket? To lie down on," Hernán said.

Without replying, tío Severo forced the truck out into the road with a jolt that threw Hernán against the side of the truck bed. The tailgate rattled. Hernán rolled around once, suddenly finding himself looking up into the bleak dark blue of the sky that had snapped down like a heavy lid.

PISTOL LOVE

Jesse   4:35 a.m.

Jesse tossed the calico cat off the bed and reached over Amanda's deep indentation on the old mattress for the watch. He still had another thirty minutes of rest. Amanda was in the shower washing herself off; she had not resisted his dawn-inspired urge, but he knew it was for the sake of keeping him appeased about her indiscretions.

He opened her nightstand drawer and dug out the hand pistol. Small and feminine with its silver and ivory lining, the pistol was deceptively heavy, smuggled in from México for Amanda's protection: there were too many crack heads sneaking around in the after-hours at the trailer park. Amanda kept the gun unloaded, lost in a pile of cosmetics and old mail. The tiny copper-tipped bullets rolled forward with the pencil eyeliners. He pulled out the empty cartridge clip and stuck his pinkie in the casing, and when Amanda dropped the soap in the shower the thud excited him.

They had been married for eight years and Amanda had always been discreet about her affairs, but lately she was being deliberately sloppy: a hickey on the neck, a bruise on the inner thigh, tooth marks on her breast. She wanted a divorce but he couldn't agree to it. To end the marriage would only realize the failure his father was expecting of him ever since Jesse first brought Amanda home.

"She works in a cantina?" Jesse's father nearly fell off his chair at the disclosure. His mother simply withdrew into her seat, staring into space, her face dead of expression, never to speak to her son again.

"You got yourself an overworked old owl from a cantina?"

"It's not what you think, Papá."

"Good for nothing, as always." His father paced around the living room, unable to make up his mind about what to do with his wandering hands. "No school. No job. No sense. You take this woman back, Jesús, and be back by supper and *maybe* we'll forget what you just did. Almost thirty years old and I still have to wipe the shit off your ass."

Jesse had tried to explain but it was useless. He stumbled over his own words so that in the end it was better to leave without saying good-bye and without a blessing from his parents. He would have receded completely into humiliation had it not been for Amanda who after a lengthy silence in the car touched his cheek and said, "What does it matter, corazón? We've got each other."

Jesse's eyes watered whenever he remembered the words that had given him back his dignity. From that point on she became the boss: she dictated what, when, where, and how long it should take him. She was aggressive and stalwart as a fist, and exact as the kisses she firmly planted on his flesh: always at the right moment, in the right place. His saving grace.

But now this, Jesse thought as he awkwardly swung the pistol inside the circle of his thumb and forefinger. Now she was determined to be rid of him. He aimed the pistol at the bathroom door, then at the calico cat as it tried to jump on the bed again. It scurried out of sight at the threat. Jesse brought the pistol down on the covers when he heard the showerhead go off.

For eight years he had let Amanda wear the pants. "No brats," she said; "my body's too old for childbearing." *Fine.* "Don't expect much of a housekeeper or cook," she said, "I only know how to work in rough places: cantinas, prisons, factories, warehouses, fields." *That's fine too.* "And I don't care how much of a stud your scrawny little ass wants to be, never from behind!"

For eight years he satisfied himself with surges of private power, like the time he got to her unemployment check in the mail first. Amanda had become anxious at not having received it. She made angry phone calls. Yet for two days he secretly rubbed the envelope flat between his hands, tracing the outlines of the sealed flap and sniffing the address window when Amanda's back was turned. He had flicked the sharp corners into dullness before returning it to the mailbox. When she found it his handprints were all over it. But she kept quiet, letting him keep his two days of reverie in the small act of having controlled the fate of this money, and by association, Amanda herself.

At work their contact was limited; he was the foreman, she was the tallier. Yet everyone seemed to know who made her husband take her boots off after work and give her a thorough foot massage. Jesse heard the jokes, the mock lip-smacking. And with Naro walking around telling everyone what he saw the times he spent the night at their trailer, there was little chance of the grape pickers running out of things to ridicule.

"Jesse, are you awake?" Amanda called out from the bathroom.

"I'm awake."

"Make sure you use fabric softener on the towels next time; I'm drying myself with sandpaper here."

Jesse pointed the pistol at his head and pulled the trigger, feigning a blow to the skull and collapsing on the pillow.

"Did you hear me?"

"I heard you."

"You've been on Mars the last few days. What's the matter with you?"

"Oh, nothing. Just worried about the way things are going at work, that's all."

"Have a drink after work or something. Relax," Amanda said. "You know it's shitty in the middle of the season."

"Yeah, but there are rumors of a strike and—"

"Let them strike. We'll get rid of each one of them if we have to. They're all dispensable, for crissake. My God, is that all? You're even making Trabalenguas nervous. Has she been fed? Don't think I don't know you kick her around when I'm not looking, you brute."

Amanda's voice rattled in Jesse's head as he pictured himself pulling the pistol on Naro and scaring the shit out of him in front of the grape pickers. If it cost him his job it was worth it. He needed a change anyway. And most likely, with the supervisor's connections, he'd simply get transferred. Merengue would understand after he explained to him how Naro had fucked his wife and that he was simply saving face. No doubt Merengue already knew. Jesse grabbed for a handful of bullets from the drawer, then changed his mind and threw them back in. He stuffed the pistol under the mattress before Amanda slid open the bathroom door.

"What are you doing?" she asked. Her black hair wet and flat, she stood with a green towel wrapped around her waist, her breasts exposed. Stretch marks crawled out of the towel and up her sides.

Jesse reached over and pushed shut the nightstand drawer. "Looking for something," he said, slipping back under the covers to hide his flushed chest.

"Don't look through my things, you know how much that bothers me."

She walked across the small trailer bedroom and stopped to pick up the calico. "My baby, baby," she said to the cat in a high-pitched voice. She kissed it on the forehead and let it meow after her as she stepped into the compact kitchen.

"Where's the goddamn cat dish?" Amanda demanded. "She gets fed indoors, not out. I told you that I don't know how many times. And goddammit with your muddy boots!" Amanda's voice softened. "Stay inside, Trabalenguas. Baby, baby."

When the trailer door swung open, a gush of cool air invaded the small living quarters. Jesse pulled the blankets tighter against him; he missed the comfort of Amanda's heat. With the passing of time she had been slowly denying him her body: first her tongue and face, then her hands and feet, her back and breasts. She acted as uninspired as a hole in the mattress at night, and during the day she was all mouth—like a blowhole. Jesse recalled those airplane disaster movies where a punctured window sucked everything out with such force through its tiny opening. Imagining a view of the suction in progress from the outside of the plane—*that* was Amanda. Jesse snickered.

"What's so funny?" Amanda asked as she walked in naked, the towel now neatly wrapped turban-style on her head. "You're going fucking crazy." Bulky around the hips and shoulders, her corpulent body moved with such ease and familiarity through the space of the trailer. It was this self-confidence that made Jesse scared of losing her; by possessing her he also possessed her qualities. She was the other half of the bed, he thought as he extended his arm across the indentation on the mattress. She was the bone, muscle and joint of the relationship. Amanda, Amanda. There is no life without Amanda. Amanda's shadow, cast by the bathroom light, reached across the room to press against the wrinkles on the covers, against the shaky night stand, against the edge of the lampshade, and then it narrowed down to the size of a bowling ball to punch the weaker side of the trailer wall.

Papi

Cirilo   4:45 a.m.

Ninja was throwing out stink through both ends, puffing on a cigarette and farting shamelessly at the same time. He was turned on his side and when he farted he exhaled and a stream of smoke shot into the air. The noise of Ninja's butt-cheeks grating against the pressure of the gas was ruining Cirilo's sentimental browsing of his one photograph of his children, but he couldn't blame Ninja for the undercooked beans Moreno had fixed for dinner the night before. For all his feminine qualities Moreno couldn't make a decent meal when it was his turn in the kitchen. If Tamayamá were awake he would be doubling over, Tamayamaing each time Ninja broke wind, but since it was still early in the morning, he slept soundly on the floor next to Moreno, both men unaware that they too let out an occasional fart.

"The room is going to explode right in your face if you don't put that cigarette out," Cirilo said, his hands clasping the photograph over the small wooden table. In the center stood a few old examples of Moreno's skill at origami: a lion, a fish, and a seal. Cirilo sat on a plastic crate. To keep the hard surface from digging into his flesh he had flattened out a few layers of newspaper between the crate and his boxer shorts.

Ninja spoke through his cigarette, "The smoke covers up the smell."

"Well, make sure you don't fall asleep with that piece of shit in your mouth, then. You'll burn yourself alive."

"The grape's already doing that," Ninja responded. "We're getting roasted like turkeys in the oven."

"What are you, a poet? Just try to keep your holes shut. I'm trying to think," Cirilo snapped.

He turned to the photograph again, slightly ashamed that he was taking out his frustration on Ninja. Ninja rolled over on his back, his cigarette spent. Now the three men supine on the floor, one next to the other, their blankets darkened into mounds of earth, resembled a row of graves. Cirilo shook this thought away and rubbed his fingers against the sleep stinging around his eyes. It was Moreno's week to cook, but it was his week to prepare the lunches for the four of them, which meant getting up an hour earlier than the others. He didn't mind that too much today because he couldn't sleep. What bothered him was having to dig into the same undercooked pot of beans from last night. Chela would savor even these, his small miseries; such was her hatred of him for having left her after the birth of each child. He missed his children, and even though they lived just across town he was not allowed to see them as often as he wished. Chela was adamant about his absence since she planned to leave for Bakersfield or Fresno as soon as she saved enough money and she didn't want the children to endear themselves to him. She didn't want to make it that much harder for them when the time finally came.

His children leaving him instead of him leaving his children would be a new experience. And of course Chela couldn't understand why he left each time though it made perfect sense to him. The first time he simply became nervous and anxious about this child they had brought into the world of long hours and heat. Tiny Lucita wailed into the dawn with a force that pierced his dreams with nightmares and shattered his sleep. Startled awake and drenched in sweat, he grew ever more fearful of the shadows that took the shapes of those terrible configurations from his childhood. The more he tried to resist the unsettling illusions, the more powerful Lucita's cries became, spinning out of the crib like angry hornets. A solitary wasp of a thought crawled out at the very end: hadn't he witnessed his own father succumb to madness the first months Cirilo's younger sister arrived? Mariana had descended like an invasion of stingers that turned the harmony of their house into a screech-infested prison that banished their father from their lives forever. Cirilo and his mother never forgave Mariana, and the little girl grew up with a scar of blame that made her a timid silence of a woman.

Cirilo shut his eyes in hopelessness as he remembered his aversion to holding that small creature he had fathered. He refused to kiss her or even look at her, all in the guise of a male attitude that only the mother had to be responsible for the child's weaning. Only the warm touch of his wife gave him solace. Once Lucita was asleep, Cirilo insisted that Chela motivate her weary body into a muscle and limb performance that climaxed with his pushing deeper inside of her until he felt he had penetrated so far in he was swimming in her womb. But the moments of pleasure and the private conversation of murmured promises lasted only until Lucita was awake again. And with Chela's second pregnancy, even those brief encounters were threatened altogether. He didn't wait for his second rival to arrive; selfishly, Cirilo left, taking refuge with Moreno, Chela's cousin, where he would be close enough to observe, but far enough not to experience.

Only distance managed to fool Cirilo into believing that he had overcome his emotions. With Moreno on his side he convinced Chela to let him return. Lucita and Pablo had outgrown their suckling stage so Chela's bed was once again alive with an uninterrupted ecstasy that made him feel sole master of the house—until Chela's third pregnancy. Chela must have detected his growing uneasiness, his imminent shift back to the cowardly man who couldn't compete with his children's cries for attention. She reverted to her old self, to the times before their courtship softened her soul. She became edgy and short-tempered, her mouth foul with cussing and humiliations. In the weeks before she was due to give birth, she kicked him out of the house—an effortless gesture since he had already been packing his few belongings behind her back. This time however, there was a hint of finality in her voice, an irreparable rift that scared him to the point of begging her for another chance. But she wouldn't budge, not even on the day the third baby was born and she completed his emasculation by naming him Mickey, after that cartoon mouse.

"That's not even a saint? How can you name our son after a chingado mouse and not name him after me?" Cirilo demanded upon entering the hospital room. Chela was lying down behind a rollaway tray with a small dish of food. She ignored him.

"Well, explain yourself!" he persisted.

"Because el chingado mouse has more character and certainly more money!" she snapped back. She threw the tray out of her way and stood up. "Where are my chingadas slippers?"

"Ma'am!" a white nurse had rushed in. "You can't leave the bed, ma'am, you've just had a baby."

"What are people going to think? What's my sister going to say? When she had a son she named him Felipe like her husband," Cirilo said.

"That's because Mariana's an idiot who lets her husband push her around like a chingada pack mule. What does anyone including you care what I name the baby anyway. I had him."

"I fathered him," Cirilo said, self-righteously.

"Please, wetback," Chela said. "All you did was finger me in my sleep. Believe me, it wasn't such an accomplishment. I've had better orgasms popping mints."

"Sir," the nurse said, trying to hold Chela back, "you need to help me put her back into bed."

"Well, how about if you give him a middle name?" Cirilo pleaded, softening his voice.

"Mickey Cirilo? That sounds pleasant," Chela said. "I'm already cursing him by giving him your last name, what else do you want?"

"I want to come home, Chela," Cirilo said.

Chela had one slipper in her hand and her cotton bathrobe was slack over her right shoulder. The nurse pulled at her arm more aggressively. "Ma'am," the nurse kept repeating.

"These chingadas gringas," Chela said, "always in the way and raising up a stink like roadkill." Chela shoved the nurse so violently the nurse fell back on the bed.

"My goodness!" the nurse cried out in shock. She lifted herself off the bed and rushed out of the room.

"And go get some sun, querida," Chela called out after her.

"Chela, please," Cirilo said, bowing his head. From the corner of his eye he watched her stubbornly refuse to soften her stance. The only thing that convinced him there was a spark of hope yet alive was when Moreno suddenly appeared at the doorway with little Pablo in one arm and Lucita shyly poking her head behind his leg.

"Papi?" Lucita had muttered.

———

Moreno stirred in his sleep and let out a bearish groan that made Cirilo turn his head. "Is it time yet?" he asked, still drowsy. Moreno's hair was thick and sleep-tossed, with no visible hairline because he was lying in the darkest part of the room. Cirilo could barely make out his features.

"Almost," Cirilo answered finally. "Lunch is packed. I think I'm ready for some coffee. You want a cup?"

Moreno got up and brushed his shirt with his hands. "I'll heat up some water," he said. "It smells in here," he added.

"All three of you were firing cannons in your sleep, thanks to those beans," Cirilo said. "I thought all you jotos knew how to cook."

"I'll show you a joto," Moreno said. He kicked Tamayamá in the hip. "Wake up, you cocksucker."

Tamayamyá jerked his body forward once and then fell back to sleep in his original position.

"Let him sleep, Tiki-Tiki," Cirilo said, "don't be a cabrón."

"I'm letting you get away with that shit only because you're sometimes family," Moreno retorted. He walked up to the stove and searched inside the oven for a small pan.

"Peace," Cirilo declared, holding up two fingers. He turned the photograph over on the table.

"I've seen it," Moreno said, slightly annoyed.

"I know you have," Cirilo stuttered. "I don't know why I did that."

Moreno pulled out two coffee cups from the sink and placed them on the table. With one hand he grabbed the jar of instant coffee and the bag of sugar, with the other he poured boiling water into the cups. "Just like in México," he announced.

"That's true," Cirilo said. "Down there they think instant coffee is a luxury." Cirilo was close enough to the sink that he simply reached over to pull out a spoon. "I'll even let you stir first," he said.

Moreno took the spoon. "Did you get much sleep?" he asked.

"Nothing," Cirilo said. "Not even with the pills you gave me."

Moreno sipped on his coffee. He tapped his finger on the back of the photograph and said, "Don't worry, the boy will be fine."

"Chela doesn't tell me anything. It's not just him I'm worried about. She still has this crazy idea in her head that she can move away."

"That's just Chela talking. She's not going anywhere," Moreno said.

"I don't know, Moreno. This time I think it's for real. Maybe this time she's leaving forever."

"I'll see what I can get out of her today," Moreno said. "Will that help?"

"Of course," Cirilo answered. "She probably blames me." Cirilo raised his hand to cover his eyes.

"Hey, man," Moreno said, "no one's judging you."

"That's the problem, Moreno," Cirilo said. He uncovered his eyes, watery and bloodshot. "No one judges me. I should be jailed or shot for what I do to my children. I should have my nuts chopped off for what I do to my wife."

"I've read about crazies like you that castrate themselves," Moreno said. "I hear they have to piss through a straw. If I were you I'd rethink that one."

Cirilo laughed and swatted Moreno on the head. "You're such a piece of shit, Tiki-Tiki."

"Well, cousin," Moreno said. "You have to have a sense of humor about all of this. I mean, just think about it: you live in a one-room house with three farting good-for-nothings, you get paid pennies to breathe in pesticides all day, and your wife named your third child after a rodent in red suspenders just to spite you. As cousin Chela would say, that's chingado funny! Why cry about it? If you were meant to have it easy you would have been born white. Brother, your life was shit from the moment you crawled out from the brown space between your mother's legs."

"What is it with all you chingados wetbacks that makes you poets?" Cirilo said.

"I think it's the Mexican water," Moreno said. "No fluoride."

In the minute of silence that followed Cirilo thought and re-thought the words he was going to use to express his gratitude. Moreno was his sole source of comfort in times like these, which was why Cirilo was so overprotective of him. Sure it was true what people knew and said about him, but what did that matter when, in the quiet moments just after dawn, Moreno was not a freak. Moreno was the closest Cirilo had ever come to a brother. Of course, he couldn't tell Moreno he loved him, but there was no word more appropriate, or more rejected in the vocabulary of spoken appreciation between men. So in the end Cirilo decided to say nothing sentimental. Somehow he sensed Moreno knew. Instead, Cirilo picked up one of Moreno's origami animals and said: "Brother, do you mind if I keep one of these for myself?"

Flattered, Moreno smiled and nodded once.

FEVERS

Jacaranda 5:00 a.m.

After taking a shower in the coldest water her body could stand, Jacaranda ran outside in her shorts and T-shirt, completing ten laps around the house before attacking the punching bag that hung from the mulberry. She ended her ritual by shaking her body fervently to generate more heat.

"You're going to catch pneumonia," Eva warned from the window.

"In the summer? I'd be laughed out of the hospital," Jacaranda answered, tightening the bandanna that kept her long hair up in a loose bun.

"Well, just keep doing your little dance this early in the morning and you'll see," said Eva. "Mami says to drag in the garbage can since you're out there." She shut the window.

Jacaranda's long, slim neck glistened with the lights coming down from the house. In the kitchen her mother made flour tortillas like she did every morning because she didn't want them to eat store-bought brands packaged in plastic. "Who knows what kinds of germs it's been cultivating all that time with no oxygen," she reasoned. Her mother was as obsessive about cleanliness and hygiene as her father was about the Book of Psalms. From the beginning Jacaranda, Eva, and Sebastián were expected to grow up with their bodies as squeaky clean as their souls.

The clarity of dawn guided Jacaranda's way to the curb because there wasn't a street light along the highway. With the house facing Highway 86, cars only sped by and never stopped or paused. And with no neighbors for at least three miles, the family had its privacy—*she* had her privacy.

Across the highway stood the date-tree farm. When they were younger, Eva and Jacaranda snuck across to bring back palm fronds and seed sticks during the pruning season, disguising their bodies to terrorize their younger brother. Her parents had worked for the date company for over a decade. Her father pruned out in the farm, her mother cleaned and sorted at the warehouse. Sebastián had even worked in the date store for a while, keeping order in the display cases and making pulpy date shakes for the tourists. No matter what, no matter when, the family stuck together. They were stuck together. So when her father fell off the date-tree ladder because of an improperly fastened security belt, Jacaranda was not surprised that just as she was about to embark on a two-year commitment to do missionary work in southern México he had found yet another way to bind her to him.

Jacaranda's father used to be a volunteer preacher at the abandoned pink church down the road. It could hold no pews because it was the size of a small apartment. They used folding chairs with faded Corona Beer logos. The congregation consisted of his family, a few old Mexican women who called her father "Padrecito," though he wasn't an ordained priest, and a young man Sebastián had coaxed into marking the singing of the psalms with a guitar. Before Ramiro it was just Sebastián on the keyboard. After Ramiro it was Eva giggling instead of singing because Ramiro constantly winked at her as he strummed. The gathering was more like a Bible study group with an emphasis, of course, on the Book of Psalms. They read them, they studied them, they sang them, they swam toward the spirituality of them from "Blessed is the man" to "Praise the Lord"; the poetry of God was the language her father had adopted because any other language was too inadequate to express atonement and redemption.

Jacaranda's father was pressuring her to teach Bible school since she already worked with children as a teacher's aide at John Kelley Elementary. She had resisted the idea of a convent education in exchange for community college. Did she dare go against her father's wishes again? Her Bible school training had begun when she was young, when her father expected her to learn the Catholic catechism, to memorize passage after passage in the Bible, and to read book after book about virgin martyrs—all demands that hadn't been forced on Eva or Sebastián. Neither of them had demonstrated her patience and discipline. With Eva she'd act out scenes from the lives of saints. When she was Santa Margarita, Eva played the Devil who disguised himself as the executioner at her beheading; when she played Santa Lucía, Eva played the suitor for whom she had plucked out her eyes.

Jacaranda lifted the garbage can. This was the summer the farce finally ended, she thought as she dragged the can to the front of the house. Sebastián was moving out to go to college, Eva had to marry Ramiro before she began showing signs of pregnancy, and her father was going to die. Jacaranda had contacted the Baptists to let them know she was available to go to México after all. And last month Jacaranda ran across a letter her mother was writing to her sister in Texas, asking about job opportunities available to a recently widowed forty-two-year-old mother whose children no longer needed her. Somehow they had all agreed—without any of them having spoken it—to endure one more summer together, making believe that the moribund born-again Christian was not the same man who had touched his own daughter.

In the living room, Sebastián banged on the television. "This antenna is a rip-off," he said. "We can't even get normal static. Look at this shit!"

"Watch your mouth," their mother called lazily from the kitchen. The rolling pin struck the dough on the board with a thud. "Your father's sleeping," she added.

Sebastián was slim like Jacaranda. If it weren't for her long hair, they would be indistinguishable from behind. Eva however—Jacaranda observed as she came upon her sister in front of the vanity mirror in their room—was all female, all round nubs and curves, with a giggle that made men notice her. Every morning Eva played the same Selena tape at low volume and swayed her shoulders from side to side to the music's contagious rhythms.

"Let me brush your hair out," Eva said as soon as she saw Jacaranda remove her bandanna. Jacaranda took Eva's place before the vanity mirror.

Their contrast was evident: Eva was light-skinned, Jacaranda was the darkest in the family; Eva was plump, Jacaranda thin and flat-chested. But Jacaranda had the waist-length hair Eva envied.

Eva had to satisfy herself with running the bristles through the three and a half feet of fine, black hair on her sister's head because hers had never given her more than a few inches of short wavy locks—her father's genes.

Jacaranda had been an ugly child. She grew up shy and reserved, qualities her father had wanted to nurture for the convent. In elementary school the other girls, including Eva, had teased her by calling her a boy. Twice she ran away from home. Hence her father's overprotective response, hiding her in his arms and taking her with him everywhere he went. She had even taken to napping beside him, sleeping soundly against the comfort of his torso, and to keeping him company in the prayer room at the back of the house. She had become so dependent on the shield of his shadow that when Jacaranda eventually blossomed into her own form of beauty it was almost a disappointment to him.

"Your hair is so sweaty and dirty," Eva said. "I feel like I'm grooming a horse."

"I want to see yours at the end of the day," Jacaranda answered.

"Don't remind me," Eva said. "The only thing that keeps me going is that Ramiro and I need the money." Eva gathered the strands of hair to begin a braid. "But at least tomorrow is Friday. Paycheck day, Los Arcos night. And you better talk to the men this time. They're going to say you think you're too good for them. Or worse, that you're a lesbian."

"Let them say what they want. I go there to hear the music, not stupidities."

"That's exactly what I mean. You need a man, Jacaranda. What are you going to do here all alone with Mami and Papi? We women have needs, you know. And there are so many men out there, my God! Of course, the ones at Los Arcos probably won't want to look at you anymore, Señorita Muy-Muy. Except maybe that cargo truck driver. What's his name? Trino?"

"Dino."

"Whatever. The point is he's asking for you whenever he has a chance. Though people do talk about him and that Jacobo guy. Both muscle men and standing there side by side at the bar like a pair of peacocks. Maybe they're maricones. We'll have to ask Tiki-

Tiki. He knows all about that. And then there's Naro, of course. Wouldn't you just love to get a taste of him?"

I am in the midst of lions; I lie among the ravenous beasts—men whose teeth are spears and arrows, whose tongues are sharp swords. Psalm 57.

"Maybe I just won't go," Jacaranda said.

"We'll see about that."

Jacaranda smiled as Eva curled up the braid, wrapped it tightly inside the bandanna, and then stuffed the bulge into a beige beret— a simple baseball cap couldn't contain her mass of hair throughout the day. At a distance it looked like an old-fashioned train conductor's hat. The foreman and a few of the other men had taken to tooting whenever they saw her arrive at work.

"I'm getting something to eat before we go," Eva said. "Join me?"

"I'm not hungry," Jacaranda responded, tucking a few stray hairs into the beret.

"Well, I'm famished. I won't be able to lift an arm without food in my stomach, let alone pick grapes for hours on end."

"Take up smoking," Jacaranda said. "It helps."

Eva shook her head, walked a few steps back then turned around abruptly. "Say good morning to Papi. He was calling for you earlier."

After Jacaranda put on her work clothes, she crept into her father's room. The dark smelled like wood polish and carpet deodorizer with the faint odor of rubbing alcohol and tamarisk spray. No dust ever settled in this room. Her mother saw to that. Jacaranda leaned forward to check if her father was awake. Her eyes adjusted quickly, but it was the heavy breathing that let her know he was asleep.

The first weeks he was bedridden were the hardest. They had to listen to his screaming, his *Save me, O Lord, for the waters have come up to my neck!* to his reasoning that his fall had been a punishment from God for attempting to climb toward His heavens on a palm tree. He cited the Tower of Babel and the Challenger space shuttle. The Twin Towers. Jacaranda and her mother prayed with him nightly until he became too weak to keep up with them, constantly dozing off at mid-prayer.

In August she was off to México. The summer in the grape was going to pay for her escape *like a bird out of the fowler's snare. Psalm 124.* Her father had spent years praying over her body after the incident. She pretended she was sleeping when he snuck into the room, Bible in hand, reciting the psalms in a whisper, prefacing each session with Ephesians, chapter 5, verse 19. *Speak to one another with psalms.* She learned to fall asleep to the murmur of his voice. She completed verses in her dreams. She was not allowed to speak to other boys, and later, other men. Even contact with the clumsy Sebastián was limited. Her father guarded her jealously. He had censored her Bible, removing Solomon's Song of Songs. But she had memorized it and at night while he prayed over her, she turned the song over and over in her head just to spite him. *Dark am I, yet lovely.* Not good enough. *Dark am I, and lovely.*

Jacaranda knelt next to her father, saddened that he would leave this world consumed by guilt. But there was nothing she could tell him. What had happened, had happened, and he had done it all to himself. If there were a psalm, or even a word she could pronounce that would exonerate him from that night he had covered her body with the painful weight of his mouth and hands, Jacaranda would not dare utter it. In fact, she would bite down on it—suck it back into her belly to let it starve.

When her father suddenly stirred, Jacaranda moved back into the shadows. He still frightened her sometimes, though he no longer loomed. He had become as silent as the big black book that lay beneath his pillow, and he was just as useless.

THE WEIGHT OF IT

Aníbal   5:00 a.m.

Half nude for comfort despite the cold dawn, <u>Aníbal</u>, lay prone beneath the sky with the early light shining down on the smoothness of the car hood and of his torso. He considered the hot tight flesh that reached far down his body, tracing the bones on his long feet. The toe tips were thin, flat as Popsicle sticks. Behind him, on top of another car, Carmelo turned in his sleep, his weight sinking into the metal so that the indentations popped back into place as soon as he shifted. All through the night it was pop! pop! pop! All through the night Carmelo's shirt buttons scratched the metal surface. Carmelo, all night.

The rare wind pushed the slightest of scents closer to Aníbal, as if he were the center of a funnel. The air smelled of sagebrush and motor oil. He smelled the men—all body sweat, foot odor, and breath. Aníbal knew their breath because it had to be as pungent as his.

The desert was large but the men gravitated to the same area. About a dozen shared the clearing with Aníbal. <u>Some of them slept in the open desert</u> to save money since the <u>grape-picking season in the Caliente Valley was only a few months brief</u>. Others spent the night because the late work hours made it impossible to complete the commute to places as distant as Mexicali on the Mexican border ninety miles south. Whatever the reason they kept each other company. One never knew.

"What time is it?" a voice called out.

"Almost five o'clock," another voice answered.

"It's getting late!" one man hooted. Then a brief chuckle rose from yet another.

One voice mumbled a question, another voice mumbled an answer. The sound of urine striking the soft sand came from two different sides of the clearing. Someone kicked his way through the nearby brush. The spurts of sound were signs that it was time to leave. Aníbal was always awake when the first men spoke up, anxious about heading back to the fields and anticipating the pit stop at Sosa's Market for gas, a quick breakfast of coffee and fruit pies, and a prepackaged sandwich for lunch. Aníbal heated the frozen burritos in the store microwave, and then wrapped them in foil. There was always a line, but it went quickly. Three men with each turn.

"Are you still dreaming?" a voice near him asked. Aníbal was about to answer when suddenly someone else spoke up: "I should be."

"I had a nightmare," the first voice said.

"And? Do you want me to come over and give you a hug?"

"Don't be a güey, cabrón, it was serious."

"What about?"

"It was a woman."

"Did you fuck her?"

"No, she only wanted me to lick it."

"Did you?"

"I did."

"So why was it a nightmare? Was it your mother?"

"Worse," the first man said. He paused, then delivered the punch line. "It was yours." Both men broke out into laughter.

"Can you believe those güeyes?" Carmelo said from the next car over.

Aníbal's body shook with a start despite Carmelo's gentle voice. He didn't want to meet Carmelo's eyes. Not yet.

"Did I scare you?"

"No," Aníbal said, sitting upright and reaching over to the car door for his shirt. "Well, yes. I didn't think you were—"

"Listening?" Carmelo interrupted.

"Awake," Aníbal said.

"I'm awake all right. Hard-on and everything."

Aníbal blushed. The urge to look at Carmelo was strong. He envisioned the jeans, the blue fading on the denim cloth over the zipper. Carmelo suddenly pounced out of sight and directed his attention to someone else. In seconds the clearing was a commotion. Each body shifted from one place to another. Aníbal rubbed his hands against his sides, impulsively identifying the men that moved around him: Carmelo, Germán, Lorenzo, Trujillo—no, that wasn't Trujillo. That was Salomón. Or was that Sinaloa? It didn't matter. They were all the same man with the same purpose: to work work work. One ignition went on, then another. Set after set of headlights lit up. Germán's car was getting jump-started as usual. The mufflers expelled white smoke so that the air became one huge cloud of dust and pollution. Even after he rolled the window up from inside his car, Aníbal smelled the exhaust of the running motors. Voices flew out and got lost. Aníbal thought he heard his name, but nothing was visible now except the glare of the lights. The first car drove off, followed by another. After that the cars set out in pairs.

Aníbal hadn't turned the engine on yet, a bad mistake. If the engine didn't run he'd be stuck in the clearing until the men returned from work, which could be anytime between the lunch break and midnight. He'd miss work. Naro and Jesse would have to pick up the hand scale and do his job. They'd do it, but with enough resentment to get him fired. A spark of amusement went off in the back of his head as he turned the ignition key.

He paused, realizing that Carmelo didn't stay behind today, nor did he wave good-bye. The static in his brain pulled out the memory of a childhood crush—Fernando from elementary school, who only wore clothes from the gringo side of the border, just like Aníbal. When he was thirteen Aníbal decided to reject his Christian name. Fernando was better. He practiced the signature on his school notebook, on the dirt as he sat next to the eucalyptus behind his house in Mexicali. The F was large, the foot shooting down like a spear. The two horizontal lines were also exaggerated in length, with the rest of the letters in that name perched like seven birds across the shorter line. Aníbal attempted to write the name on the dusty windshield, but failed because the dust was on the other side of the glass.

The engine worked fine. Aníbal shifted the stick into reverse, then into first gear and eased out of the clearing. He waited on the side of the highway for his turn. The grape picker rush hour was about to begin. By five-thirty Highway 86 heading toward Mecca at the tip of the Salton Sea was a zoo. Aníbal stepped on the gas, released the clutch and quickly shifted into first, second, then third, passing the date-tree farm, the grapefruit orchard, the first blocks of grape fields. When 86 came upon the tangerine he instinctively paid homage to the accident that had claimed the lives of a truckload of pickers. Most of them had carried false IDs like he did. Aníbal mused at the thought of dying, wearing the name on his fake green card: Juan Carlos Macías Leyva. Aníbal Pérez Ceballos would dissolve completely, the way he had wished for long ago when it pained him that he wasn't Fernando. Or at least with him.

The stop at Sosa's Market was swift. He missed most of his companions from the clearing because they didn't all work for the same crew, though they frequently saw each other in the fields, if only from a distance. As he drove on, the sun was only beginning to show over the Caliente Valley mountain range, seeping into the sky as if slowly burning out the dawn's dark blue. Car lights winding up the Chiriaco Summit of Highway 10 were fading; the salty prints of the alluvial fans were coming into focus. Aníbal wondered at how from a distance the grape fields were dwarfed by the desert hills. But as soon as he parked his car next to the blocks, he confirmed as he did every morning that the fields were actually enormous—it was he inside his little orange Celica that shrunk down to the size of a plum pit.

To estimate the length of this year's picking season, Aníbal turned over the figures in his head: Lozano's company owned forty blocks of table grapes, mostly Perlette, some Flame, a share of seedless Thompson and a private vineyard of Black Exotic. Each block averaged ten acres with one hundred rows per block. About fifty-two grapevines made up a row. There were a few half-blocks, some double blocks, and five crews—each crew employed around one hundred pickers and packers. The crew was divided into twenty-five to thirty groups—three or four people in a group. One annoying supervisor. Aníbal's crew got stuck with Merengue, the white man Spanish-speaker who claimed to have roots in the barrio, who happened to be Lozano's cousin. Merengue had his subordinates: the two foremen, Naro and Jesse, the taller Amanda, and Scaleboy, the lackey at the bottom of the pecking order. The crews got bigger and faster each year. They had already swept through Thermal, which grew the larger part of Lozano's crop. Aníbal calculated that the grape-picking season for those working for Lozano was going to last two more weeks at the most.

This season he planned to follow Carmelo to the grape route north, to the vineyards, where it was rumored the fields were cleaner and the weather less wearisome. There was talk from the men at the clearing that they would skip out early on the Caliente Valley. No matter what company you picked for the hours were now short and unpredictable, not like in the beginning of the season. The week before, the hours had picked up but that only gave them false hope. There was also talk that the United Farm Workers was organizing to protest all the non-union hires. Undoubtedly these rallies attracted la migra. The last thing Aníbal needed was an immigration official scrutinizing his falsified documents. They'd tear his green card up and throw him back to Mexicali that same afternoon. They'd tear him away from Carmelo.

He had resisted the urge to migrate north for years, choosing to return to Mexicali and hide out with Nana between seasons. But lately Carmelo had been more aggressive with his invitation, almost desperate. Accepting Carmelo's proposition would give him more distance from the border, from Jorge and Talina, and from his parents.

Aníbal slumped down on the vinyl seat, waving back at those workers who acknowledged him with a nod. Most of them distrusted him since he had taken his post. He had wanted to remind them that Merengue forced him to take the job after an immigration raid carted off the previous Scaleboy.

A group of men started a small bonfire, fueling it with dry tumbleweed that snapped with the flame and occasionally shot off sparks. Aníbal recognized los Caraballos. One of them was Puerto Rican, the other Mexican, but they looked alike—their faces long and dark, with the sides of their skulls narrowed in. They had horse faces—Caraballos for short. Like many, los Caraballos commuted from Mexicali every day, a two-hour drive. Four hours on the road a day. Twenty hours on the road in a week. Drive drive drive. Aníbal knew the hassle of a commute, especially on Fridays when everyone was anxious to get home to México. It was better to stay in the open desert after work, relaxing under the shade of a desert willow or a palo verde or even beneath a creosote bush, like a rattler.

"Hey, Scaleboy," Naro tapped on the car window. Aníbal looked up and raised his eyebrows.

"Well, open the fucking window! Am I going to talk through the glass like you're inside some goddamn ticket booth?" Naro was a big man, with a dark mustache that disappeared against his dark skin.

Aníbal rolled down the window. "What's up?"

"What's up is that the inspectors are finding the boxes a little too light on the scale, that's what. Are you aware we have a minimum weight requirement?"

Aníbal flipped through the numbers: twenty-three pounds in a carton box, twenty-six pounds in a wood box. That's without bags. Packed with bags, that's . . .

"Just make sure you're keeping an eye on all these lazy fucks." Naro pulled out a pack of cigarettes and lit one, offering Aníbal a smoke. Aníbal shook his head. "I'll be watching," Naro said, walking off. Aníbal rolled up the window.

Naro didn't commute from Mexicali; he commuted from El Centro on this side of the border. That worked out to half an hour less on the road each way. That was an hour less in a day, five hours less in a week. Naro came to work drunk too often. His temper was a big front for his hangover. He caused little damage. It was Amanda and Jesse who gave Aníbal a headache. They gave everyone headaches. He imagined them resting their cold hearts together in bed. They were perfectly matched like ice cubes in the freezer.

When Aníbal heard another tapping on the glass he expected to see Naro again, but was surprised to see Tinman the mute walking off. Tinman was los Caraballos' packer. He was six feet tall, with a white face that didn't redden in the sun. He was the stiff, pointy-nosed giant that reminded everyone of the metal guy from *El Mago de Oz,* and of that popular, silver-masked wrestler from Mexicali who wore a funnel for a hat. Tinman turned his head around suddenly and motioned to the opposite side with his chin. Through the rearview mirror, Aníbal watched Merengue's truck pull in with the water tanks and a load of brightly colored oversized umbrellas. A cargo truck followed closely with the shipment of metal packing tables, each with a single wheel at one end for easier transport on the sandy fields. The workers gathered to pick out materials.

Aníbal quickly rushed over to Merengue's truck, lunch sack in his pocket. He had to check that the hand scales worked properly. It was fifteen minutes past six o'clock and the crew would start work late again because of Merengue's delay. By seven o'clock it would be eighty-five degrees. By eight, ninety, then ninety-five, one hundred, one hundred five.

"Get the yellow umbrella, the yellow one's a good one," someone called out. Los Caraballos toot-tooted when they spotted Jacaranda and her sister walking into the fields.

Aníbal checked to see who it was but the voice was lost in a crowd of hats, bandannas, caps. Only Tinman stood out, hatless and towering above the rest.

The procession of ice chests, lunch bags, and radios turned the corner into the avenue of grapevines, where pallets of empty boxes awaited distribution. He hid his lunch behind the large soda chest Merengue hauled in the truck bed. He pulled the water tanks forward, the spigots facing out. The portable scales were stacked on the side. He took one and pressed down on the flat metal plate over the clock-like measurer. The pointer made one full circle. And when Aníbal removed his weight, the pointer jumped back to zero.

PART TWO

Viña

THAT R

Merengue   6:20 a.m.

Merengue relied on Naro to huddle the workers together before addressing them. He had to descend on all of them at once. He watched the crowd from a distance, making sure his balance was in check before approaching. The last thing he needed was to stumble or trip. He was the supervisor; he couldn't laugh it off the way any of them could. The walkie-talkie let out a spurt of static.

"Aijodesutamayamá!" Tamayamá's voice carried clearly though the avenue. Merengue had been spotted. He straightened his back and thrust his strong chin upward, showing confidence and dignity, like a rooster taking stock of its coop. If only he hadn't had his feathers ruffled the night before. He pushed his sunglasses up with his index finger knuckle and wiped the drop of sweat that lingered at the rim of the right lens. Tears and sweat were very different fluids, he concluded. When he sweated the drops felt heavy, reluctantly making their way down the sticky skin. But tears sprung off the face, anxious and hasty. Sweat slipped like a chunk of fat on the grill; tears exploded like firecrackers.

Last night at Tati's funeral he had been reluctant to grieve the way he wanted to, unsure of what was permissible for a non-blood relation. Until last night he thought he knew who Tati was and what Tati knew of him. This morning he woke up brain-heavy with the D.T.s, still furious at Tati's betrayal. All night he thought about Arrocito, his childhood pet. For weeks his new puppy endeared itself to him, cuddling close at night and nipping at his toes in the mornings, eager for attention. Then one day, on the dog's first time out of the house, Merengue released it from his arms and Arrocito seized the opportunity to run and run until his high-pitched barking diminished into a permanent silence.

Merengue felt a rumbling in his stomach, so he sidestepped behind a wall of lush vines and slowly crouched down in case he vomited. The bile coated his throat, but nothing more. He spat. He looked sideways, bent down low enough to see the field of grapevines from a different angle: row after row of trunks with the barks slightly peeling; the ground look unsullied, beautiful. He wondered how many of these bastards who owned these blocks had even taken the time to appreciate the precision of the spacing. He spat again, rose, temples throbbing, and continued down the path toward the workers. En route, he straightened the hat that completely covered his blond curls. He adjusted his sunglasses, exposing his light-sensitive eyes for one brief moment, enough to make him squint. His eyes were blue. Rarely did he allow any of the workers to see them. Even when the crew was sent to the warehouse and night fell he kept the glasses fixed to the bridge of his nose.

As more people turned to face him, Merengue called out "Merengue!" signaling the workers to get to work. "Send the boys over!" he added. As he searched for a few grape samples from a nearby vine, the walkie-talkie at his hip pocket broke out into more bursts of static.

"School for escuintles!" Naro yelled with one hand cupped over his mouth. "Send over your goddamn brats!"

The older workers took over the gathering of the boxes and box cushions, and the packing set-ups at the ends of the rows. The boys gathered around the supervisor, each barely distinguishable from the other beneath baseball cap visors and bandannas that flowed down from the caps, kepi style, to protect their necks and ears.

"Pay attention!" Naro called out. The boys moved in closer. The ones standing in the back stretched out their necks.

"See this?" Merengue lifted a bunch of grapes up in the air. His forearm was thick, with wiry yellow hair crawling up to the freckles on the knuckle. "If they're this big, just clean them up. Like this." He snipped away at the bottoms with a pair of clippers. "If the bunches are any smaller than this, leave them on the vine. If I see anyone of you sticking something like this in a box—" Merengue showed them a second bunch; the Perlette was small, round, and green, and to inexperienced eyes there was only one shade of green, not ripe green and green green—"you get to stay home to watch cartoons."

The more confident boys let out a chuckle.

"Okay," Merengue said over the static of the walkie-talkie, "Merengue."

"Back to work," Naro said.

"Did you get a good look at those shirts on doña Pepa's boys?" Merengue asked. "Are they trying to be comedians?"

"I'm watching those little clowns closely," Naro answered. "I catch them goofing off I pull them out by the ass hairs."

Merengue grabbed Naro by the arm and pulled him aside before he could leave. "One more thing," he said. Naro leaned over to listen carefully. "There are rumors going around that the Chavistas are organizing a strike."

"A strike? Here? But we only hire non-union labor," Naro said.

"And that's why. They're already causing problems for Freeman. Lozano's afraid they'll come here next."

"These people are loyal to us, you'll see," Naro said.

"You can never be too sure. They see those red UFW flags flying around in the field and they get carried away. You know how these people are."

"Not to worry. We know how to handle them. Did you tell Jesse and Amanda?"

"That's your job. But be discreet." Merengue let go of Naro's arm.

After Naro took his place along the row of packers, Merengue shut off the walkie-talkie. If headquarters wanted to reach him, Naro or Jesse would let him know. He didn't want to hear from that nose-picker cousin of his, not while he was trying to sober up from last night's drinking binge after the funeral.

He walked absent-mindedly through the dirt path, a row of vines on either side of him. Jesse and Amanda would keep the workers in line. That's why he asked for that pair of stingers year after year, for days like this when he couldn't focus. He paused in front of one of the groups and blindly rummaged through a box don Manuel was already packing.

"Your women do fine work!" Merengue said loud and clear for the benefit of the partially deaf don Manuel.

"Only one of them is my woman. The other belongs to someone else, no matter what you've heard," don Manuel responded with a sly smile.

Merengue laughed, let go of the grape and walked away. The Mexicans joked with him but they distrusted him. That was all right. It was part of the job not to be trusted, though he suspected much of that came from his being white and being fluent in Spanish. He was almost like one of them. He had even married into their kind, and Sara had turned out to be as money-hungry as his white ex-wife. Twice as fertile. Now he was going broke paying child support for the half-breeds as well. About the only good that came out of that second marriage was that Sara's cousin Arturo Lozano offered him this comfortable position with his company. He had no previous experience, but it didn't take a genius to identify ripe fruit and to herd Mexicans around like cattle.

"Merengue!" he yelled out. It relieved his stress.

"Merengue!" one of los Caraballos responded, then let out a shrill whistle.

"Merengue!" another voice echoed.

They had named him Merengue, too long ago to be bothered about it anymore. He had been angry at first, trying to figure out who and why. He even sent out Jesse and Amanda to spread the rumor that he was offering a three-hundred-dollar reward for that information, but no one came forward, except for Jesse and Amanda, who only offered suspicions and speculations. So he decided to keep the nickname he couldn't get rid of, using it as a signature expression. How much more Mexican could he get?

Merengue was better than his previous nickname, the one Tati gave him when he was a child. He loved being called Tato because he thought it was a derivative of his Mexican grandmother's nickname. She was really his babysitter, but Tati held him in her arms the same way she held her brown grandchildren—pressing him into her flesh, swallowing him up, and protecting him.

There were so many reasons to love Tati. She cooked from

scratch, she had perfected his Spanish, shown him to appreciate a spicy Oaxacan sauce as much as the sound of a trilled r. She taught him to eat ice cream on a stick and still keep his hands clean. Tato moved away from Gringo, Fantasma, Güero, Bolillo, Gavacho— the snot-nosed kid from the trailer-park white-trash Lockwoods who spent their welfare on booze and GPCs and who made him eat pasta from a can every day. By the time his alcoholic mother had noticed he was not around much, Tato had all but moved in with the brown people.

At Tati's wake, it was all Mexicans. Tía Elvira threatened to throw herself into the grave. The old women from the neighborhood pulled out their rosaries and came over in an invasion of black that draped most of the floor. The men drank all night and he was allowed to join them since he was, after all, a part of Tati's life. He even attempted to contribute a Tati story of his own, standing against the wall like the rest of the men, a row of beer cans glaring with the streetlight.

"She named me Tato, you know," he said, teary-eyed, his tone heavy with sorrow.

Out of the darkness he heard a burst of laughter. Celedonio, one of Tati's true grandchildren, stepped out of the shadow of a pickup, wiping the beer froth off his lips.

Merengue was shaken. "What's so funny?"

"You dumbfuck," Celedonio said. "You stupid, stupid dumbfuck."

The men turned to Merengue, who felt as if he had been pushed. "What the hell's the matter with you, Celedonio?" A few men tried to muffle their laughter, but not too hard.

"Dumbfuck! Don't you know why she named you that?"

Merengue's face tingled. He racked his brain trying to fit some logic into Celedonio's words.

"Remember that TV midget, Tattoo? Tati pronounced it Tato. She named you Tato because you lisped!"

When the men erupted into a commotion of jeers and laughter, Merengue stormed off amid Celedonio's drunken imitation of *De plen, both! De plen!*

Merengue stopped in the middle of the dirt avenue to set his watch alarm for nine o'clock, lunch hour. Lunch half-hour to be precise, that's all they needed. Mexicans were a people with endurance. Tati did the cooking until she could no longer hold a soup spoon. She had been worn out. She had given up the task of setting apart brown face from white face, frequently mistaking Merengue for one of her grandchildren. Secretly, it pleased him, though there was always someone like Celedonio around to point out her mistake. Leaving the wake hurt twice as much as going to it. Merengue's body quivered all through the night from the anger. And to make things worse this goddamn strike was sneaking up behind him. All he needed now was for those Chavistas to show up to the fields to poke fun at him, a white man walking among Mexicans. They were all the same in the end: unforgiving and cruel.

"Merengue!" he called out. His gringo accent crept into the r but it didn't hurt to say it so he said it again, "Merengue!"

RIGOBERTO
GONZÁLEZ

CHINGADA

Chela   7:45 a.m.

"Merengue. What merengue? I don't know about you, Francisca, but this is the last time I work for this chingada company. The very last time. No more, never, nothing. I'm joining up with the union, too. Get my due," Chela said, clearing a space in front of a grapevine.

Francisca was hidden on the other side by the long growths of branches and leaves. "You say that every season, Chela," she said.

Chela pushed the box against the irrigation tube sticking out of the wet sand on the ground. She bent down to peek at Francisca but only managed to see pink leg warmers covered with foxtails and green clusters of nettles.

"Yes, yes, but this time I mean it. By the heat of el chingado sun I mean it," Chela said. "This entire week we started almost an hour after all the other crews, that gives us one less hour of morning weather. Not to mention a smaller paycheck. It's bad enough the hours stink like goat piss. And I've got a town full of ungrateful sisters that won't look after my kids for free, so I take the kids to daycare, might as well. You know how expensive daycare is nowadays?"

"My daycare burdens were over ages ago, thank God," Francisca said.

Chela straightened up and continued picking, recalling the scene at the daycare center at dawn: car after car pulled in, dropping off each child wrapped in a warm blanket, tight as a taquito. A single mother, Chela took two of them. Her third, Lucita, walked herself to the summer school migrant education program a few hours after Chela left for work, a heavy key knocking against her breastbone as she skipped to school. By three o'clock in the afternoon, the neighbor, a reluctant babysitter, gathered them all up until Chela got home.

Chela stuck the clippers in her back pocket, and then balanced the box overflowing with grapes on her head as she walked to the end of the row, to the packer beneath the umbrella. Conversation pauses lasted only until she finished dropping off a load, or until one woman asked the other if she had an empty box on her side, or until both women agreed to take a water break, or a pee break—especially a pee break since the portable toilets were always far away and it took two to get motivated to make the long trip. Chela had made her complaint repeatedly, but the gringo supervisor and his peon foremen wouldn't know the strain of walking to the end of the block since they could just stick their peckers into any of the vines and get it over with. She had even approached Amanda about the matter but that woman probably pissed standing up by the way she just kept scribbling in her little notebook as if Chela had suggested a shuttle service. But as soon as the end-of-the-season party preparations began, there was fat Amanda, chingado notebook in her hand and a *What are you going to be bringing for us?* crawling out her grin because she played administrator and all the other women were the volunteer cooks, chingados aprons and all.

Valentín picked at the vines behind the packing cart to complete a box. As soon as he saw Chela he removed the empty box from the metal table to make room.

"How are the grapes farther in?" he asked.

"It's a good crop," Chela said. "How about in the end?"

"Chingado. It's going to get time-consuming clearing off this part, so as soon as you two work your way here go on ahead to another row. I'll finish up, otherwise we won't make anything out of piecework."

Aníbal stopped to level the hand scale on the loose sand. He took a packed box from the stack and weighed it.

"How are we doing, Scaleboy?" Valentín asked.

"Perfect," Aníbal responded, then walked away.

"How many hours did we put in last week?" Chela asked.

Valentín pulled out a flattened paper cup he used as a record book and read off his entries: "Eight hours on Monday, five and a half on Tuesday, a full day on Wednesday plus six at the warehouse. Only four on Thursday."

"And nothing on Friday," said Chela, dusting off an empty box as she picked it up.

"It's still better than this week."

"I'm not counting on this week to afford me a piece of paper to blow my nose, chingado," Chela said.

Chuckling, Valentín turned to pack the new load. Chela headed back to the middle of the row, mumbling to herself. If the hours kept getting shaky, she was going to have to pull out of the group. She hated to do that, but if she was spending all her paycheck on daycare and thank-you bonuses for the neighbor she might as well stay home and look after the kids herself.

Lucita was the one who worried her the most, waking up each morning after the rest of the family had disappeared. Lucita had been the one to call her teacher Mami, which nearly gave Chela a heart attack because Chela had thought Lucita was referring to her in the third person whenever she pointed to something at K-Mart and said, "That's for Mami. Buy that for Mami."

Once, at Lucita's request, Chela bought a two-dollar music box. "Are you giving that to Mami?" Chela asked her, coyly.

Lucita nodded. "Yes," she said. "Tomorrow at school."

Teacher had become Mami.

Chela wanted to be part of her daughter's schooling but las chingadas teachers all thought the Mexican mothers backward, especially after that school uniform debate which wasn't Chela's idea but it sure made sense to her since it worked for México all those years. Those teachers were just like Amanda, women who spoke as if they were squeezing the words out through a straw and who only came around shining polite and nice during potluck planning when they needed someone to sweat it out in the kitchen.

Chela repositioned herself where she left off. She pulled out the clippers and started cutting, then grinning. She had taught them a lesson though, right after the time all the better-off kids got the giant inflatable pool and all the farm workers' kids got the water hose because the pool belonged to some uppity chingada mother who didn't like the way the chicken pox scars shone on brown skin. So the very next time Lucita came home with one of those homemade dish requests for the PTA meeting, Chela gave them what they deserved: a *mole poblano* with enough laxative in the sauce to make those teachers flush the next two school terms out of their chingadas nalgas! Chela couldn't keep from laughing out loud.

"What's so funny?" Francisca asked.

Chela plucked a grape out of a bunch and bit into it to coat her dry mouth. "My mischief," she answered, letting go of another burst of laughter.

"There must be plenty of it," Francisca said.

"I know where to crack my walnuts," Chela said. She stepped back to stretch. After the picking season she was taking a few months of unemployment insurance until the date-packing company was ready for her. When that ended she'd seek out the carrot and corn warehouses. The breaks between jobs were Lucita's time, and Pablito's and Little Mickey's. They were going to have their good schooling despite the rumors that no children of Mexicans were going to get free school anymore. Chingados administrators! They said many things but accomplished so few, locked up in their air-conditioned offices and going from one building to the next encased in their car coffins.

"Don't think too much, Chela," Francisca spoke up, breaking up Chela's train of thought. "Keep your hands going, not your head."

"How about my mouth?"

"If you don't use your fingers to open and shut it, go ahead."

The flashes of conversation were not enough to lighten Chela's mood. She was here to prove even the social security workers wrong, but chingado, it was getting harder every year: more restrictions, more paperwork, more cutbacks, and the same bug-eyed secretaries looking down at her as if she'd just gotten off the sofa long enough to walk her overfed nalgas to the welfare office. They treated her like she made those three babies all by herself, *Why don't you find yourself a man and keep your ass out of government assistance!* their typewriter keys seemed to scream when they struck the application, *Go back to your man!* her sisters advised, as if that would solve anything. Sometimes she wished she had made her kids all by herself just to avoid meeting up with that no-good wetback that used the children as a round-trip ticket to her bed.

A few days ago Cirilo came knocking on her door, sweet as a Tootsie Roll, with a smile on his face so thin, she could read the need for sex on his teeth. But she straightened him out fast: she gave him the usual rosary of chinga, chingar, and chingados, leaving him outside to stare down the porch with those droopy eyes of his that wanted the door to take pity on him and open up all by itself. That shameless mierda came by pretending he was concerned about Little Mickey and his case of measles. It's true what they say: when bad shit arrives he brings his whores with him. That same night she was treating Little Mickey with an itch-relieving ointment, coloring in the measles so that they wouldn't scar when the boy scratched, when all of a sudden he blacked out for a second and fell face first on the rug. She couldn't figure out who panicked last because before she knew it she was running out with a screeching child, all four limbs flailing against her arms all the way to the hospital. Of course, those doctors must specialize in white children because as soon as she brought in her afflicted brown child they couldn't figure out that the thermometer goes up the asshole and the Popsicle stick goes into the throat. She might as well have been given a Band-Aid and vitamin tablet for all the good their diagnosis did. "Just keep an eye on him," they said and patted him on the head. For once she wished she had given birth to a rabid Rottweiler and not a boy.

But enough was enough. By the end of the season she was going north to the cooler climates. Far from that thorn in her brain named Cirilo and closer to better job opportunities. She needed to show her children there was work outside of the fields. Maybe in the hotels or in the kitchens. A different kind of burden no doubt, but different nonetheless. Come August they were out of there like cats with firecrackers tied to their tails. Oh yes, grape picking ended here in the Caliente Valley and with her, Chela la Chingada.

"Che-la?"

Chela lowered her head to find Francisca's eyes through the leaves.

"I think I'm about ready to water the end of the block," Francisca said.

"Merengue better watch out then," Chela said, putting her clippers away in her back pocket. "I'm letting loose the second flood."

On their way out Francisca stopped to whisper to Valentín that they were headed for the toilets. Valentín nodded once and stuck to his task.

"You've been quieter than usual," Francisca said, as soon as they were out of earshot. Francisca walked with a slight limp, dragging one pink nettle-covered leg along.

"You know," Chela said.

"The kids?" Francisca said. Chela nodded.

"I need to spend more time with them before I turn around and they don't even recognize me. Even the babysitter can locate their birthmarks faster than I can."

"You need Cirilo to help you out, Chela, like it or not. If you're going to do this alone you're going to wear yourself so thin, your children are going to see right past you. I mean, you suffer because you want to. Your man is standing right over there." Francisca pointed at Cirilo with her pair of clippers.

Chela chuckled, "I'm done spreading my legs for that son-ofabitch, I'll tell you that, Francisca."

"Then find yourself another. Children need a father, and a woman can't live without a man. We come in pairs, see? Like the portables ahead. Man and Woman," Francisca said, pleased with her analogy.

"Chingado," Chela muttered, studying the two stalls locked together at the base. Dependency is what Francisca was getting at. Everyone wanted to make her dependent on a man, and that burned the hairs right off her chin. She couldn't imagine Cirilo or any man matching her role in the sturdy and upright partnership of Francisca's vision. There was no husband, there was no father, there was only Chela, the real Mami. And those two portable toilet stalls up ahead, in this light, at that distance, squinting the way she was doing now, Chela envisioned a bikini top flat on the sand with the cups facing skyward—keeping her red self company.

SILENCE

Don Manuel   8:15 a.m.

Refusing to wear a hearing aid allowed don Manuel to block out the noise around him and to concentrate on his task, but not even the partial deafness could lessen the pitch of the declaration he had made the night before: *Joaquín Murrieta was, has always been, and forever will be exclusively Mexican.* It rattled in his brain as he walked to the water tank to fill his canteen, then it distracted him when he asked to borrow box cushions from Group 23, and now it followed him back to the packing table.

Don Manuel's youngest son Leonardo attended that fancy school in Los Angeles, and each time he came home on vacation from classes he brought with him some crazy idea those Chicano professors had put between his ears. Last Easter it was about questioning the church, its holy mystery of Juan Diego and la Virgen de Guadalupe. "It was just a ploy the Spanish missionaries used to convert los indios to Catholicism," Leonardo had said, expecting him to believe it just like that because some intellectual had declared it in a stuffy room at the university.

"It's a phase," his wife Ramona said. She protected him. "All the college kids go through it, look at Pepa's grandsons," she said; "it's a Chicano thing."

Don Manuel had let it go, but not after a good finger-shaking warning about blasphemy. True, they didn't attend mass on Sundays, but that didn't mean he was out of reach of the wrath of God. This time around Leonardo had his mother roaming the house with a tape recorder and talking nonsense in the early morning hours. If Ramona encouraged her son's tarugadas that was her business, but he was damned if he was going to let Leonardo ruin his peace of mind. As soon as he drove in from the university Leonardo started rummaging through his briefcase, plucking out paper after paper and scattering every document all over the place like a stack of corn husks for tamales. And just last night he tossed this precious jewel across the dinner table: "Joaquín Murrieta might have been from Chile."

Don Manuel adjusted his heavy glasses and tipped his hat forward, unfolding the cushion in place to complete the final box he was going to pack from this row. He fitted one bunch at a time, holding the grapes in place with his left hand as he filled the box with his right, careful not to shine the grape. A swift, steady hand never rubbed the sulfur off the fruit so that it looked untouched. The stems all pointed down, except for one row of three, carefully spaced from top to bottom and evenly spaced apart. When the inspector opened the lid, he'd be struck by the meticulousness of the packing. But how to explain this sense of fulfillment to an overgrown schoolboy that college had turned into a vegetarian?

First impressions were critical to prospective buyers. Don Manuel took pride in his work because he knew that he contributed to a process that climaxed at the warehouse, where the company owners and corporate representatives finalized all transactions. He was present at the weight test, the sugar-level test, the aesthetic value test, the tension and disappointment when the first few samples failed inspection. The entire cargo had to be unloaded and spread out across the expanse of the warehouse floor to be repacked in time for the second inspection. If the next round of samples passed, the pleased expressions on the sellers and buyers were contagious enough to make even the weary don Manuel breathe in, then let out a deep sigh with satisfaction because he had done his part toward that success. The workers restacked the entire shipment back on the pallets and went home, a little more fatigued, but congratulated for a job well done.

On Fridays don Manuel snuck a little grape out in the ice chest to share in the celebration of a good harvest. He liked to enjoy a nice bunch of salted grapes while watching *Cristina* on the television. But at this too, Leonardo had found cause to object.

"*I* support the boycott," Leonardo said in response to an offer of grapes.

Don Manuel clarified the situation for his son: "*I* picked these grapes myself, pendejo!" Eating the bowl by himself wasn't as satisfying, especially with Leonardo looking on from the kitchen.

"You're falling behind, Manuelito!" Ninja called out through the cigarette in his mouth. Ninja wheeled the packing table forward to catch up to his group, something don Manuel now prepared to do as he gathered his materials: spare boxes, cushions, extra grape, umbrella, clippers, a pencil for keeping a work record, the cross-shaped bag hook in case a shipment called out for bagged grape, his canteen and, of course, the spare ice chest he kept full of beer.

Tamayamá squeezed through the vines. "Hey, don Manuel," he whispered.

Don Manuel pulled his glasses forward.

"Leave me a you-know-what before you go." Tamayamá held out a dollar bill through the leaves. Don Manuel looked around, and finding it safe he took out a beer and slipped it to Tamayamá.

"Aijodesutamayamá!" Tamayamá said and then snuck back out of sight.

Suddenly a second figure stuck his head out through the vines, a set of eyes poking through like two wet fish heads. Tinman. Don Manuel rubbed his thumb and index finger together but Tinman simply withdrew back under the vines.

"Safado," don Manuel said under his breath. He stepped out of the row to pull the packing table out, turned it around facing the direction of the crew, then pushed past Group 25, past Naro and Merengue, past Group 7, past the beeping cargo truck, past Group 16 where he paused to say hello to Felipe and Felipe's boy, past Group 12, and so forth until he reached the sign Ramona had propped up at the end of the row's post marker: the number 10 written at the bottom of the box, using the juice from a grape and a handful of dirt.

He pulled out his canteen and took a long swig. Tinman passed by with his own packing table, looking down at don Manuel with narrowed eyes.

"Safado," don Manuel repeated under his breath as he set up the table. There was no simpler way to say it. That bookworm Tinman was definitely a few beads short of a rosary. Don Manuel worried that Leonardo would end up that way with all that schooling since it was a known fact that too much education made a person crazy. Like Macario el Memorizador back in Jaramillo, Michoacán. Macario was always chosen to speak at the dieciséis de septiembre school assembly because he was the only one who didn't need to read a speech out of a paper, stumbling over the printed words. He had such an awesome memory. He recited lists from the catechism as well as from the periodic chart—by elemental order no less. He was fought over by opposing teams during Sunday afternoon rote tournaments at la parroquia. Over the years don Manuel never bothered to verify which list of virtues had five entries: the theological or the cardinal? But then, Macario wouldn't be able to either, not after having pursued a promising career as a student of law. Macario studied and memorized, studied and memorized, until one day he started wandering through the streets, chewing on his books and talking gibberish, mixing up the words in his mouth with the words on the pages. After that he ceased being Macario el Memorizador and became the man people pointed to with apprehension, whispering the warning: "That's what happens when you stuff too many things into your head."

All set up, don Manuel began to pack the boxes his wife and doña Gertrudis had already picked before he arrived. He glanced over to the packer behind him, and determining that he'd match the stack in no time, he couldn't help whistling with delight.

"Moving along," Felipe said as he passed by with the packing table. Behind him his wife Mariana carried the ice chest.

"Moving along, don Manuel!" Felipe repeated.

Don Manuel heard his name. "Felipe! Moving along?"

"There's no other way," Felipe said.

When don Manuel saw Felipe's boy pass by with a high stack of empty boxes, he nodded in approval. Watching the younger boys at work gave don Manuel a pang of nostalgia—a longing for the days his own sons worked side by side with him, as he had done with their grandfather. Don Manuel understood times had changed. Leonardo was the youngest of his children and had never worked a day of his life in the fields. But Leonardo had built up resentment toward something he knew nothing about. Even worse, Leonardo wanted to educate him about what life in the fields was really all about—exploitation of labor, oppression of the farm worker, violation of workers' rights. Pendejadas!

Leonardo was an intelligent boy, but stupid in many ways: he could fill out an income tax form and find the lowest fares down to Guadalajara on that small computer contraption of his, but the boy couldn't light a grill with a gallon of gasoline and a blow torch. He didn't know how to tune a guitar, or how to tinker with a car engine. Most of his visits home coincided with the times his little red Nissan truck was due for a tune-up or an oil change. For years he had been trying to coax Leonardo into learning to replace a spark plug, but to Leonardo that wasn't as important as spreading those books open like a pair of hands and reading the palms for hours on end like a hypnotized gypsy.

"You should read more often and watch less television," Leonardo, book in hand, advised don Manuel before dinner last night.

Don Manuel ignored him. His legs were stretched out and the remote control rested safely on the reclining chair's armrest. On the screen, Cristina was interviewing male cross-dressers.

"It dulls your brain and it's bad for your eyes," Leonardo persisted. In the kitchen two pots were cooking: one with beef picadillo, the other with Korean noodles—a food Leonardo had attempted to introduce to the family but which had disgusted don Manuel because it tasted like soggy celery.

"Besides," Leonardo continued. "Can we really trust what television tells us? Why do we believe everything we hear, especially from that Cristina Saralegui and her ridiculous program? I mean, look at that? Who watches that?"

Don Manuel yelled out with a burst of energy that made Leonardo drop his book. "*I* do! *I* watch that show. This is *my* house and *my* time to relax and those jotetes are prancing around in heels just for me. I don't have the energy or desire to sit around reading books after my long days. You would know that if you knew anything about work in the fields."

"Manuel, what's happening?" his wife called out from the porch.

"Breathe in deeply, Pa," Leonardo said, using hand gestures to coach his father's rhythm. "I've got the perfect herbal tea for high blood pressure. Don't move!"

"Tea? Tea? Do me an even greater favor and get me another beer!"

"Herbal tea can take care of alcohol dependency as well!"

Don Manuel took a step back from the packing table and stretched. His hands appeared to reach so far away from his body that for a moment they didn't look like his hands. On a hot day like this last summer when everyone's strength was slowly draining the foreman announced that the shipment they were packing was headed for Canada. The news pumped new life into the crew because now the fruit had a specific destination, they weren't simply filling box after box to be stored and haggled over at the warehouse. They had a larger goal, a bigger purpose, and that made all the difference. How could Leonardo understand something like that?

He brought down his hands and considered the liver spots, the dark, leathery skin on one side, and the calluses thickened between the grooves of the joints on the other. Leonardo's hands were smooth as book covers, his face tight and unscarred by the hardships of the fields. Leonardo didn't know horsepower from horseshit but that didn't keep his mouth shut. So when he said to him in the spirit of good dinner table conversation, *Pa, I read this article that claims Joaquín Murrieta might have been from Chile*, it was just one sentence too much, one pendejada too many. Don Manuel had used those hands to reach across the table, his fingers trembling when he flung his body forward, his heart heavy with regret when he shredded those words to pieces inside Leonardo's mouth.

CUT

Doña Ramona   8:35 a.m.

Manuel was working with a pair of eyes, a pair of hands, a tight-lipped mouth, and no ears. Not much disrupted the mechanical way he packed the grapes into the shipping boxes, except a bee buzzing around his line of vision and even then only when it finally landed on the rim of his hat. Doña Ramona watched him weave the quick swatting motion into the rhythm of his hands. She felt shooed away herself when she asked twice, "Do you want some more water in your canteen or something?" and he kept at his task in front of the shaky packing table. She turned to doña Gertrudis in her orange hard hat making her way back to end of the row. She was still within earshot but she didn't feel like raising her voice so doña Ramona decided to wait until their next shipment drop to get water. A few steps forward she glanced at the pocket watch around her neck and changed her mind, turning back toward the avenue subversively, without her best friend and without her husband. The pocket watch dangling from her neck pressed against her chest like a medal. And although this act startled her at first she liked the taste of it and washed it down with the first gulp of water from the tank.

Chela and Francisca came up behind doña Ramona. Chela surprised her with a soft jab on her side with the handle tips of the clippers.

"Leave some for us, doña," Chela said; she sat on the lowered tailgate to take her drink.

"Is that how you spend the day, behaving like a water pipe?" doña Ramona said.

"I don't understand you, Ramoncita," Francisca said.

"You know," doña Ramona said. "Sucking it in through one end and then flushing it out through the other."

"Doña Ramona," Chela said, giggling uncontrollably. "I didn't know your clippers were that sharp."

After taking her drink of water, Francisca suddenly reflected out loud: "It's so hot this morning. I should have stayed home."

"And why didn't you?" Chela said just before she sneezed.

"Bless you," doña Ramona said. The three women started walking back to the rows of grapevines. All along the avenue the stacks of packed boxes were quickly growing tall.

"Neither of you have to come if you don't want to," Chela persisted. "I don't know why you put yourself through this chingado heat. You should stay home and learn to knit or something." Chela pointed down at Francisca's leg warmers. "You could make yourself a nicer pair than those pink rags you have there."

"That's Mexican women in México, Chela," doña Ramona said; "we're Mexican women in the United States of America."

"Then maybe we should dye our hair blonde at least," Francisca said.

"Not that!" said Chela. "Then we would have to marry gringos and learn to have sex with the lights off or else go blind."

Doña Ramona shook her head in amusement as she separated from Chela and Francisca who ducked into their row. Valentín nodded to her as she passed by, and so did don Nico, Felipe, and a few of the other packers as she made her way to her row. The foremen were whispering to each other and looked suspiciously at her from the corner of their eyes. She looked down at her pocket watch. It was then that she realized she might have taken too long at the water tanks. She sensed the other women scrutinizing and mumbling behind their bandannas, glaring and shifting their eyes at each other like thieves in complicitous agreement: there she was, the lazy one—the one who shoved onions and tomatoes into one of those fancy dicing machines. When was the last time she cut her finger chopping vegetables? When was the last time she held a knife?

She could show them all her cuts: from the caesarian to the scar on her head. Better yet she could show them who had caused them. There in one room was Leonardo, born nineteen years ago and still a pain in her side sometimes. And there in the other room was Manuel, still a headache after all this time. Leonardo was too young to remember and the others were now old enough to forget how Manuel used to come in late at night, all fury and fists. She had called her mother in México the morning after she woke up on the kitchen floor, her head wound clotted but still on fire. Her left cheek was numb from having been pressed to the cold tile all night. A few feet beside her the rolling pin lay defeated with a thin stain of blood and a hair stuck to it shaped into a grin.

"And what do you want me to do, pendeja?" her mother had replied. "You married him. Now hang up before you get another whack on the skull for making such an expensive call!"

She had expected her mother of all people to be more understanding, especially since she was married to a violent drunkard herself. Maybe her mother could share with her those magic words or that miraculous prayer that made the suffering tolerable. Instead all she got was a dial tone that drilled a painful accusation in her ear: she had married him.

When she reached Manuel he looked at her with scorn. "What did you do, dig the water well yourself? Doña Gertrudis already brought me another box and I can hear you laughing away with that chingada welfare mother all the way over here."

"I'm here already, aren't I?" doña Ramona snapped back nervously. She picked up an empty box. Dissatisfied with its condition, she tossed it aside and chose another.

"What's the matter with you?" her husband asked. She didn't answer.

The Sunday after he had knocked her unconscious with a blow to the head, she waited for him at the door, rolling pin in hand. She hadn't washed the stain off the wood, though the hair had fallen off on its own. As soon as he stumbled in, ready to bark orders and raise his hand when they were not executed fast enough for his taste, she swung the rolling pin with both hands and struck him dead center in the ear. Had he not collapsed she had planned on taking a swing at his other side as well, but that first hit had floored him for the night and well into the next morning. His hearing was never the same since. Neither was his urge to lash out with violence. Last night with Leonardo was one exception. And deep down in the recesses of her love for her youngest born, it pained her to admit that perhaps he had it coming. Still, the wrath in her husband's hand had been temporarily shaken awake, and it had made her nervous.

"Ramona," doña Gertrudis said in greeting. "You're not the same this morning."

"Too much in my head," doña Ramona said.

"It's not good to think too much in the sun," doña Gertrudis warned, "makes your brain boil over like beef stew."

Doña Ramona liked that metaphor and made a mental note to tell Leonardo's little black box about it. She suddenly remembered his most recent unusual request.

"Oh, I've got something special planned for us today, Gertrudis," doña Ramona said.

"A story?"

"Maybe later," doña Ramona said. "But we're going to have us some fun doing this." She ducked down and pretended to snap a photograph from an imaginary camera.

"Santos cielos," doña Gertrudis said. "And won't your husband get angry?"

Doña Ramona dismissed doña Gertrudis's concern with a wave of the hand. Of course her husband might get angry and so what? What was he going to do, hit her? Those days were so long gone they might as well have happened to someone else. In some other country even. What did she care what Manuel or anybody else thought or said? In the end she had the upper hand.

Now on the occasional Sunday afternoon, Manuel asked that she clip the hairs in his ear. Coarse and black, they were almost obscene, but he rested his head on her lap anyway and waited patiently. She used the barber scissors, long and sharp as an ice pick, and guided the tip carefully inside his ear. Open and snip. Open and snip. The sound was so fine it made her cringe. It bothered her even more to know her husband couldn't hear the metal blades grating. It was as if he didn't recognize the danger of the delicate procedure. Had she been any less skillful, any less calculating, she could cause irreparable damage. Indeed, an accidental jabbing could make him permanently deaf, or even kill him. She imagined the ear canal led directly into the internal tissue of the skull—the vulnerable brain perhaps.

To test her theory, doña Ramona reached into the vine and

plucked a bunch so tight it was almost a knot. She held it in place against her thigh as she pushed the blades of the grape-cutting clippers into the center. She ruptured the skins of the outer layer and immediately the juice began to scurry down her pant leg. Suddenly she couldn't stop herself and pushed the clippers farther in until she felt the sharp pain of the tip digging into her flesh. She imagined the blood leaking out to mix with the grape juice, a thick consistency that was both sweet and bitter.

THE GOOD SON

Severo   9:00 a.m.

When Hernán came up to drop off a load of grapes, Severo was about to tell him to lift the box up on the packing table when a bunch of grapes came flying out through the vines, striking Hernán on the side of the face. Ernesto, who had remained hidden until then, popped his head up over the vines, cackling with laughter. Severo chuckled. Hernán wiped the juice off his face, picked up an empty box and walked away in silence. Ernesto came around the vines with another load. "Merengue, merengue, merengue," he mocked.

"Just don't make him cry again," Severo said. "He'll slow us down."

"Don't worry about it, all right," Ernesto snapped back.

Severo cleared the table and Ernesto placed the box neatly along the metal frame, making the table wobble.

"How much longer before lunch?" Ernesto asked, licking the sweat off his mustache.

Severo looked at his watch. "You still have half an hour."

"Shit, I'm starving," Ernesto said. He looked around him before reaching under the table. Stealthily, he pulled out a tangerine from a lunch bag.

"Make sure you share that with Hernán," Severo warned. "It's his."

"He can nibble on the peel," Ernesto said as he walked away with an empty box in one hand and the fruit in the other.

When he heard the beeping of the cargo truck, Severo stuck his head out to see how fast it was coming. It was backing up slowly in reverse about twenty rows down; Amanda was only a few steps ahead of it, taking down in her notebook the number of boxes packed per group. Severo decided to try to finish up another stack of ten packed boxes before the truck arrived, or before they called the lunch break, whichever came first. He might make it if Ernesto and Hernán got busy picking. They were clean pickers for the most part; he didn't waste precious seconds cleaning up the grape before packing it. He looked at his watch to time himself.

A packer had to set goals to keep from falling back from boredom and exhaustion. Pickers could stand, kneel, and even squat if they could reach the grapes on the vine. They got to walk back and forth through the length of the rows, stretching out their legs. Packers stood the entire season. At the end of the day Severo's knees were swollen, cramped because the bones had been pushed down to the joints, nerve tissue crushed in between, like pieces on a wall of stones.

While he looked around to check that he had an adequate supply of lids and box cushions, out of the corner of his eye, Severo caught a black object soaring down from above, rustling the leaves where it finally landed.

"A chanate has come to pay us a visit," doña Gertrudis said. Doña Gertrudis came to work wearing a construction worker's orange hard hat. Ernesto once pointed out that from a distance she looked like a teakettle.

"Is that a type of bird?" Severo asked.

"It's a black bird with red shoulders," doña Gertrudis said. She stepped back from the barrage of vines at the end of the row and pointed with the tips of her clippers. Severo nodded as if he had spotted the bird, but he saw nothing perched on the grapevines. "Oh," he said.

A black bird with red shoulders, Severo mused as he turned back to the table. How the hell was he supposed to look for shoulders on a bird? These old women had imaginations the size of the Gulf of California. Like Mamá Patricia, believer in ghosts, possessions, limpias, loterías, and in making invocations to San Antonio, finder of lost things.

Before the death of Papá Patricio, the family accepted her harmless superstitions with amusement. But after his death she became obsessed. Many nights she woke up wild-eyed and drenched in sweat, gathering her fortune-telling toys around her in a fever of immediacy, attempting to grasp the final strands of inspiration. On her better days she struggled to predict natural disasters or winning lottery numbers, but most of the time she was frightened and confused, attempting to guess at the day of the week or the number of fingers in her hands. On a number of occasions, when she became frustrated, Severo had to cradle her until she tired and fell asleep. She hummed herself into peacefulness.

Mamá Patricia had learned to consult astrological charts, the Tarot, the Naipe, the Ouija board, the Celtic runes, the *hexerei* of the Pennsylvania Dutch, the grimarios of Albertus Magnus, the Book of Revelations, the Magic 8 ball, and that Walter Mercado psychic hotline that ran up the phone bill each month. Severo had seen it all. Her most recent craze was a correspondence course in phrenology from an institute allegedly located at the top of the unreachable hills near the Guatemalan border. Severo suspected it was a bogus operation but humored her. Last week Ernesto walked in on Mamá Patricia feeling for bumps on Severo's head. "What? Does he have lice?" he asked.

Severo humored her but she was fast becoming a burden. He had stopped going out with his friends and started staying home to look after her. He couldn't keep a steady girlfriend, and unless the doll-sized women on the television screen started making eye-contact he wasn't expecting to be noticed by a female anytime soon. Sometimes the pain of his loneliness struck him hard and he became angry. He hid his mother's toys to punish her, but quickly brought them out for her as soon as she began to plead or cry.

In the garden Mamá Patricia had set up a series of altars: one for la Virgen de Guadalupe, one for the Buddha, and a third for Agabo and Malaquí, the biblical fortune-tellers. At night she lit them up with blinking Christmas lights. People came to stare and wonder about the woman who spread *aceite de paraíso* in the rosebush, making the garden smell like patchouli oil, vanilla extract, and sandalwood. Sunday mornings Severo discovered offerings and milagros pinned to the white altar cloths. Sunday nights he collected them, tossed them into the dumpster.

Some neighbors thought Mamá Patricia a lunatic. They suggested clinics and types of medications. He refused to hear any of it. Papá Patricio had been firm about her care before he died. Severo was the oldest. It was Severo's duty to protect her. As soon as Ernesto moved out, Severo planned to find a smaller place, a more private space for himself and Mamá Patricia. He even considered returning to Sinaloa—to Culiacán. Maybe he could complete his university studies, which he had to abandon because Papá Patricio had finalized their immigration papers and sent for them to join him in California. With no knowledge of English, farm work became Severo's year-round occupation: celery and asparagus in the winter, citrus and bell pepper in the spring, onion and grape in the summer.

Severo took in a deep breath as he cracked his spine by moving his sore shoulders back.

"Merengue!" Merengue said as he passed.

Once Severo considered releasing Mamá Patricia of her madness. Severo's skin tingled at the memory of the incident. He had ground Papá Patricio's old medicine pills and tablets into fine powder, and then mixed it into the Pepto Bismol, relying on his mother's craving for mint after a lengthy mouth-souring nap. He remembered shaking up the pink liquid and then watching it ooze along the bottle wall, thick and—he hoped—fatal. He left the refrigerator door wide open, then sat down to contemplate from the living room sofa as the pink bottle, snuggled between the mustard and soy sauce, glowed with the refrigerator light. At that instant not a sound came from Mamá Patricia's room: not a snore, not a single mumbled word, not a deep dream-inspired sigh. It was as if she had read about his plot through one of her divining tools and had decided to oblige him by sinking into the silence he had wished her into. Suddenly, an attack of panic struck Severo so he rushed into Mamá Patricia's room and forced his face inches apart from hers, anxious to receive her soft, living scent and to respond with his own breathing. For a month afterward he became overly concerned with her health, running to her side at her slightest cough or sneeze. And after that afternoon he too began waking up in the middle of the night, wild-eyed and drenched in sweat, horrified not at having attempted to poison his mother, but at the self-fulfilling prophecy of her death.

Ernesto walked up behind Severo, another load in his arms. "Almost lunch time?"

Severo glanced at his watch. "Almost. In one more load."

"Fuck," Ernesto protested, dragging three empty boxes behind him.

Severo quickened the speed of his packing as the beeping truck approached; Mamá Patricia still spun inside his head. Mamá Patricia had been a mathematics teacher in Culiacán, and last night she roamed the garden, murmuring incantations to the full moon. "It's a Gemini sky," she explained. She dressed up in her blue huipil in honor of Nuestra Señora la Reina, the lady of the twelve stars, ruler of the moon in Gemini.

"Just don't set off any fireworks like last month," Severo chuckled from the doorway.

"How can you joke about this, Severo?" she said. Her hair was loose, fanned out across the back like a gray collar. "The summer solstice approaches and the moon is dry. This is earthquake weather," she declared.

"Mamá," Severo said, "this is California—any weather is earthquake weather."

"Carry your San Elías in your wallet just in case," she said, then resumed her murmuring. "Tomorrow the foundations of the earth will tremble for some of us."

Severo needed one more box to complete the stack. He leaned forward across the packing table to reach for a box cushion, and just as he spread the cushion out Merengue suddenly yelled out "Quebrada!"—a call that los Caraballos responded to with a flutter of whistling that frightened the chanate out of the vines. When the bird came into full view, Severo realized that the coloring on the black bird's feathers did resemble shoulders. He tried to follow it as far as he could, but then the chanate launched itself directly into the glare of the sun. Severo didn't know whether the bird had swooped down to rest on the vines of some other block, or if it had shot straight into the sun like an arrow, determined to get to the other side.

La Quebrada

Aníbal   9:30 a.m.

The workers ate their lunches at the ends of the rows, beneath the vine canopies for shade, each group with its own colored ice chest. Still a crowd gathered behind Merengue's truck to use the water tanks and to buy generic soft drinks for fifty cents a can. Aníbal had just squeezed in through the cluster of bodies to reach for his lunch when a violent tug forced him back.

"Check the weight on some of these boxes before the cargo truck hauls them off," Jesse demanded. "We've been getting complaints from the warehouse so make sure today's first shipment is perfect."

Jesse walked off with the static-ridden walkie-talkie bouncing against his hip, his combat boots hitting heavy against the ground. Flat-footed, he left behind a pair of parallel prints, like tire tracks.

Aníbal scowled, muttering under his breath but conscious about being heard by the pickers. The scale boy earned a salary, the pickers worked for hourly wages and piecework; what was he complaining about?

"I'll have the piña colada, a piña colada, bartender!" el Caraballo Uno yelled out to the amusement of those around him. He pushed his way to the front.

"Mexicans go first, boricua," Ninja said through his cigarette. Pifas, also annoyed, muttered, "Pinche puertito."

"There's plenty for everyone. Back away. Don't crowd," Naro said. He and Amanda took charge of the soda sales for Merengue.

"Small bills only, Sebastián, this isn't a bank," Amanda said.

"Is this diet? I hate diet," someone among the crowd complained. Aníbal only saw the hand raised up and waving the can of soda in the air. He missed the soda rush. It was the same chaos and excitement as with the paycheck rush on Fridays—everyone pushed and shoved, but politely made way for the person exiting the mob. Minutes later the dust settled at the scene of the soda sale. The volume on a transistor radio went up. Cornelio Reyna and his accordion took over.

"I want to hear Juan Gabriel!" somebody complained. The complaint was answered with jeers and whistles.

When he bent down to lift a box from a low stack near Group 15 Aníbal smelled chipotle sauce. His mouth watered. The scale read twenty-two pounds. Aníbal pressed his thumb down the plate to complete the minimum twenty-three-pound weight requirement.

"No lunch?" don Nico asked.

Aníbal smiled back at the old man and shook his head. "I'm on a hunger strike," he said.

"He's trying to keep his weight down," doña Ramona volunteered, biting into a crisp corn tortilla while using her free hand to blow into a miniature battery-powered brasero.

Doña Gertrudis removed her orange hard hat. The damp strands of hair stuck to her skin around the hairline. "Santos cielos," she said, "working through the break. The Union would never put up with this."

"Here we go," said doña Ramona, tapping her finger against her temple. She had replaced the pocket watch around her neck with a camera with its cap dangling from the lens. She broke a chip off the toasted tortilla to dip into her bowl of rice and sauce.

"Grape picking back in the seventies with Chávez," doña Gertrudis began, staring out into space, "the Union was so strong we could have had the gringo owners feed us with their own hands."

"Don't exaggerate, comadre," doña Ramona said. "You sound like those women that come down from San Joaquín, telling us the grape pickers there get two one-hour lunch breaks through the Union. Tonterías!"

"One-hour lunch breaks?" don Nico laughed.

Tamayamá, sitting just behind don Nico, let out a quick "Aijodesutamayamá!"

"We should be so lucky to get some decent hours working," don Nico said.

"Well we need the Union," doña Gertrudis said. "I heard talk about a strike down at Freeman's company. They'll show all of us how it's done."

"Strikes don't work anymore," said don Nico. "Not like they used to."

"That's for sure," doña Ramona said. "It's not the same nowadays, not down here in the Caliente Valley."

Aníbal walked farther down, the sun already pressing down hard on his back. He had been looking forward to getting out of the heat, at least for the short duration of the break since he spent the entire morning walking back and forth down the length of the block. As soon as one of los Caraballos saw him coming, he elbowed the other.

"Well, well, look here, Demetrio," el Caraballo Uno said. "The scale boy came to look at us. But I bet he likes me better than he likes you."

"That's because he thinks you have the bigger cock," el Caraballo Dos said. "But just wait until he gives me a chance."

Aníbal ignored them. Los Caraballos were loud and obnoxious, mostly harmless but annoying just the same. From the corner of his eye he noticed Tinman observing from a distance. Tinman never ate. He only drank four of Merengue's cheap sodas, enough to let out a belch the entire crew could hear. During the break he read his book, his long hair brushing both sides of the open cover.

"The pretty boy's getting mad, Estanislaus," el Caraballo Dos said, making mock prissy gestures as he made his list. "Blowing up like the bullfrog. Glaring like the glass. He's going to break like the firecracker. Aim like the gun. He's—"

"He's scheming, Demetrio. Look at him. What's he thinking? What does he want and how bad does he want it?"

Aníbal checked the reading on the scale.

El Caraballo Uno kept goading in a whisper. "I bet that ass is real tight."

"It's this tight," el Caraballo Dos whispered, making a fist.

"Enough, already!" Aníbal said, hoping that an outburst would settle them down.

"Easy, easy," el Caraballo Uno said. "What do you think, Tinman? Should we let this pretty fish go?"

Tinman put his book down, pressed his hands together and imitated a fishtail plunging back into an imaginary surface. Afterwards he released his belch.

"Tinman says you're not that good a catch," el Caraballo Uno said between chuckles.

"But at least an appetizer," el Caraballo Dos chimed in, puckering his lips and throwing Aníbal a kiss. "A nice sweet mouthful." He grabbed for his crotch.

"And we can net ourselves Tiki-Tiki for a main course," el Caraballo Uno said. "Where is that jotete?" Behind him, Tinman stood up and swayed his hips, his wrists limp.

"Does anyone here have salt?" Eva came up behind Aníbal. Both Caraballos quickly scrambled for the lunch bag.

"I've got your salt, Evita," el Caraballo Uno said. "Take your grimy hands away, wetback!"

"I brought the salt, pinche boricua. Let me see!"

"I'll let you see it when I find it. Move!"

Aníbal seized the opportunity to sneak away, but was stopped by doña Pepa in her bright red sweatshirt with an offering of a piece of sandwich. "Take it," she said, bringing the slice of folded bread up to his face.

"No, thank you, doña," Aníbal said with embarrassment.

"Take it, take it. You're going to thank me later."

Aníbal quickly stuffed the bread into his mouth. It soaked up the last traces of saliva, which nearly made him choke. He wasn't starving, but he wanted to please doña Pepa, whose oversized glasses reminded him of Nana back in Mexicali.

"If you get dizzy suck on a lemon," doña Pepa advised.

Doña Pepa sat on a box turned upside down. Grape boxes weren't made to withstand the weight of a human body, but doña Pepa was petite, frail-looking yet as strong as any other worker. Aníbal had seen her lift boxes of grapes that were twice as full as those that her grandsons carried.

"Your grandsons?" Aníbal asked to be polite.

"They're back there pissing," she answered. "Cochinos. I told them not to wear those propaganda shirts. What's Merengue going to think? That we're troublemakers? That we want to strike?"

Doña Pepa was the crew's abuela. Everyone knew she was beyond retirement age, but she came back to pick every year using her daughter's social security number. This year she brought with her the two pocho grandsons who weren't very popular with the crew because they spoke broken Spanish.

"Tell your packer the boxes are a little heavy," Aníbal said. Doña Pepa chewed her food slowly. Los Pepitos, her grandsons, pelted grapes at each other farther down the row.

"Scaleboy!" Amanda yelled. Aníbal turned to meet his reflection on her sunglasses. "We finally got the identification stamp," she said. She handed him the metal numeral stamp and inkpad. "The shippers will stamp what's already been loaded; you need to stamp what hasn't. Start at the other end."

Aníbal looked to the end of the block. The bright umbrellas stood out, adjusted against the sun. As he walked, he considered that this would be over for him in a few weeks. It was the heat that was killing him, not Amanda or Jesse or los Caraballos. The heat was beating them down as well.

When he reached the end of the block, he bent down to begin stamping each box above the label. The inkpad was dry so he spat on it. In the absence of workers, the sandy avenue between the blocks widened, framed by the neat stacks of boxes and the litter of damaged covers and torn cushions. Aníbal knelt down in front of a stack. The vibrations of the electricity cables hummed from the end of the block. With his body pressed low to the ground he imagined himself camouflaged, his eyes following the stamp, roving like the anxious horned toad.

"It's actually a lizard," Carmelo would clarify. Carmelo was fanatic about desert wildlife, especially birds. Aníbal could only point out the roadrunner from the quail; Carmelo knew shrike from mockingbird.

"It's all in the black bar along the head, see it?"

Carmelo had stood behind him that time, his arm propped over Aníbal's shoulder and pointing into the spindly mesquite. Aníbal's vision had blurred with excitement. Bird or no bird, the instant Carmelo's muscle touched Aníbal their entire bodies connected.

Aníbal caught the glare of the sun on the metal stamp each time he turned his wrist. He was careful not to make contact with the metal, or else it blistered his skin.

What Aníbal liked best about life in the fields was the privacy. Despite the occasional trouble from los Caraballos, no one really cared who he was when he wasn't a grape picker. There was no prying. In Mexicali, he could never lose himself among the network of neighborhoods that knew him, his parents, and his parents' parents. Once a well-to-do family settled on its property it engraved itself on the map. There was little chance of escaping mention in the gossipy society columns. The unwritten rule was that if a man had roots on the border he maintained them. Only poor migrant campesinos from southern México actually crossed it; if they lived on the border they did so in ejidos, the barren outskirts of the city, with no running water and no street names. They didn't live anywhere and nobody really cared. But if a long-time border resident took that extra step into foreign soil then everyone would wonder: no money? no pride in México? no place to hide?

Aníbal's parents were scandalized after he made the decision to become a field worker in the U.S. "A slave," quipped his father. They wanted him to stay and repair the damage he had done. For years he had worked as an assistant accountant for his father's construction business, saving up his money for Talina, the daughter of two lawyers. His mother anticipated the union, and the subsequent climb up the social ladder. And just when the engagement was about to be printed in the papers, Jorge came forward. Silly, romantic, and beautiful Jorge came forward, pleading with him to call off the engagement, to run away with him the way they fantasized after making love. Aníbal and Jorge. Forever. In an act of desperation Jorge revealed everything to Talina, who revealed everything to her future father-in-law.

"Who's Jorge?" his father had asked. And within minutes the room exploded into stuttering and incoherent explanations. Then the cover-up: *Talina had a change of heart; Talina's too young to marry, say parents; Young Pérez Ceballos needs to secure his future first.* Finally, the escape: the move out of his parents' household and into Nana's, the resignation from Industria Pérez, and the jump across the international border, without Jorge who had betrayed him. And then Aníbal became Juan Carlos Macías Leyva who became Scaleboy, one transformation after another as if that took him any farther away from the shame.

But enough of shame. This afternoon Aníbal was going to tell Carmelo he was joining him on the grape route north, to Sonoma and San Joaquín. The understanding was clear, but left unspoken. Carmelo would keep his girl on that side the border, and his male companion on this one. Last month Carmelo had Aníbal take pictures of him standing outside a house with a nicely kept lawn. And then more, standing next to some stranger's Cadillac. The best ones Aníbal took were shot at the downtown shopping mall, where Carmelo asked the blonde from the ice cream parlor to pose with him by the indoor fountain. Aníbal imagined the look of envy on the faces of those who saw those pictures across the border—a deception that probably compelled others to seek similar fortunes. Little did they suspect that it was the eye behind the camera that saw the truth, the whole truth, the necessarily hidden truth.

Aníbal kept one of those photographs with him at all times for comfort. Carmelo's smile was his. Only one side of his cheek perked up when he smiled, revealing the crooked canine. After his meals, Carmelo sat hunched on the hood of the car with a plastic case of dental floss. Aníbal followed the green string from the case to Carmelo's mouth to the ground. He studied the waves and loops of its design, kinky as chest hairs.

Suddenly Aníbal heard a rustling through the leaves in the row in front of him. He crouched down even lower and peeked around the stack. Moreno and Pifas were each sneaking off with a box of grapes.

"You go out first and check if anybody's coming," Moreno said.

"It's safe," Pifas said. "Get the trunk open."

The two men crawled out by ducking beneath the grapevines, stashed the grape, and then crawled back into the field. Aníbal remained motionless, afraid that they might see him, and not trust him to keep their secret.

"Thanks, Pifas," Moreno said.

"No problem, Tiki-Tiki," Pifas said.

"What's the matter with you, compa?" Moreno objected.

"I'm just playing with you."

"Well, that's heavy, Pifas."

"I said I was just joking, Tiki-Tiki—I mean, Moreno."

"Never mind," Moreno said. "Can't get a break even during the break!"

The huge cargo truck pulled up, its noisy motor and beeping drowned out the sound of the two men cutting through the vines. The driver shut off the engine.

"Take your time, paisa," Dino said as he swung open the door. "No hurry."

"We might as well lunch," Jacobo said. Jacobo stood in the back of the truck on a stack of pallets. He was slim and muscular, unlike Dino who was stocky with plenty of hair on his body that soaked his T-shirt with sweat on all sides.

"What did your mother make?" Dino asked.

"Potatoes and chorizo. She forgot to pack the jalapeños though. You have any?"

Dino searched his bag as Jacobo jumped off the truck. He pulled out a raw chile serrano and showed it to Jacobo.

"I want one in vinegar," Jacobo said.

"Hey, would you rather look at the complete menu?" Dino said, displeased. Aníbal let out a small laugh.

"You find that funny, huh?" Jacobo snapped.

"Leave him alone," Dino said. "He's just the scale boy. What does he know?"

"I'll give him something to laugh about. Maricón," Jacobo said. "Where's that goddamn jalapeño?"

Aníbal began stamping carelessly. In seconds he was far away enough from the truck to slow down. Too often the shippers left him stranded out in the field when he was sent to stamp in other blocks. They drove him there, promised to return for another shipment, then forgot about him. With a fifteen-minute drive to and from the warehouse, and a ten-minute forklift job per pallet, Aníbal calculated at least a two-and-a-half-hour wait. There were twelve pallets per load, eighty boxes per pallet, and the possibility of an overstocked warehouse, especially if the grape wasn't selling fast enough. Shipping trucks idled in the lot for hours with a full cargo waiting for refrigerator space and in the meantime Aníbal was stuck in grape hell.

He came upon the portable toilets in time to see Jacaranda walk out of the women's side. She walked past him as if dazed, unmoved by the sound of the stamp striking the wood. Then the men's door swung open and Felipe's boy jumped out. "Is it still lunch time?" he asked.

"It's almost over," Aníbal answered coldly.

Felipe's boy stood near Aníbal, adjusting his belt. "What time do you think we get home today?" he asked. He sniffled.

"I don't get told those things," Aníbal said. He fumbled with the stamp in his hand and almost dropped it. This made him angry all of a sudden.

"But you hear the foremen talking. Did you hear anything?"

"Get moving, boy," Aníbal said without disguising his irritation. "I don't get paid to answer stupid questions and you don't get paid to ask them."

Aníbal turned away from the boy, slightly ashamed. He spat into the inkpad again but only managed to spit out a dry sound. The boy rushed off. Aníbal's stomach growled. The odor of urine wafted toward him, making him nauseous. Down the block, one of the foremen honked the horn to signal the end of the break. Merengue yelled out "Merengue!" and los Caraballos let loose a blitz of whistling. Bodies merged one last time at the path between the blocks, scrambling to steal one last drink of water before heading back into the sulfurous rows of vines. At his end, Aníbal felt like the solitary woodpecker that no one sees or hears but that everyone knows has been around because it pecks pecks pecks, leaving its mark behind. Peck peck peck. A distant knock so faint it remains unnoticed when it ceases, as if there had been no knock at all.

NO SHADE BETWEEN
BLACK AND WHITE

Eva   10:40 a.m.

"Chingado!" Eva cried out through the blue bandanna veiled over her face. She had accidentally snipped the skin off the tip of her index finger.

"Did you hurt yourself?" Jacaranda asked, and afterward came the sound of bunches of grape being dropped into an empty box.

Eva ducked. "You already filled the other box? Are you in a hurry?"

Sebastián came from behind to replace a filled box with an empty one. "The foreman says you're picking green crop," he said, dragging a box out from under the shade. "Goddamn this is heavy, Jacaranda, are you trying to give me a hernia?"

"Which foreman complained?" Eva asked.

"Naro," Sebastián replied as he walked off straining with the box over his shoulder.

"You know what that's all about," Eva said. She balanced the clippers across one of the leveling wires that ran from one end of the row to the other connecting all the grapevine trunks. She knelt down to clean the blood off her finger with the water leaking out of the irrigation tube.

"He's married, Eva," Jacaranda reminded her, progressing rapidly to the next vine.

Eva sucked on her finger. "So? Men leave their wives for other women every day," she said, giggling.

"And there are those men like Naro who don't bother to," Jacaranda said. She withdrew into silence.

Eva raised one eyebrow. She pressed her fingertip against the palm of her hand to stop the flow of blood. In the next row over, Dino the shipper had walked down to talk to the women in Group 18. Eva perked up her ears when she heard him mention the grape season.

"They say two more weeks," Dino said. "Maybe three."

"Why such a short season this year?" Francisca asked.

"I don't know, sister. I heard talk over at the warehouse that there are crews over in Indio already done picking Flame. Freeman's company is on hold waiting for the Thompson. Whatever's left of it."

"I heard talk that Freeman's company had a walkout," Chela's voice reached over the row.

Dino craned his neck to respond. "Rumors. Nobody strikes in the Caliente Valley anymore. Not in the grape anyway."

"It all sounds pretty suspicious to me," Francisca said. "How come we don't hear anything on the radio?"

Chela laughed. "Do you think those chingado companies don't have any influence? They're all in it together with the chingado government."

"Ay, Chela," Francisca rolled her eyes.

Dino lowered his voice. "So what do you say, sister? Can you spare a few or not?"

Eva spied Francisca reach inside her blouse to remove a few bills tucked inside her brassiere. She handed them to Dino; he pocketed them, patting her on the rear.

"And don't forget to ask the foreman if it's true we're getting sent to the warehouse!" Francisca yelled.

"Yeah, yeah," Dino responded without much enthusiasm.

As he walked by, Eva reached out through the vines and touched his arm. Startled, Dino grabbed her at the wrist.

"Hey, beautiful," he said once he recognized Eva. "Where's your sister?"

"She wants to know if we're headed for the warehouse," Eva said. Jacaranda took a reprimanding swipe with her hand on Eva's shoulder.

"Well, you tell your beautiful sister that if she wants to talk she knows where to find me Friday nights." Dino took a few steps forward, turned, shrugged his shoulders and mouthed the words, "I don't know."

"You're incorrigible, Eva," Jacaranda whispered once Dino was out of earshot. Eva giggled.

Despite the unsatisfactory answer, Eva felt a sense of relief. The tiresome picking season was getting shorter and shorter each summer, but that was good the way she looked at it. She wasn't like Ramiro who worried too much about money. Ramiro worked for a different company and the workers there had been complaining about the hours as well. Sometimes the foremen sent them home before the lunch break, which disheartened Ramiro because his paycheck was smaller than hers at the end of the week. He made up the difference taking the night shift at the adult video store.

"You wouldn't believe the number of losers that go in there in one night," he said to her at one of their weekly strolls down to the outdoor swap meet. "It's the one place you don't have to worry about the language barrier. The videos come in English, French, Italian, Japanese, and I bet you not one man goes into the store knowing anything but Spanish."

"What do these men look like?" she asked, curiously.

He stopped and swept one arm across the vicinity. Eva looked in surprise as if for the first time at the people surrounding them— people no different than her co-workers who bore the same burdens in the fields that she did. She could see it on their tanned cheeks, and in that sluggish gait caused by weary hipbones and knees.

Eva didn't have to ask to know that Ramiro himself watched pornography. All men did. Sebastián had a collection of magazines under his mattress that would frighten the Holy Ghost right out of Mami. And ever since Ramiro started working at Pezones, he had become more daring, experimenting with her body in ways that made Eva want to see the video herself since Ramiro was a bit vague with his directions. But she let him think he was performing like an expert. He was already insecure about her putting in an application at the ammunition factory when she turned eighteen a few months ago. "For the steady income," she had explained, which didn't rub off the look of defeat on Ramiro's face.

"Goddamn, can it get any hotter?" Sebastián said as he approached. His long-sleeve cotton shirt was stuck to his thin frame. The indentations between his ribs showed through.

"The radio announced this morning that it was going to be one hundred five degrees," Francisca in the next row offered.

Sebastián acknowledged her. "Lucifer's on the loose, chingado."

"Complete Jacaranda's box with mine if you need more grape," Eva suggested.

"I'll carry my own out, thank you," Jacaranda interjected. She lifted the box, bringing it up to hip-level with the use of her knee.

"What's the matter with her?" Sebastián asked.

Eva shrugged. "You know Jacaranda as well as I do."

"Is Ramiro still on for Los Arcos tomorrow?"

"Of course," Eva said. She rolled her eyes. "But we still need Jacaranda, otherwise you don't have a ride home and I don't get to spend time with Ramiro."

"Don't worry," Sebastián assured her as he walked with a full box, "she'll go. She went last week."

The previous Friday Jacaranda sat at the table in the corner, observing the band the entire night, stoically refusing invitations to dance and smoking an occasional cigarette. With a pitcher of ice water at the center of the table, Jacaranda sat motionless; a black choker around her slim neck held her head up stiffly. Sebastián sat at the bar as usual, guzzling away with a crowd of other underage drinkers, while Eva snuck out with Ramiro. The arrangement worked for everyone: Jacaranda drove the intoxicated Sebastián home, then waited by the bedroom window to help Eva sneak in by dawn. Everyone had his or her fun, everyone got home happy. Except maybe Jacaranda.

When Jacaranda returned from the water tank, she held out a paper cup. The cup felt cool to Eva, who received it through the vines. As she gulped down the water, she watched Jacaranda's bony dark hand rigid around the clippers. Eva imagined those hands at task with the Bible shoved away under the pillow. Book by book, each verse had been underlined in ink, with figures scribbled all along the outer margins, which Eva had deciphered as dates and times. Jacaranda had been keeping a log of her reading, an obsession that frightened Eva. Jacaranda was strange. At times Eva detected a hint of desperation in her eyes, in the way she sat at the dinner table and contemplated the people around her with a disconcerting silence, picking at the food on her plate because pickings were all she would allow into her body. Jacaranda was anorexic again. And Jacaranda would overcome it. Again. She was, after all, Jacaranda— the middle ground and safety zone in that insane asylum they called home, the house of the mad and the moribund.

The cold water made Eva lightheaded, nauseous. She walked a few grapevines back, expecting to vomit, but didn't though her stomach cramped.

"Are you sick?" Eva heard Jacaranda. Eva waved at her to come.

When Jacaranda crossed the vines to comfort her, Eva began to sob because that was part of the arrangement: Jacaranda, the life-saver; Jacaranda, who sacrificed her time and strength so that Eva could walk through the path that had been cleared for her. It was understood that Eva would leave and Jacaranda stay, that Eva would have the new family and Jacaranda take care of the old one—of lonely Mami and sick Papi. Day and night. Left and right. Some lived and others died. Some ate and others starved. The cycle had to go on. To disturb that balance now, Eva realized as she stood upright to swallow a breath of fresh air, was to shatter the delicate threads of those roles they had sewn together. Jacaranda could never do that to the family, to Eva. Jacaranda could never leave.

A Man's Man

Moreno   11:20 a.m.

"The bad news is that it's indigestion," Moreno said to Ninja, who was doubled over behind the packing table. "But the good news is that it's not diarrhea."

"Get the hell away from me, you sonofabitch, Tiki-Tiki, joto maricón," Ninja retorted. "I should put my cigarette out on your nose and give you another hole to stick your finger in." He let out a loud fart.

"Goddammit, Ninja," Merengue said as he walked by. He took his hat in his hand and waved it in front of his face. A few of his blond curls were stuck to his receding hairline, wet and darkened. "What the hell have you been putting in your tacos? Dead rat?"

Don Nico was packing in the next row. At the sound of Ninja's flatulence he walked over and chimed in. "What you need is a good purge."

"Jesus Christ hole sucker, look at what you started!" Ninja said, admonishing Moreno. Moreno displayed a toothy grin and shrugged his shoulders.

"Back in Monterrey," don Nico said, scratching the back of his ear, "we had a beautiful mare that got clogged up eating grass. We thought she was getting big with colt until the neighbor pointed out there were no crap droppings anywhere in sight."

"No crap droppings around here, either," Merengue said as he looked around jokingly.

"He taught me the secret to the best purge," don Nico concluded. "In less than a day that mare was spilling down to the floor so quickly I thought she was going to shit her own stomach out."

"And what was the secret?" Ninja asked.

"Cricket," don Nico answered.

Merengue lowered his sunglasses to look down at don Nico. His blue eyes glared when he asked, "Cricket?"

"I don't understand," Moreno said. "He made cricket powder and mixed it into the mare's water? Or did he feed her a live cricket?"

"It was a live cricket all right," don Nico said, deadpan. "Except it went in through the other end. Chingada mare had her anus tickled so much it stimulated the muscles in her shit hole all afternoon." Don Nico opened the palm of one hand, and with the other plucked a kicking cricket out. "Who wants to take care of the job today?"

"It's all in fun, Ninja," Merengue said amid all the laughter. He patted don Nico on the back, a friendly gesture to send him back to work. As soon as Merengue walked away, Chela appeared.

"What's all this racket? All of a sudden we're getting friendly with big boss, Mr. Ghost?" she asked.

"Nothing," Moreno said. He picked up another box of grape and placed it on the packing table. "Ninja's got an upset belly."

Chela rubbed Ninja's stomach. "Why doesn't Buddha go pick some grapes while I talk to Tiki-Tiki? I'll get you a pill from Francisca in a minute. She's got a whole medicine cabinet in her lunch bag."

Without objecting, Ninja traded tasks with Moreno. Chela then took her place beside Moreno, helping pack the grape. Their hands were the same dark shade of brown, a testament to their kinship—his father and her mother were brother and sister. And like their parents, Chela's and Moreno's shoulders were broad and naturally muscular. Yaqui shoulders, Tata Nacho used to say. They were pure tough Indian, built to carry the cold rock pitcher of the moon and the hot copper cazuela of the sun.

"So what's the emergency, Moreno? I only have a few minutes before Valentín begins to complain to Francisca," Chela said, her voice sharp and peeved. "So if you're speaking up for that chingado beaner, you tell him that the only way I'll look at him again is if he's bought himself some of that old white man's pito medicine."

"Viagra?" Moreno asked, puzzled.

"That's right," Chela said. "If he's going to fuck with me again he might as well make it worth my while and not get off after ten minutes, leaving me all hot and bothered to take care of things on my own."

"Now don't get all excited all of a sudden, I just want to say a few words," Moreno protested.

"Chingado," Chela said, shaking her head. "Just because you dress like doña Furibunda doesn't give you the right to act like the metiche."

"Aijodesutamayamá," Tamayamá said as he dropped off a box of grape. "There's a black widow spider in this one. Make sure it gets a free ride."

"He doesn't believe in killing insects," Moreno explained. "Karma."

"Anyway," Chela said as soon as Tamayamá was gone. "What does he want?"

Moreno shook his head. Even as children Chela could be as cold as a wasp. No one ever won a fight with her, female or male, because she could fight like either—hair pulling and scratching or punching and kicking. And if it was a shouting match, her opponent didn't stand a chance because no one could spit hot poison out of the mouth the way she could. Tata Nacho once said that after Chela was born, any soul condemned to hell was met with silence because she had stolen the devil's tongue. Her rabid-dog temper and quick-to-bite-back ways only grew worse with time. It had nearly gotten her excommunicated at the tender age of ten because she had burned the priest with a candle. When Tata Nacho asked for an explanation she said he had tried to burn her first for giggling during Catechism class. The priest wanted her to sample the eternal fires of damnation so he grabbed her by the wrist and tried to hold her finger steady above the flame. All she did was pull out and down to offer the priest a taste for dining in and one to go. Even Tata Nacho couldn't hold back a chuckle.

But deep down inside Chela was a lonely woman, an outcast of the family much like himself. Yet even he had his time to shine when he performed as a cross-dresser in the red light district of the border. Unlike most of his family, Chela made an effort to drop by. Since women didn't frequent these establishments, everyone thought she was one of the local bull dykes. It didn't help that she could drink like a man and when she hung around to the late hours of the night she didn't object to having a young woman sit on her lap.

"Chingada Chela," Moreno admonished her one night after he had changed out of costume. "You're causing more of a scandal than I am."

"I'm getting all confused, cousin," she replied, slurring her words. "The men are blowing kisses at you and I've got a girl asking me to touch her tits."

"Chingado!" Moreno yelled out. He held his make-up kit in one hand and held his drunken cousin up with the other. The journey home was unsteady and slow.

"I just want to ask you one thing, Chela," Moreno said. He placed the lid on a packed box while Chela fitted an empty one with a paper cushion, ribbed side facing down. By the time he returned from adding the box to the stack, Chela had already brought a freshly picked box to the table and had started packing it. "Are you really ready to leave Cirilo for good? He's worried sick he'll never see you or the children again." Chela kept nodding her head. "I mean, think about it, Chela. What was it about Cirilo that made you invite him into your heart in the first place?"

Chela laughed. "You make it sound like a romance," she said. "We're the working class, not royalty, cousin. Men like Cirilo wouldn't know love and affection if it came in a can of beer and if he drank the whole case of twenty-four, you should know that. They just come up from behind and swing their clubs. Small clubs at that. Besides, I don't have room in my heart for anything else except the constant ache of worry. I worry about the children, about money, about my job, and when this chingado comes around with his itchy weasel stuffed inside his pants, I worry I'm going to end up with another kid to worry about. I go to bed worrying so much I worry that I'll sleepwalk to the railroad tracks to say hello to the train. I worry about this heat, and that one day I'll be picking grape, thinking that I need to buy tampons after work, and suddenly I'll suffer a brain hemorrhage and never see my babies again. I worry about all those things and everything else because my faith is running out, Moreno. I come to work praying this is the last day I have to put up with this chingado sun, and right after that I pray that I can come back the next day so that I can pray to go home again. Well, I'm almost through with praying because this chingado wheel of hell has been rolling long before I crossed the border and it's going to keep on rolling long after I'm dead. So what's the point in staying? I'm packing up my Salvation Army mierda and my babies and making one-way tracks out of the Valley, whether anyone likes it or not. You tell that chingado that if he's got something better, I'm right here within reach because the day's moving slowly, but if he doesn't, he should move out of the way because when the time comes to burn rubber I'm plowing through so hard and so fast that if Jesus Christ himself were to hold up his hand to try to stop me, I'd rush right through the hole in the center without making the sign of the cross."

Chela, her eyes red with emotion, wiped her hands on her sweatshirt and turned to leave, but just before taking the first step into the avenue she added: "You tell Cirilo that life's tough. That's what being a chingado Mexican in gringolandia is all about. Only a man's man can make it. And I may not have anything dangling between my legs, but I've got legs and two feet, and I can stand and walk and run and keep up with any wetback around here. See you later, cousin."

The hairs on Moreno's nape stood on end. He stood frozen, stunned by Chela's mouthful of words, which had just charged at him like a runaway bull. Suddenly he realized what an imperfect match she and Cirilo were. Chela moved forward, and when obstacles got in the way she moved to the sides and around. She adapted, adjusted, tailored her actions with the same skill as she wove together her words to speak in sentences that made such indisputable sense and showed such keen awareness of the world. She was a survivor, very unlike Cirilo, who fled and feared and failed, who needed a planet of a woman like Chela to drag him along by the force of her gravity. And maybe he was no different in his own apathy, resigned to the bad luck and bad breaks that had been plaguing him from the moment he left his haven at the nightclub on the border. Chela had will, guts, balls. There was no doubt about it. She would outlive them all.

In that instant a slight tickling on his hand startled Moreno out of his trance. The black widow spider had crawled out of the box. At the sight of the insect he acted on instinct and slapped it off, underestimated his strength, and smeared it dead on his skin.

"Mierda!" he said, just as Ninja returned with a box of grape, Tamayamá and Cirilo close behind.

"Poor little spider," Tamayamá said. "It's going to return from the great beyond to kill you back."

SWEAT

Naro   12:00 a.m.

By noon, Naro observed, there wasn't any sun—only heat. And sweat. Sweat under the armpits and in the crack of the ass. His back was drenched and his aviator glasses kept slipping down the bridge of his nose. When he tilted his head, the lenses caught the sweat. Even his mustache felt like any other piece of excessive body wear, like the belt tightening around his waist and the watch gripping his wrist. It didn't help that he had just done a line. Crystal made his body sweat even more, but he had to stay aware.

He climbed inside Merengue's truck, leaving the door open and letting his leg hang out over the metal step. The grape pickers had slowed down—they always did at this hour, which was fine since they had already swept through most of the block by midmorning. Their speed would continue to wind down until two or three in the afternoon, which was late for quitting time but there was no way around it today. It was the crew's turn to repack. Lozano had already radioed from the warehouse that a shipment had fallen. Dirty grape. It wasn't a shipment from this group otherwise Naro and Jesse would have to harass them all afternoon. They deserved it too if they were being sloppy to keep up with the piecework. At any rate, Naro would have to stay behind as well. He'd stay at Jesse's and Amanda's overnight again, which was better than driving all the way to El Centro just in time to eat, get up and turn the car back around.

He turned the volume down on his walkie-talkie because the static was mostly Jesse calling all over the blocks asking what crew was doing what and how fast, like it fucking mattered in the one hundred degree heat. Jesse had leaked to Lozano about his drinking on the job but Lozano didn't give two shits. Naro got a half-assed warning from Merengue and everyone knew that white boy had drinking problems of his own. This morning they both showed up with hangovers. Naro had offered to share his line but Merengue said he didn't like to snort on weekdays. Naro had tried to explain that he didn't either but Merengue just waved him away.

Naro reached for the small flask beneath the driver's seat: charanda—strong and sweet as the maguey from Jalisco and the sugar cane from Michoacán. He took a drink to bring down his high, and then stuffed the flask back under the seat. His bellybutton hole felt like a pool. He imagined the hair swimming like seaweed. This was definitely the last time he mixed his drugs.

Through the sideview mirror he saw Jacaranda approaching the water tanks. Her height and slim torso gave her away in spite of the long-sleeve shirt, the funny hat and the layers of bandannas disguising her face. As los Caraballos would say, *Toot-Toot!* Simply stated, Naro wanted to fuck her. She was the first to resist him that coldly. He suspected she was teasing, getting him worked up to the point of begging. But he never had to beg. Women knew he could make them happy. It was written all over his hairy arms, in the tough skin of his knuckles, and in his heavy walk. Even Amanda who was hard to please didn't complain. During the season she had to have him at least once a week or she became irritable.

"Does Jesse fuck this good?" he once asked Amanda as she bounced on top of him, her tits clapping against his hands.

"Yes," she answered, out of breath. Bitch.

He waited until Jacaranda reached the tanks to get up and greet her. He surprised her wetting a bandanna with the drinking water.

"Hey, baby. If I catch you doing that again you start bringing your own water. We have the toilet tanks for that," he said, trying to catch a full view of her dark brown eyes, almost black.

"It's for my sister; she's not feeling well. And it's too far to go to the toilet tanks," she said. She gathered the drenched bandanna in the palm of her hand. She grabbed for a paper cup.

"I just saw you come down not ten minutes ago," Naro said.

"That was for me," she said.

"Are you all that thirsty over there? I can have a tank sent over to your group to make it easier for you." Jacaranda ignored him.

Naro's head pounded. A bead of sweat ran across his cheek to meet his lips. He resisted the urge to suck it into his mouth, so he wiped it with a slow stroke of his hand. He walked up behind Jacaranda and reached around her body for a paper cup, deliberately brushing his elbow against her arm. The touch was electrifying. She moved to the side. He moved in closer and managed to whisper, "I bet your sap tastes like the honey off the maple, so sweet and sticky."

Jacaranda laughed. "You like trees? I've got a mulberry outside my house," she said. "You can come over while I'm gone and lick it clean." She walked away, paper cup in hand.

Naro smiled. The bristles of his mustache prickled his cheeks. She had flirted. She was coming around. Slowly. Then he'd pounce and fuck her. He filled up the paper cup and drank, crumpling the cup afterward.

He sat back in the truck to watch the dirt avenue through the sideview mirror. When the heat reached this intensity, the workers started to pretend they were busy by moving back and forth between the avenues from one block to the other.

"Naro."

Silvania startled Naro at the passenger window. He grimaced at her teary eyes. He looked around for witnesses.

"I've been trying to talk to you all morning, cabrón," she said.

"Make it fast," Naro said. "I don't want Merengue to see you talking to me looking like this."

"You mean Amanda, hijo de puta," she spat out.

Naro leaned over. "Keep your voice down, bitch! What are you trying to do to me?"

"You bastard. Do you think you can play games with me like that? Here's your fucking money!" Silvania threw a handful of crumpled bills at Naro's face. "It's all paid off, cabrón. Get your pussy some other way." Silvania stormed off, pulling the bandanna over her face.

"Goddamn cunt. Couldn't this wait until after work?" Naro muttered as he picked up the bills that had fallen off the seat.

"Dissatisfied customer?" Amanda said, notebook in hand.

"Fuck off, Amanda. Go keep your records. I'm not in the mood today."

"Well you better get in the mood," she said, puckering her lips. "You're spending the night since we're headed for the warehouse after work." Then just before she turned around she added: "And make sure you bring the powder. That is if you didn't sell it all to Silvania. I want a good fuck tonight."

Naro watched Amanda move away in the sideview mirror. These fucking cunts. They had him by the nuts and pulled one to the left, the other to the right. Even Diana his wife. Pussy-whippers all of them. Wild cunts. Naro felt his erection against his zipper. The sweat down there, between the scrotum and the thigh, made his body tingle. Sweat was sweet. Sweat was good. His mother-in-law ironed in a stuffy room to feel the entirety of the trails of sweat streaming down her face. He thought she had finally lost her mind, bored senseless after being forced to retire from the sewing shop after forty-five years. But now he understood. The face was only the beginning. Like a good fuck, a full body sweat was about waking up every sleeping fold and cleavage. Naro squirmed on the seat of his pants. It was about his body kicking him back and reminding him he was still alive.

IMMACULATE CONCEPTIONS

Mariana   *12:10 p.m.*

Picking grapes was boring work, especially with partners who refused to talk because talk, according to Felipe, was expensive. With bills to pay they couldn't afford it, not at work, not at home. Mariana looked across at her son who yanked and cut with a quick pace. At the end of the row her husband gathered the fruit into the boxes at an even quicker speed, his arms flexed and extended as if plagued with muscle spasms. She pictured his eyes jerking around in their sockets in the same manner they shifted when he sat behind the wheel: they jumped swiftly from mirror to mirror to road to mirror, seized by the paranoia of coming across a policemen or la migra. She shook her head. Her mother had advised her to find a man who was hard working, loyal, and strong. Felipe encompassed all three. He was all man, which left very little room in his time for what was not male.

"A good man," Mariana's mother persisted, "should be as solid and reliable as molcajete stone." Standing over the kitchen counter she chopped the onions then placed them carefully away from the diced serranos and the boiled tomatoes. The young Mariana crushed the garlic. Her mother reached across to pick up the stone pestle out of the molcajete's bowl. "I mean, look at this!" She weighed the pestle in her hand. "When will you ever see the end of this stone?"

Mariana weighed a tight cluster of grapes in her hand, squeezed it firmly between her fingers until she felt the first grape pop open inside her hand. She preferred the company of women. Trying to have a conversation with Felipe was like throwing rocks to the clothes on the line—reaction and resistance.

In the winters Mariana worked in the date-packing warehouse, where it was mostly women—gossip and giggling. There were two men, the old stuttering foreman and the timekeeper, who was young and effeminate—plucked eyebrows and silk shirts opened to midsternum. His chest muscles were deep lines of tanned flesh. The more daring women pinched his skinny rear when he passed by to announce the break or the lunch hour. Once she had attempted it herself. She had barely grazed the denim of his pants, but when she quickly withdrew her hand she jittered with excitement as if she had exceeded the challenge. Felipe would have been appalled. He would scoff at every one of them—at the women for cussing like men and talking explicitly about sex, at the timekeeper for being such a joto. Felipe hated jotos. But to Felipe, any man who wasn't like him was a joto. Her brothers—jotos, especially Cirilo who got his woman pregnant every other year and forced her to survive on welfare. The gas attendant—joto, because he worked under the shade all day. Merengue—gringo joto. Naro and Jesse—jotos for running around like hens after that marimacha Amanda. El pendejo presidente Fox—joto joto; el pendejo presidente Bush, son of that other pendejo presidente Bush—joto joto and a half; the Pope—holy joto. And don't even start him on that Tiki-Tiki fellow who some people say still dresses like a woman on the weekends. Even though he was kin to her brother's wife, she couldn't say for sure if it was true or not.

Felipe didn't entertain vices—or friends; their home was free of alcohol, tobacco, and guests. Afternoons at home were all about cleaning up and resting for the following day of work in the grape fields. House rules were clear and somewhat simple: wash your own dish, make your own bed—laundry was done on a rotating schedule and so was the cooking; no television except for the evening news and maybe *Cristina* between six and seven; no radio except for the morning news before work; no singing, not even in the shower. Felipe was obsessive about order and routine. It wouldn't surprise Mariana to find out he shit in perfect circles, like a rabbit, each dropping an exact replica of the one that had plopped down into the toilet water before it. By eight in the evening everyone was expected to be in bed. At that point Mariana zeroed in on the neighbor's chatter, sometimes contributing to their conversation in her mind while Felipe tossed and turned, mumbling protests at the obnoxious and inconsiderate people next door.

"That's exactly what I thought, comadre." Last night one of the neighbors had high-pitched from across the lawn. "She should not have gone to that party without her husband. That's adultery!"

"They're indecent, these young women nowadays," another woman responded.

"No decency, and so disrespectful," a third woman interjected.

The second woman completed her say: "A married woman stays home unless she's with her husband. What are people going to say?"

They're not going to keep their stupid mouths shut, that's for sure, Mariana retorted in the spirit of the women at the date-packing warehouse. She shifted on the mattress, gently brushing up against her husband's shoulder—a signal for him to turn around and slide his hands under her nightgown. But Felipe's arm only stiffened, and then he rolled over with his back to her.

Mariana sighed as she wiped the sweat off her chin. The clippers bore the strong odor of rotten fruit—a smell that haunted her in the morning hours when she couldn't sleep, or when she could, the smell followed her into the secret recesses of her dreams. "More grape!" Felipe shouted from the packing table.

Felipe seldom touched her after their only son was conceived, condemning sex for pleasure as perversion and as an act that weakened his body and robbed it of its valuable energy. It was no great pleasure to begin with, she wanted to tell him, but she felt the yearning in her blood. Her women friends all talked about it candidly—the need and the desire. She imagined herself in their place when they spun their lascivious tales with beds so drenched in passion they burst into flames. She was, after all, a woman. She blushed when she realized her son was still picking in front of her. He was a photograph of Felipe's youth come to life. It gave her chills to think that he would adopt his father's work ethics, become hard working, loyal, and strong, completely and precisely filling out the name his father had given him: Felipe Antonio—Junior.

Suddenly from above the fields a trilling of a propeller disrupted the dead calm of the air.

"La migra!" someone yelled.

"Aijodesutamayamá!"

Mariana looked up to see the familiar avocado-green of the INS vehicles. The plane was a retired crop duster now employed to locate the farm workers and facilitate immigration raids.

"Get your green cards ready, people! Get your green cards!" one of los Caraballos yelled out.

"To the mountains!" someone else joked.

Mariana giggled. At the date-packing warehouse the women were wild with fantasy. During the desert wars there were always rumors going around that the U.S. military was plotting a siege at the warehouse to net enough women into the service. Why them? They were Mexicans—they could cook and clean in an assembly line the same way they sorted and packed dates at the warehouse, keeping up with the speed of the conveyor belt. They were also women with a high tolerance for the heat, and the war was taking place in a landscape not too different from the Caliente Valley. The date trees, she had learned from the stuttering foreman, had come from the Middle East—smuggled into the country, the roots growing successfully within a familiar terrain. The siege made perfect sense.

"The situation is critical," doña Rosalva warned the women at the lunch break, the wrinkles around her eyes amplified into deep canals behind her glasses. "I got a call from Presidente Bush himself telling me that any day now . . . vámonos!" She imitated the helicopter lift-off with a swift lift of her hand.

Women from both sides of the conveyor belt broke out into laughter.

For weeks afterward the women discussed the imminent invasion, some with the nervous hint of fear, most with skepticism and light-heartedness, and some, like Mariana, with anticipation. The sands of the Middle East. She didn't know where that was exactly but it was somewhere in the middle—not the clumsy beginning, not the cruel end. The middle.

"I'm as eager as a vibrator with fresh batteries," Ex went around saying. Other women didn't like Ex. It wasn't the profanity or the constant sexual innuendoes that annoyed the women, it was her divorced status and how she squeezed in her ex into every other sentence. "My ex won't ever find me in the Middle East," Ex added.

Mariana clung to the noise of the propeller plane as it trailed away. Then she heard the crackling of dry leaves getting crushed behind her. Two women smiled at her: doña Ramona with a camera in front of her face, and doña Gertrudis who wiped the sweat off her orange plastic hard hat.

"What's this?" Mariana asked. The camera clicked.

"It's for a glamour magazine," doña Gertrudis said.

Mariana turned to look at her son through the vines. He only stared back with disapproval.

"My son's college project," doña Ramona said, snapping another shot from a different angle. "Hold up a bunch of grapes in your hand."

Laughing, Mariana complied, adding to the pose a clear view of the clippers aimed at the grapes.

"Tiki-Tiki! She's a natural, comadre," doña Gertrudis said. "Are you sure you've never modeled before?"

"Well—" Mariana began to speak but her husband's booming voice interrupted her.

"Mariana! What's going on back there?" Felipe shouted.

"We're doing a fashion show, Felipe," doña Gertrudis answered. "Come on back here and take off that ugly hat."

Doña Ramona shifted position and snapped a shot of Felipe. Mariana couldn't resist a giggle as her husband shook his head and turned away.

"And what's your son doing with the pictures?" Mariana asked.

"He's going to show his teachers," doña Ramona said. She pushed Mariana back against the vines and took another shot.

Doña Gertrudis added, "They've never seen grape pickers I guess."

Young Felipe let out a groan. Mariana rolled her eyes and pointed over her shoulders with her clippers. "He loses money when I get distracted," she explained.

"He's a hard worker," doña Gertrudis said, winking at the boy.

"Is he staying in school or is he staying under the sun for the rest of his life?" doña Ramona asked.

Mariana shrugged, a serious expression on her face.

"That's enough, comadre," doña Gertrudis warned, pushing doña Ramona away. "Merengue, merengue!"

As soon as her visitors had disappeared through the vines, Mariana felt the pangs of solitude. It was quiet again, with only the squeaks of the contracting metal spring in the clippers. She would have to make those same sounds with the bed springs soon, before more time passed making it impossible to fool Felipe into believing the baby growing in her belly was his. She smiled coyly. If only the women at the date-packing warehouse suspected that the feminine timekeeper had such potential given the chance.

Mariana's eyes jumped on a worm crawling on the vines. Lime green and long as her finger, the worm crept onto the blade of her clippers. Her son noticed she stopped working.

"Now what, Mamá?"

"Look, Felipe," she said, "a grape worm." She egged it forward to her work glove. The hairs on the worm's back pointed up as it inched its way across her hand.

"They're ugly," Felipe said. He resumed working at a steady pace. "They harm the grapevine. Kill it."

Mariana knelt down and let the clippers drop. She watched the worm make an effort to crawl from one hand to the other. *Mamá? Mamá?* She thought she heard her son pleading. His voice was the shrill of a girl, but it would thicken soon, and he'd learn to inhabit the cold and stoic man's world of his father. She was determined to have a daughter. She could feel her taking shape inside of her—raw and real. Her daughter would know the beauty of the grape worm, and appreciate the crickets that chirped early in the mornings in the fields. She had shared with her son the knowledge that the crickets stretched their song well into daylight, but he took this information with disinterest, almost confused about what to do with it. When the propeller plane returned, once again sweeping across the skies above the blocks, the fields exploded into whistles and catcalls. She looked up and imagined herself in the pilot seat looking down at the specks of life, the sediment in the pit of the molcajete bowl.

HELLS AND SPELLS

Hernán, 12:50 p.m.

The brief visits by the INS plane set the field humming with stories about encounters with la migra. Hernán managed to catch snippets of the chatter in Group 2 as he wove in and out of the row, replacing the empty boxes. A pallet of boxes with the Flame label had been accidentally shipped to their block where the crew was picking white grape, not red. Although Hernán was not the only one who made that mistake he was sure no one else had gotten the knuckle on the head.

"Hurry it up," Ernesto demanded.

Hernán tossed the unusable boxes into a pile in the middle of the avenue where Jesse stood with his mouth against the walkie-talkie, arguing with the static.

"How about taking these also?" Ninja, Group 2's packer, smiled through his cigarette. His top incisors were missing, so he clamped down on the filter with his gums, making the cigarette bounce when he spoke.

Minutes later Hernán took his place across from Ernesto, the grape-vines between them, and unlocked the safety hook on the clippers. Talk in the next row was still going strong; it had managed to grab even Ernesto's interest; he kept quiet instead of bothering Hernán.

"How many times did you say your uncle got bounced?" Moreno asked.

"Twelve times," Cirilo said, "before he finally gave up, and only then because he broke his ankle."

"Jumping over the fence or running away from the border guards?"

"No, chingado. He was buying a hamburger at McDonald's and he slipped on ketchup. The manager turned him in to avoid a lawsuit."

"Chingado."

Hernán heard Ernesto laugh softly. It bothered him suddenly that no one else knew that Ernesto had found it funny. He felt like Ernesto's accomplice and it pushed a bitter taste up his throat.

"How about you, doña Pepa?" Cirilo called out. Hernán looked back and caught a speck of the tiny woman's bright red sweatshirt through the vines.

"Did you ever have a run-in with la migra, Nana?" Moreno coaxed her further.

"Once," doña Pepa said in a squeaky voice, "about ten years ago." Her grandsons worked ahead of her, busy with their own conversation.

"Well what happened?" Cirilo asked. Throughout the rows bunches of grape dropped into the boxes created an interlude of thuds.

"I'm minding my own business picking and picking," doña Pepa began, "when the people around me just let go their clippers and shoot off like rockets through the vines. It catches me by surprise but I don't want to be left behind. Madres! I see everyone heading one direction I don't go the opposite way. Well I trip and shred the palms of my hands but I would have crawled on my elbows like a lizard if I had to. God only knew what was back there: some mountain lion, or some madman with one of those guns that drills you full of holes, or maybe even el chingado chupacabras, I didn't know. My heart beat so fast I could feel it want to spin right out of my mouth."

"Aijodesutamayamá!" A few vines down Tamayamá let out his cry.

"Well about two minutes into the stampede I wear out my strength thinking I was bleeding to death. I just look up at the sky and start praying to the Lord to take me before whatever is back there finds me. Well a woman a few feet away from me takes pity on me and comes back to lift me off the ground. *You can make it, doña Pepita,* she says to me with tears in her eyes. I look at her and bless her with all my heart but I know I will only slow her down so I tell her, *Go on without me, mija, save yourself.* Well she looks at me with that sunken face of hers, holding my shaky body up with her shaky arms and says, *I can't let la migra take you! God only knows how they'll treat you.* Well right then and there my body springs to life all on its own and I shove this stupid girl off me so hard she nearly falls. *Hijos de la chingada!* I yell at the bunch of fugitives, and I drag my old skin back to the blocks as I pull my green card out of my brassiere."

Rows of workers broke out into laughter, including Ernesto who cackled away until he met Hernán's smiling face. "Get to work, bitch!" he commanded.

"I *am* fucking working!" Hernán snapped back. He hid behind the wall of leaves. Around them the drone of conversation subsided, pressed by the weight of the heat. Hernán's throat was parched. It pulsated as if his words had leapt out of his voice box too quickly too soon.

On his journey to the packer's table, a box of picked grape in his hands, Hernán felt pain on three parts of his body: his lower back, his stomach, where the edge of the box pushed against him with each step forward, and his head. There was little he could do to avoid the damage to his back and stomach—if he balanced the box on his shoulder he risked an even bigger ache; if he carried the box on his head his neck would feel the strain all night. But the ache that locked itself inside his skull was dehydration. He laid the box down next to Severo's feet.

"I'm going to get a drink," he told Severo. Severo nodded once. The heat had disparate effects on his uncles, Hernán observed: Ernesto became edgier, Severo sullen and downcast.

What gave Hernán strength to get through the day was the knowledge that he was making money with each passing hour. By the time the break came around he had already made a little over fifteen dollars; by noon the total had more than doubled. Each passing hour of sweat and grief added to his daily earnings. Still this was the first and last summer he was picking grapes. By next summer when he turned fifteen he'd be old enough to apply for a job at the mall. At this point he didn't care if he got a job scrubbing toilets as long as he worked indoors, away from the stink of sulfur and closer to the scent of girls. At morning picking lessons with Merengue, all the underage grape pickers were male. His father had explained in his own awkward terms that grape companies didn't want girls because they weren't strong, and because menstruation during puberty made them susceptible to fainting spells.

Hernán thought back to the high school girls and couldn't recall one incident of fainting, except for Analí, who was rumored to have been pregnant. No one knew for sure because she dropped out of school soon after, but that only fueled the gossip. She stopped frequenting the malls and refused to accept phone calls or visitors, even him. The curtains of her bedroom window remained shut. And when they finally reopened Hernán discovered a different occupant, someone who favored solid colors and abstract lithographs. Analí's pastels and Maná posters had vanished with one dramatic sweep of the curtains. Not even Mamá Patricia's astrological locators could pinpoint Analí's whereabouts: "The needle wants to pivot south," Mamá Patricia pronounced as she enclosed her hands around a compass by the light of the stars. "Maybe México. Maybe Guatemala. Maybe Brazil."

Hernán stood at the water tanks and drank one cup after another. The horizon blurred. It was like looking through the wavy invisible fumes of a flame. The foremen Jesse and Naro were nowhere in sight, Merengue the supervisor was in his truck with his head pressed against the glass as if he were asleep, so Hernán took his fill of fluid, leaning lightly on the truck.

After Analí disappeared, Julio went around saying he had made her a woman. He said it proudly: he had popped her cherry. The other guys, Hernán included, crowded the locker room to hear his stories.

Did it pop?

Did it bleed?

Was it pink?

Julio answered each question with tantalizing detail and sound effects that echoed through the high-ceilinged locker room, the humid air dizzy with fantasy. Hernán himself found it hard to swallow with the lump in his throat growing by the minute. So for weeks afterward Hernán followed Julio to the arcade after school. He marked the exact route—he skipped over the same cracks on the sidewalk, swerved to the left around the streetlight on the corner of Towne and Main. At the arcade he placed his hands on the buttons and joysticks Julio had just released, in an attempt to absorb the last traces of warmth. Hernán trained himself to listen carefully for Julio's voice, clinging to every lilt and shrill in the words that fought for space among the buzzers and bells of the pinball machines. Once he managed to occupy the racecar simulator right after Julio's time ran out. Hernán jumped in to breathe the raw smell of Julio's excitement and defeat. Hernán was satisfied he was pinning Julio down— he knew about the clumsiness of his grip, the weak ankle that betrayed him at the racecar simulator, the insecurity of his language that depended on profanity to lift itself out of his dry mouth. Hernán concluded with satisfaction that Julio had lied—he had never touched Analí, not in the same way that he had.

Was the emptiness he felt without her called love? Hernán's head was too heavy to shake from one side to the other, so he imagined himself shaking his head, just as he imagined himself done picking for the day. He must be done because vine after vine in the row had already been stripped clean of grape. He couldn't see Ernesto, nor did he remember seeing Severo on his way into the block. Everybody was gone as if swallowed up by the earth. No clippers clipped, no leaves rustled. Nothing moved except the field itself, which jerked beneath his feet to propel him forward. His aching head was playing tricks on him. Minutes ago the sand was hot, seeping into his sneakers despite the laces wrapped tight around the high-tops. Now he couldn't even sense the grains between his toes.

"Ernesto," he muttered, realizing too late that he had reached for the most hopeless name, that the names that could have saved him— Analí, Mami, Mamá Patricia—were like the loose grapes in the box, rolling back and forth from side to side, destined to be left behind. The burden of those names imploded in his brain. The sky went dark. The field slipped out from beneath his feet, stood up, and struck him flat in the face.

The Disquieting Grape

Pifas   1:15 p.m.

Each time Pifas took a load of grapes to his packer don Nico, he breathed in deeply before proudly declaring: "Hand-picked by Pifas." He worked alone yet he matched the labor of two pickers, so his two-man group never bothered to recruit a third member. He brought down his two boxes, cleared his throat and was about to make his statement when don Nico suddenly said: "They're taking the boy to the hospital."

Pifas craned his neck out to the avenue. "Whose?"

"Severo's."

"Is he dead?" someone asked. Los Caraballos expressed their disapproval by whistling. Other workers also looked on curiously as Severo and Naro lifted the sick boy's body into Severo's truck. Only doña Gertrudis hovered close to the scene, her orange hard hat glaring like a beacon in the sun.

"What are you, Gertrudis, a curandera? Get to work!" Amanda's voice rose among the murmurs.

Pifas slapped his hand against his leg. "Bites like a viper!" he declared. To stay close by he grabbed the box don Nico had just emptied and shook the sand off the bottom. "That's the second one this season," he said.

"Merengue, people, merengue! There's no show here!" Merengue waved both hands at the workers to send them back into the grapevines. Behind him the truck sped off with Ernesto sitting in the back, his face disappearing with the trail of dust.

Don Nico bent down to mark the packed box with the group number. He wrote 12 in large clumsy figures. "The second what?" he asked.

Pifas set the box down and started to fill it up with grape from the end of the row. "The second incident. Remember Chencho?" As don Nico nodded, Pifas imagined the long grape branch stretched across Chencho's path. One foot slid under it, the other stepped on it. Chencho fell on top of the box of grape and he broke an arm. "Carelessness," Pifas asserted.

Don Nico puckered his lips. "No, not carelessness," he said. "It was just his turn."

"If he had watched where he was going he might have seen the branch."

Don Nico clipped the bottom of a bunch too long to be packed. "You sound like old Tereso. Remember him? He watches the news and scolds the victims of accidents and terrorist attacks: *If they had stayed home instead of boarding that car that was going to crash; why did those people have to go into those skyscrapers when there were hijacked planes on their way?*"

"But those are the big things, don Nico. Only God can save a person from one of those tragedies. I'm talking about the small precautions He leaves to us."

"Even then," don Nico said. "I remember the time the safety clip in my clippers broke. I didn't even feel the blades open in my back pocket, so when I reached back to take the clippers out they sliced clean through the palm of my hand. Now don't tell me I was careless then? It was just my turn."

Pifas cleared his throat and scratched the back of his scalp, just under the baseball cap that made him itch when he sweat, and went back into the vines to resume picking. He didn't like to contradict don Nico so he left the argument alone, even though he thought of another example: Ilia Mendoza.

Pifas wanted to pose to don Nico the following scenario: If Ilia Mendoza had walked into the portable toilet knowing that it was facing the highway, then shouldn't she have been more careful when she stepped out? Instead, Ilia jumped out just as a car was speeding by too close to the shoulder, and off she went, struck dead at the age of thirty-three. She had no control over the speeding car, or over the location of the toilets, but she had control over how she maneuvered her body. Didn't she hear the car approaching? Couldn't she have waited? Why did she jump instead of climbing down like a decent person? Pifas imagined these questions coming up in court when Ilia

Mendoza's family was suing the company. He became a little ashamed. Don Nico would have reproached him for lessening the importance of her death. To the company, all Ilia Mendoza meant was an inconvenient lawsuit and an enforced regulation: PORTABLE TOILETS MUST FACE THE BLOCK, NOT THE ROAD.

Taking two more boxes of picked grape, Pifas said "Hand-picked by Pifas," but don Nico was too distracted, his back to the packing table and Naro standing next to him.

"I'm not sure what happened," Naro said. "The boy wandered into the wrong block, dazed and cross-eyed. Severo went looking for him when he didn't come back from the water tanks."

"Heatstroke," don Nico lamented. "So young, too."

Pifas chimed in. "I was telling don Nico that that's the second incident we've had this season."

"Third," Naro clarified, lifting his aviator glasses to wipe the sweat off the bridge of his nose.

"Third?" Pifas asked.

Naro drew in closer and lowered his voice. "Jesse and I found a dead body at the beginning of the season when we were first checking the blocks."

"And?" Pifas said anxiously, his mouth open.

"And nothing. No one knew who he was. He had no identification on him and nobody reported him missing, so it was as if he never existed."

"A Mexican?" don Nico asked.

"A farm worker by the way he was dressed. About forty years old. Jesse and I couldn't figure out how he died. It looked like he just took a nap under the vines and never woke up."

"Maybe it was el chupacabras," Pifas said.

Naro winced at Pifas. After wiping the dripping sweat off his sideburns, he tapped don Nico on the arm and walked away.

"Imagine that," said Pifas, clearing his throat. He lifted a box of grape to the packer's table. "Hand-picked by Pifas," he said. He walked out into the avenue to search for more empty boxes. His lanky body cast an equally lanky shadow against the dirt path. "Imagine that," he repeated under his breath.

Pifas found a stack of boxes, grabbed a few and slowly made his way back to his row. Doña Pepa's grandsons stood at the water tanks, both wearing matching black caps and shirts with a silk-screened image of a bunch of grapes behind a large blood red X. The bilingual inscription at the bottom read: NO COMPRE UVAS/ DON'T BUY GRAPES. He chuckled uneasily because the slogan took him back to the incident at the community center.

On the day César Chávez died, the news struck the Caliente Valley like a blazing meteor April 23, 1993. The grape-picking season hadn't yet begun, but that weekend plenty of farm workers gathered for a small memorial service at the community center. Impromptu speeches were made about the boycotts, pesticides, the marches and huelgas, the strikes. Afterward the service quieted down to personal reminiscences about brief encounters with Chávez, or with Dolores Huerta, or with the Teamsters. The energy became contagious. Stories were embellished and romanticized. Pifas, who had never met Chávez nor was a member of the United Farm Workers Union couldn't help feeling nostalgic. For what, he wasn't sure. Then suddenly, out of the candlelit vigil an awkward sleepy voice spoke up: *Federico was dead two days in his own house before anybody even noticed.* The great hall's solemnness descended on Pifas. He looked at the drunken man's face lit with a skeletal glow. Both men stared at each other, the trance unbroken until a child woke up from a nap and uttered a cry of surprise at the stillness around her.

Walking past don Nico, Pifas thought to remind him about stopping at the post office to mail a letter to México, but decided not to. If he waited one more day, one more month, or one more year it didn't make a difference because there was no one to open it wherever the letter found its way. He only made sure that it didn't come back to him, that the illusion of correspondence remained intact. Pifas knelt down on the hot sand, a box beside him, and began to pick.

"Are you writing to Margarita?" don Nico made an effort to ask whenever he discovered Pifas laboring over a piece of paper on the table. Pifas didn't move for a moment before answering as if paralyzed by his concentration, one end of the pen pressed against his upper lip.

Yes, he was writing to Margarita but Margarita had no time to respond. She stood on that balcony overlooking a field of rushes. A pair of ocas grooming their feathers reflected the whiteness of Margarita's lace-embroidered dress and the delicate aura of her profile. A black strand of hair plunged dramatically across her cheek; the wet tip stuck to the soft curve of her chin. Margarita's face glistened with the humidity, but Pifas was certain somehow that even as the movie screen faded into darkness, she would not lift up that fan hanging from a string around her wrist unless it was to spread it open in greeting the man who had come all the way from the north to love her.

The version at the matinee was much more romantic than the parting shot at the run-down bus station in Guadalajara twelve years ago. Margarita, ten years older than the woman in the film, stood at the edge of a puddle of discarded motor oil as the station roared with the chaos of engines and people overlapped against the walls of the waiting room. Margarita's tears cleared a path on her exhaust fume–tainted cheeks, her hands clasping her purse tightly, just as he had advised her because the bus station was teeming with pickpockets. She wore her apron, on break from the kitchen of the mercado down the street. She was embarrassed to have stepped out from behind the counter—she had a pair of runs on her nylons. Pifas smiled through the green glass of the bus, thanking her for the packed lunch by waving it in front of the window. He wasn't sure she had seen him; he was sure he would never see her again.

As he moved sideways on the hot sand, without a partner on the opposite side of the vine to keep up with him, he imagined the man who came to take his final breath beneath the grape. Pifas imagined all those people on the other side of the border who *did* know who the man was and who consumed their nights thinking up explanations for his disappearance. He imagined a Sunday suit growing thinner each week, a chair left empty at the dinner table, an unfinished chicken coop in the back lot. Was there a mother or a wife? Perhaps a sister, hefty yet gentle like his own sister Eloisa, but with a husband who didn't beat her, who instead offered his arm in comfort. What a solution to a sad problem, Pifas concluded as he dropped a heavy bunch of grape into the box, if he simply walked into that man's house to wear his suit, occupy his chair, and announce to everyone he would complete the chicken coop after dinner.

Dirty Old Man

Don Nico   1:40 p.m.

Don Nico sniffled a few times before he realized he was having a nosebleed. He pulled out his handkerchief, soiled with sweat and dust and pressed it against his nose. A quick glance to the side confirmed that there were no witnesses—the foremen were chatting with the cargo truck driver at the far end of the avenue and Merengue was already sitting quietly in the comfort of his truck, Amanda by his side. It wasn't that nosebleeds were uncommon in the fields, but usually boys got them, like the one who got hauled off to the hospital half an hour ago. Seasoned workers like him were not usually susceptible to those effects of heat. Embarrassed, don Nico picked up his clippers and scurried down the row, lifting up vines off the ground until he found Pifas.

Pifas looked up in surprise. "What's the matter?" he said. "Are we going home?" He craned his neck to take a closer look at don Nico and then grinned.

"Just go pack for a while until it goes away," don Nico whispered, his voice sounding disguised behind the handkerchief. Pifas obliged him. As he walked off to the packing table, don Nico contemplated the back of his shirt worn so thin with sweat and wear that it was almost transparent. Through his own sleeves he could see the dark brown of his elbows. Scratching at the loose skin through the cotton was like scratching to the bare bone with the sharp fingernail. He imagined Eloisa, embarrassed for him as he came toward her. With the shirt drenched in sweat and stuck to his chest, he exposed his black nipples, the leathery skin between his ribs and the ribs themselves protruding out of his sparsely haired flesh. An old man is what she saw. He saw the same thing each time he took the dull razor to his chin, the scraping of the rough skin reminded him of shaving the pigs after the slaughter. The chore was usually quick and not too thorough, otherwise the seasoned pork eater would find it lacking to consume chicharrones without the singed hair or pork rinds preserved in vinegar without the prickly stubble. He felt at his chin with the back of his hand and concluded that he should shave more than twice a week.

Don Nico twitched his nose. The blood had dried and flaked off when he pushed a finger into the left nostril. The passageway was clogged but he didn't want to blow his nose for fear of starting up the blood flow again. He had no choice but to breathe through his mouth while he worked. He imagined the air building up in his stomach and the ache he would have to reckon with by the end of the day.

In the next row over, he could see Francisca's pink leg warmers snug around her calves. Chela worked opposite her, both picking at a steady pace. When Chela bent down to lift a box of grape, don Nico shifted his head to the right to get a better look at her buttocks tight against the jeans. *What a dirty old man you are,* he thought to himself. He couldn't help shifting his head again to search for an opening in the vines that would allow him a glimpse of Francisca's cotton shirt pushed up into her belly when she pressed a box of grape against her. The two women shuffled out, giggling at each other as they kept losing their footing on the soft soil beneath their feet. There was something about a woman dressed in full grape picker wear that excited him more than the scantily clad cholas at the mall or than the bare midriff models in magazines. On a farm worker every wrinkle on the cotton was a cleavage snuggling dust. Each collar, each sleeve, each pants cuff, contained a secret: an orgy of smells gathered about her—the sulfur, the heat, her perfume. Interior clothing held no mystery for him and was no match for a woman's bandanna wrapped around the bouquet of her hair. The fabric touched the more delicate sweat glands: her low hairline, the cartilage behind her ear, the soft valley of her nape. Of course, the more he lingered on the femininity of work clothes the more the image of Eloisa came into focus. Sweet and plump Eloisa.

Eloisa's frequent afternoon visits to the apartment were also gestures of unspoken gratitude to don Nico. To this day neither of them had told Pifas the true circumstances of that accident that had crippled Eloisa's husband. All Pifas knew was that Tenorio damaged his arm one hot summer afternoon and then spent each afternoon after that hurling his rage at his wife, frustrated with his useless limb. A one-armed farm worker was not a farm worker at all, maybe not even a man.

"I need a big favor, don Nico," Eloisa said. He was already in the passenger seat of her car. Pifas had been left behind to babysit because he was an impatient driver and passenger on any road trip longer than thirty minutes. As far as don Nico was concerned he was accompanying Eloisa to the dentist in Mexicali, just across the border. She needed someone to drive her back in case the anesthesia took time to wear off.

Don Nico didn't hesitate to respond, imagining that she would want to borrow money, nothing more. "If I can help you, Eloisa, I will," he said softly, his dreamy eyes locked on her face.

"We're not really going to the dentist," she said.

"Then where are we going?" don Nico asked, no suspicion in his voice.

Eloisa kept driving for a few more miles on Highway 86 before she built up the nerve to explain. Don Nico waited patiently. Tenorio's sister and her two daughters were going to cross the border. No, they weren't jumping the fence or crawling through the long stretch of desert—those were the old dangerous methods. Nowadays the border patrol officers were on the take. At the right time and with the right officer, a carload of people could cross, flashing fake green cards for effect, and no one would know the difference except the border patrol guard who kept an accurate count. He would meet up with the coyote later and charge his fee. It was smuggling on credit. For this crossing, Tenorio would drive through with the three women. He was already waiting on the American side for Eloisa and don Nico to arrive with the car. Tenorio crosses into México, picks up his family, crosses back into the U.S. and meets up with Eloisa and don Nico.

"As simple as that?" don Nico asked.

"As simple as that," Eloisa said. "However, there's the second inspection station coming into the Caliente Valley. But that lazy migra is hardly ever there. What we need to do after Tenorio gets the girls across is drive all this way to make sure they can get into the Valley without any trouble. If there is no migra around we drive back and pick the girls up again."

"What if the migra *is* there?" don Nico asked, intrigued by the whole plot.

"Then we drive through like normal and send word to Tenorio to wait for another day. Once the girls get across they have to be patient."

Crossing the girls was the easy part. Eloisa and don Nico waited at the park on the American side for Tenorio. Within a few hours he arrived with three nervous women in the car. Another car followed and parked right behind them. The stressed look of Tenorio's face made both Eloisa and don Nico chuckle.

"It wasn't that bad, was it?" Eloisa asked.

Enraged, Tenorio grabbed Eloisa by the shoulder. Eloisa squirmed and suppressed a cry of pain. Don Nico turned his head.

"Bitch," Tenorio said. "It's not that funny. We have a change in plans."

"Why? What happened?" Eloisa asked.

"The border patrol guard raised his fee. We need to gather some more money before the coyote will let the girls go."

Don Nico tilted his head to catch a glimpse of the second car and understood immediately. It wasn't as simple as that. Tenorio joined Eloisa and don Nico on the long drive back to the Valley. He was anxious so he asked Eloisa to drive. He took the back seat in order to lie down for a while and think. They needed to access the cash inside their mattress and to check about the second inspection station. The border patrol was posted that afternoon. This only angered Tenorio even more. He commanded Eloisa to step on the gas as soon as they passed immigration, slapping her once on the side of the head. She caved in under the pressure and jerked the car to the side of the road. The car came to a violent halt when she hit the brakes, the front facing a ditch. She burst out into tears, her hand gripping the gear shift. The incline was sharp. The car was balanced at a precarious angle.

"I'll fucking drive, you stupid bitch, before you kill us all!"

Tenorio yelled, spittle escaping his mouth. He climbed out of the back seat through the right side of the car. Don Nico watched as Tenorio walked to the front to survey the damage. Bent over with his hand on the hood, Tenorio kept shouting profanities and threats.

"I'm going to beat the shit out of you if you fucked up the alignment!" he said.

The next few seconds seemed to stretch out into minutes. From the corner of his eye don Nico saw Eloisa's face harden. She became pale, and stiff as stone. She shifted into neutral and released the brakes. The car inched forward easily, taking Tenorio with it into the ditch. The damage was done: Tenorio was crippled for life, his shoulder going numb with the weight of the car; his sister and nieces were returned to México; and Eloisa began to work in the fields to make up for the meager disability check Tenorio received each month. When the police and paramedics arrived asking questions, don Nico told them the truth: Eloisa had lost control of the car and nearly driven them into a ditch, and when her husband climbed down to check the wheels, his hand heavy on the hood had shimmied the vehicle into forward motion. The explanation was good enough for the police but it didn't quite convince Tenorio, who from that day on relied on the bottle for comfort, and on the hostility of his good arm for emotional release.

At the hospital, Eloisa was crying into the same handkerchief don Nico now held close to his nose. Through his one clear nostril he could still identify the faint traces of her scent since he had refused to wash the piece of cloth after she gave it back to him. He carried it in his pocket like a talisman, or a love letter, and had only used it now out of desperation. And yet he could romanticize this happenstance as well—their fluids were now united. Her tears and his blood had come together, offerings in the sacrifice of love. She had cried for him, he had bled for her. He spread the handkerchief over his mouth and nose and breathed in slowly and deeply, his usual habit. However, this time the air filtered through the cloth stung his good nostril and he sneezed, releasing a small mass of reddened mucous. *What a dirty old man you are*, don Nico said to himself. He crumpled up the handkerchief, stuffed it into his back pocket and continued picking grapes.

LAS INVISIBLES

Doña Gertrudis 1:45 p.m.

"This is the last one," doña Ramona said to doña Gertrudis as she tilted the camera to the left and prepared to snap the shot. She had parted the branches of the grapevine and leaned into them to keep them spread open for a cleaner view.

Doña Gertrudis cast an annoyed look beneath her orange hard hat. "Santos cielos, comadre, now's not the time," she admonished. "We've just had a near fatality on our hands."

Doña Ramona brought down the camera. "What fatality? Are you still thinking about that boy? He'll be fine, comadre. You said so yourself it was only a minor heatstroke. A young boy like that will be back picking grapes by Monday morning, guaranteed. Look at Manuel: fifty years older and four strokes ahead of the boy." She positioned the camera again. "Come on. The last one."

Doña Gertrudis had no choice but to humor doña Ramona. She pulled two tiny bunches from the vine, each with only a few mature grapes dangling from the long thin stems that made them look like white cherries. "Earrings," doña Gertrudis said as her picture was taken. The supple tendrils twined around the stems added to the effect.

"You'll look better than in your company ID, that's for sure," doña Ramona said. "Those are prison mug shots." She took her weight off the branches and they came together again into a wall of leaves separating her from doña Gertrudis.

Doña Gertrudis laughed, shaking the dust off the narrow plastic rim of her hard hat. "Remember how Eva and Silvania and the other young women demanded the pictures be retaken?"

"What a waste of time. Who was going to look at them anyway?" doña Ramona said. She wound the string around the camera and stuffed it inside her shirt pocket. Afterwards she worked in synch to doña Gertrudis's cutting motions.

Doña Gertrudis bit her lip. She had secretly cheered on that uprising by the young women, it was the closest she had seen to an organized movement, let alone collective bargaining. Gone were the Union days in the Caliente Valley. All the activity was up North. So it was refreshing to see some excitement in the otherwise dull fields. Besides, her own ID made her look at least ten years older than her fifty-seven years, and no matter what her daughter-in-law said about women over fifty with growths of white hair, it still made all the difference. That week she even called in for a skin care treatment from that beauty expert on Spanish television, Samy. When the package arrived she tried to hide it from her daughter-in-law but Carina could whiff out a penny embedded in a piece of shit because that afternoon she waved the face creams in front of Daniel and whined: "Daniel, look at what your mother has been throwing her money at!" Daniel had calmly unbuttoned his blue groundskeeper work shirt, revealing a thin torso, and ignored her. Frustrated, Carina raised her voice in English and hurled the creams on the sofa. Then Daniel yelled back and soon the fight was between the two of them. Doña Gertrudis gathered her creams and took them into her room. The tape player greeted her from the dressing table, both items purchased from Goodwill. She set the creams down, flipped the cassette over and let Chavelita Vargas drown out the bickering with her throaty croon. The bickering always lead to the same watering hole: *Return her to México*. Carina resented sharing breathing space with her husband's mother, especially the kitchen. Doña Gertrudis didn't exactly dislike Carina's cooking, but she couldn't help making suggestions for improvement here and there: a little more salt, a little less oregano, and how about chopping the tomatoes instead of mutilating them in the blender? Suggestions, nothing more. And not once did she ever ask her daughter-in-law about her inability to produce a child after six years of marriage. Now if Carina happened to walk in on doña Gertrudis having a phone conversation regarding the subject, well that was an entirely different matter. And despite Carina's suspicions, doña Gertrudis never once eavesdropped on the private activities unfolding in the next room. Carina's voice simply carried. It pierced walls. Whisper, sob or moan, Carina's was the high pitch of a neurotic soprano. But she knew how to get back at her mother-in-law with that household budget of hers that combined their three small incomes. The Golden Rule: NO LUXURIES. No fancy jewelry, no Lotto tickets or Scratchers, no top shelf liquor, and no vanity products, including cosmetics, hair dyes, and those herbal eye pads doña Gertrudis wore to counter puffiness. In short, no simple pleasures for doña Gertrudis. Daniel allowed the squabbles to bloom and wither around him without taking much interest. Like his father before him. And sadly, doña Gertrudis suspected, he escaped to his job, working double shifts and overtime, refusing to take time off. Like his mother.

Doña Gertrudis sighed. The plastic band inside the hard hat made her head itch.

"Are you tired already, comadre?" doña Ramona asked.

"No, comadre," doña Gertrudis answered. "Work has been so slow lately that I hope we get the late shift at the warehouse soon."

"My knees are too weak for kneeling all night long checking boxes. If we have to repack I'll drop you and Manuel off and come pick you up at midnight."

"I heard talk that we *are* going to repack tonight," a mousy voice behind doña Gertrudis said.

Doña Gertrudis looked over her shoulder at doña Pepa. The coloring of doña Pepa's cheeks behind the pair of oversized glasses reminded doña Gertrudis of the sun-burnt juicy raisins often found at the ends of the grapevine rows. "Are you going to join us?" doña Gertrudis asked.

Doña Pepa shook her head. "My lazy grandsons won't go."

"Neither of you need to go!" doña Ramona scolded. "And I'm not letting you go either, Gertrudis. We're too old for that."

"I'm not an old woman yet," doña Pepa said. She pulled back the sleeve of her bright red sweater and offered doña Gertrudis her biceps. "Feel this," she said. "Go ahead, go ahead. Touch it."

Reluctantly, doña Gertrudis squeezed the soft tissue. "Woman, you could be Popeye's mother!" From across the vines doña Ramona laughed.

"I used to box and play soccer with my grandsons. Now they're

too ashamed to get beaten by their own abuela made tough as iron."
Doña Pepa swung a left hook, her head dodging an invisible punch.

"Santos cielos," doña Gertrudis said. "You better be careful with
that loaded weapon." Doña Pepa quietly turned around and continued picking. Doña Ramona gave doña Gertrudis a wink through
the vines.

Doña Gertrudis felt for doña Pepa. Twice she had gotten lost
within the block. The first time she was located the foreman laughed
it off, especially when an outraged doña Pepa denied in her squeaky
voice that she had ever been lost. But the second time Naro had to
organize a small search party. The supervisor strongly advised her
to stay close to her grandsons and to retire after the season. Doña
Gertrudis remembered stepping back into the crowd of onlookers,
afraid that the supervisor was going to single out other older women
in the crew.

"She reminds me of a woman I once heard talk about," doña
Ramona whispered.

Doña Gertrudis raised her eyebrows. The cargo truck started
beeping in the distance.

"This woman . . . let's call her Cleotilde," doña Ramona said.

"Cleotilde. Of course," doña Gertrudis stated, matter-of-factly.

"I like that name," doña Ramona explained. "All the women I
hear talk about deserve a name. I like Cleotilde."

"Go on, go on," doña Gertrudis said, drawing circles in the air
with the clippers.

Doña Ramona focused on each bunch as she cut it down from
the vine. "Cleotilde," she began, "was a hard-working woman who
didn't remember a day that didn't start at three in the morning.
Although she didn't have a family, there was always some chore to
do around her own house before she went out to clean other
people's houses. Her schedule was tightly packed with places she
cleaned every other day, every third day, or once a week, or only on
weekends—every job at all hours of the morning, afternoon and
evening. The poor woman's hands were bleached white under those
rubber gloves she wore. She never took them off in front of her
employers because of the rash of welts on her palms and in the
spaces between her fingers—"

"My neighbor's niece suffers from overworked hands too," doña Gertrudis interrupted. "She works at a bakery, spreading the frosting on cakes. Her index fingers don't bend anymore and they're always pointing out like this." Doña Gertrudis demonstrated.

"Yes, well, anyway . . ." doña Ramona paused ". . . Cleotilde was always on the go, day and night, sweeping, dusting, mopping, spraying, polishing, scrubbing, rinsing, wiping, gathering, separating, washing, drying, folding, ironing—everything! She was going bald from all the chemicals she was exposed to, but that too she kept hidden by wearing a bandanna around her head. Her eyesight was getting blurrier and more sensitive to the light so she wore tinted glasses, a stronger prescription each year. To ease the arthritis on her knees she stuck hot compresses behind her kneepads. And to keep all those cleaning supplies close at hand, she designed and sewed her own work apron with a pocket or belt loop for each of her cleaning tools. Cleotilde looked like a janitor's closet come to life."

"Santos cielos!" doña Gertrudis proclaimed.

"Coming home for Cleotilde was like arriving to yet another work place since she didn't spend any more time in her own house than she did in any other; everything looked just as vaguely familiar and temporarily under her care. Well, eventually her body couldn't bear the stress anymore and her employers began to notice discrepancies and oversights in her work: a water spot on the wine glass here, an untreated collar stain there. Even she had to admit the time had come to stop."

"To retire?" doña Gertrudis asked in a low whisper, aware of doña Pepa picking grapes behind her.

Doña Ramona nodded. "Cleotilde finally had to stay put in her own home for a change, settling among her belongings that stared back at her like a room full of strangers. For the first few weeks she kept waking up at the usual hour, so she forced herself to take her time with the household chores, stretching them out as long as she could. But a woman living by herself finds very little in her home to keep her busy for too long. So Cleotilde began to give herself things to do: she always left a dirty glass out to come back to a few hours later; she became more critical when she made the bed, undoing and doing the linen repeatedly until she was satisfied she had reached perfection; she stopped taking out her shoes before entering a house so that the carpet demanded to be vacuumed more frequently; and to insure that she had plenty of laundry at the end of the week, she changed clothes three, sometimes four or five times a day."

"Santos cielos!" doña Gertrudis said.

"Believe it," doña Ramona insisted.

"That was a good one, comadre," doña Gertrudis said. "Now let's take the grape before your old man starts to complain."

Each woman took her filled box and walked her path down to the packer's table at the end of the row. The story of another woman spun inside doña Gertrudis's head at the moment, but she didn't dare compete with doña Ramona. Or with Cleotilde. The woman she once heard talk about was named Gertrudis: Gertrudis lived in an apartment with a son who wouldn't think to offer her a glass of water unless she was a car engine overheating. To keep his widowed mother completely out of his way, the son married and brought home a wife. But instead of a companion, Gertrudis now had two flighty grown-up children swirling around the living room, ignoring her into invisibility. That nasty suggestion bounced off the walls: *Return her to México.*

Daniel and Carina were not going to make her disappear so easily; Gertrudis was taking care of that. She would buy her bus ticket to Jalisco at the end of the grape-picking season, of that she was sure, but not before planting tiny reminders here and there of her existence: a knot of dark nylons dropped inside Carina's hamper; her old wedding photograph slipped between the stack of papers in the glove compartment of Daniel's car; a dab of her arthritis treatment smeared on the vinyl sofa; a white hair plucked and carefully extended between the folds of the TV Guide. She would be daring and leave behind her thumbprint on Carina's diaphragm—a double message!

When doña Gertrudis finally reached the end of the row, doña Ramona came around the other side. Doña Gertrudis had carried the box on her left shoulder, and doña Ramona on her right, so that when they came face to face on the opposite ends of the packing table, each woman reflected the tired, dust-covered body of the other.

SEVEN

Despite the air holes at the top, the portable toilet didn't get enough light. Sebastián was locked inside the near dark with the smell of piss and salt water, trying to keep his breaths short. Each bead of sweat prickled as it slowly made its way down, heavy as mercury against his skin. The plastic toilet lid kept shifting underneath his wet buttocks.

What a contrast to the spit-shined restroom at home where every new flake of mildew met its end under his mother's fierce scrub brush. She was protective about her clean house. After work he and his sisters had to leave their dirty clothes outside to be washed and pressed by the following morning. She especially followed him around, coating his scent with air freshener all the way to the bathtub where she kindly reminded him to use the pumice stone against his ankles. The soap she made herself, grinding rosemary leaves and jasmine into a cup of laundry detergent, then sprinkling the powder with baby oil until she had one big clump. She packed the clump tightly and rubbed the surface until smooth, finally setting it out in the sun to bake like brick, which is what the damn thing felt like in the shower.

The shower was a whole different point of contention because it clogged up so often. He blamed it on his sisters who shed so much hair it surprised him not to see them bald; Jacaranda's hair was so long he could use it as kite string. But Eva blamed it on the sticky substance that lodged itself in the drain, and when he asked, *What sticky substance?* Eva clarified without hesitation, sending Mami reeling back in shock. Sebastián just rolled his eyes, at both Eva's crassness and Mami's prudishness, but he had to appreciate Eva's attempts at breaking the spine—no offense to Papi's broken back—of the moral codes that hung inside the house like a neon sign that flashes on and off, day and night, week after week, so that after awhile it's nothing but an annoying reminder of the neon itself.

It had been Eva, as a matter of fact, who taught him the ins and outs of the flesh. Pun intended. They were only children then, fascinated with the likes and unlikes of their naked bodies. As if playing with their Lego blocks, they experimented inserting their fingers, their tongues, and his baby carrot–sized penis into their dark orifices. And it had been Jacaranda who put a stop to their explorations when she caught them rubbing their bare asses together. She was solemn in her warning against indulging in corporal pleasures. The corporal part he understood because of the seven corporal acts of mercy Papi made them memorize, but the pleasure part didn't kick in until years later when he was too old for kiddy Bible school and was moved up to the young adult section, where hands and feet groped and grabbed blindly under the tables. The challenge was to keep a straight face during opening prayer as somebody's fat toe poked his scrotum. That was also the year Susie Thompson asked him to drop his pants behind the church and then recoiled in horror after stroking the foreskin of his uncircumcised cock. *Aren't they all the same?* he asked her, and she said, *Hell, no! You've got a Mexican dick.* He went home angry and hurt, convinced that his parents had done this to him to make sure he didn't go around chasing the white girls and that he ended up marrying somebody like his sister Jacaranda, self-righteous and ugly as a foot.

But marriage was not something he was looking for so it stayed lost in the sack of improbabilities along with career. Sure, he was going off to college in the fall, but so were half the knuckleheads from the high school, even Pecas, who got expelled for sniffing glue in the gym. Sebastián received a modest scholarship from a national Hispanic organization touched by his essay on how he was the son of a palm tree pruner and he wanted to better himself through an education, to stop doing farm work in the summers. Come this fall, no more grapes, no more heat, and no more watching television at night with headphones because the house had to be still as a mausoleum for Papi to get his sleep. No more Papi. Each night after the television finally went off and he walked back to his room in the dark, Sebastián always missed the doorways and bumped into the walls. There was no memorizing the house after all these years. Perhaps he had always known his stay was temporary. When Papi took the family to a house swallowed by a grove of date trees, the only person who wanted to stay for good was Papi. Poor dying on the bed Papi.

During the first weeks in the new home, Sebastián kept recalling the gingerbread house from the storybooks. Falling asleep to Papi's doomsday prayers gave him nightmares about floating through space into adobe ovens. It didn't help that his mother covered the wood and vinyl with her homemade spray polish of fruit extracts and cinnamon tea, a solution whose smell didn't wear off. Instead it penetrated anything that came into contact with it. When he woke up, his heart racing with fright, he smelled the gingerbread furniture and couches.

Sebastián reached for the roll of toilet paper. When he placed it back on its stand the roll kept the damp indentations of his fingertips. The plastic toilet lid preserved the ring of sweat made by his butt cheeks. He kicked open the door and welcomed the stale air. The hot daylight struck his eyes with such force he had to shield them with an open hand. The side of his hand stuck to his forehead from the grape juice that seeped between his fingers when he packed it. He was considering heading over to the water tanks when Dino the shipper stopped him.

"Have you heard?" Dino asked; a grin on his face.

"No, what's up?"

"Your crew's going to the warehouse."

"Sonofabitch," Sebastián said. Dino patted Sebastián three times on the shoulder and walked on.

"And say hello to your sister for me," Dino shouted back.

Sonofabitch, Sebastián kept repeating the rest of the way back to his row on the block. The warehouse meant backaches and a stinging of the lungs as each box was tossed to him to toss to another man until the entire cargo was down. The pain didn't go away for days, so he expected to take the warehouse with him to Los Arcos. Hopefully he would lose it there among the empty shot glasses and sweaty Budweiser bottles. That was the key: leaving places behind. He had learned that from the maps.

When Papi first bought the used car way back when, he showed off the fancy features none of his previous cars had had. The family gathered around the panel and when Papi turned on the air conditioner, every hand sought an outlet to receive the flow of air. The window didn't have to be rolled down—the glass descended at the push of a button. And the right sideview mirror could be adjusted from the driver's seat without the need to stretch across the length of the car. But it was Sebastián who discovered the stack of maps forgotten under the front seat. He snuck them away only to unfold them in the privacy of his room. The paper was worn and soft, but the real evidence of their use lay in the routes outlined in shades of red and black. Sebastián spent hours tracing the plotted itineraries and discovering new ones, his small finger plowing through the names of unpronounceable towns and swimming swiftly across bodies of water. And when the long lines he drew ran off the page, he knew that there was a larger landscape that not even this puzzle of scribbles and letters could contain. There he was, inside this hollow dot called Caliente, California, and there was the spider web of paths pointing out the many exits.

Moving along the block, he took a place behind the metal table to pack the last few boxes of grape his sisters left behind. They had taken the number sign with them. They were Group 7, lucky seven, catechism seven: sacraments, virtues, sins and gifts, the seven deacons, the seven joys of Mary, her seven sorrows, the Book of Judges, the Sabbath, July, days of the week, the seven senses, the seven altars, seven bulls, seven rams, the seven-year famine, the seven-year-old king, the seventh seal, The Seven Year Itch, Seven Brides for Seven Brothers, House of the Seven Gables, Seven Against Thebes, Sinbad of the Seven Seas, the seventh heaven, the seven sisters, the seven wonders, 7-11, Seven-Up.

Once done, he collected his tools and prepared to push the packer's table to his group's next row when he suddenly realized he didn't know whether Eva and Jacaranda had gone to the left or to the right. His head had emptied completely. He was left disoriented. He stalled, reorganizing his materials as he tried to detect the direction the crew was moving by the way the bodies shifted, by the tone of their voices. But the workers weren't going anywhere or saying anything in that precise moment. Like Sebastián they stood firm, quietly rooted to the scalding earth.

FOOTPRINT

"Where the hell is he?" Eva asked. She and Jacaranda had each brought down a box of grape. With their feet they shoved the boxes under the shade to protect them from the sun. The grape darkened, opaque in the shadows. "Is he still taking a shit?"

"Disgusting, Eva," Jacaranda admonished. She plucked a grape from the vine and once rubbed into near transparency she popped it inside her mouth to coat her dry tongue. Across the avenue Merengue started up his truck. A man coughed at the dust blown by the muffler. Jacaranda could make out don Manuel toiling over the packing table, his arm over his mouth, and behind him doña Ramona threw the necklace pocket watch over her shoulder before she bent over to pick up an empty box.

"How old do you think she is?" Jacaranda asked, no energy in her voice.

"Amanda? About forty," Eva replied. Jacaranda noticed Amanda had suddenly come into view after Merengue moved his truck a few feet forward.

"I meant doña Ramona."

"About eighty. One ages faster in the fields. Why do you ask?"

"No reason," Jacaranda said. She dug her fingernails into the side of her neck to scratch. "I'm bored and there's nothing better to look at than an old woman who has picked grapes all her life."

"Well, there's always Dino tossing the boxes up on the cargo truck," Eva said.

"There's more poetry in the old woman," Jacaranda said, heavy on the sarcasm.

Eva rolled her eyes. "You're hopeless," she said, then added as she looked down at her watch: "It's almost two-thirty. I'm not picking anymore. Come on, let's go."

Eva put away the clippers in her back pocket and led Jacaranda by the sleeve to the middle of the row, to the stake painted white. They both kneeled on the hot soil beneath the leaves. Jacaranda didn't resist, remembering clearly all of those humid afternoons they had to stay behind after quitting time to help Sebastián pack the last few boxes. The foremen didn't allow the workers to leave grape off the vine. The rule was clear: You pick it, you pack it. Through the vines Jacaranda could see others hiding out in the rows as well. The soft murmur of conversation carried.

"How are you feeling?" Jacaranda asked Eva.

Eva looked back at her sister. Her eyes were bloodshot and Jacaranda suspected hers looked just as irritated.

"I'll be fine, considering," Eva said. She sighed.

Jacaranda thought about stroking Eva's cheek with her hand, but had reservations. They were affectionate toward their mother but not with each other, ever since Jacaranda had caught Eva and Sebastián fondling each other as children. It seemed a disgrace that the innocent act had grown into a shameful secret that made all future physical contact avoidable, deemed a forbidden act. She blamed herself for it. She had taken a self-righteous stance. For months she lorded over them with the threat of exposure. Eva did Jacaranda's chores when their parents were at work and Sebastián gave up the money he was collecting from leaving his baby teeth beneath the pillow. While Eva cleaned, Jacaranda prayed for their souls and every quarter left by the Tooth Fairy was dropped into the collection basket at church. At night, she prayed alongside her father in the back room, which he called the prayer room because it was isolated from all the heathen distractions in the rest of the house. His was a fervor that excited her. He sweat profusely before the votive candles and his hands trembled with a passion that matched the vibrations of his voice as he read the Gospels. She wanted to feel the intensity of his heat, enter into the zeal of his trance, so she pressed her small body against his as if by osmosis the currents taking possession of his soul would travel into hers. Eyes shut, she could feel the transfer taking place. She felt his heat, his sweat, his breath, his heartbeat, his hands, his mouth. Their intimate sessions in the prayer room, before the cross of Christ, became filled with an ardor that spun her mind in circles, at first provoking dizzy spells and later blackouts. Jacaranda couldn't remember how long the ritual of the prayer room went on before her mother demanded that prayer take place in the openness of the living room. The cross and votive candles were replaced by the new washer and an elaborate assortment of cleaning products that made the back room look like a supermarket aisle. Neither could she remember when she realized that her father's possessions were very corporal and not spiritual. He was a man, not a saint, and like any man his body responded to the earthly pleasures first, the heavenly rewards, second. And like a flawed man, his soul succumbed before his body did. The strap coming loose around his waist caused his fall. But he was already a fallen man.

"What are you naming your firstborn?" Jacaranda blurted out. Eva did not flinch.

"We're thinking of naming him after Papi."

"It's a boy?"

"Only a male can be such a pain in the ass," Eva said. They laughed. Jacaranda pulled out a cigarette box from her shirt pocket. "I'm not even showing yet and already I get morning sickness."

At the sound of a whistle, Eva stuck her hand out to wave at Sebastián. When he finally reached them he shoved a few vines to the side and ducked his head, his face red and wet.

"Pick about another box and a half and no more," he warned. "I heard talk that we're quitting at two-thirty." He looked down at his watch.

"Finally," Eva said. "What's the point of this game? No one's even working anymore? Why are we still here?"

"They're not letting us go because they're sending us straight to the warehouse," Sebastián said.

"We're not going home?" Eva complained. "Mierda!"

"Let me have one of those," Sebastián said, pointing at Jacaranda's lighted cigarette. Jacaranda blew out a breath full of smoke and handed her brother the cigarette box.

"Can you guys blow your smoke somewhere else? My God," Eva said. She waved her hands in front of her face theatrically.

"So pack about a box and a half and no more," Sebastián reminded them before walking back to the packing table.

"It won't be that bad," Jacaranda said. "We need the hours anyway. Besides, you know we don't do any loading and unloading. We just sit around and wait." Praying, the foremen called it, because everyone repacked the fallen shipment on their knees. Some even referred to the trips to the warehouse as visits to church.

"It's not that. I just want to get home and shower and eat. Aren't you starving?"

The awkward silence that followed was the incentive they needed to start picking again. Eva crossed underneath the vines to work on the opposite side. She raised one leg over the leveling wire and then the other, careful not to get her sneakers caught. The rustling of the leaves as her body came out on the other side was a familiar, jarring sound to Jacaranda. She bowed her head and her eyes locked on the deep footprint Eva had made in the soft earth. The image reminded her of the last time she remembered her family at the height of their happiness and functionality.

It was a particularly humid night in the desert. Everyone was lying around in their underclothes, Papi in dark blue boxers and a white tank top. Sebastián pouted on Papi's lap. Mami wore her silky yellow slip. She was in the kitchen refilling the ice trays. Eva and Jacaranda had not offered to help their mother make the iced tea. Later, Jacaranda would try to measure which of the two was the bigger disappointment: her uncharacteristic lack of courtesy or Papi's overlooking it. When Mami came into the living room with a tray heavy with five servings of cold sweetened tea, Sebastián climbed off Papi's lap reluctantly, and Papi was the first to help himself to a tall glass.

After they took their first sips of iced tea the room went dead with silence. This made Papi uncomfortable. He sprung up off the couch and announced to the family that there was to be a dance.

"A dance?" the two sisters said in unison. Mami shrugged her shoulders, a soft smile on her face that made her look unaffected by the oppressive temperature.

Papi switched on the radio. It was the first time he had ever done so since he condemned the evocative lyrics written for popular music lately. Usually it was Mami or Eva who listened to the radio at low volume. Papi turned the volume up. A Sonora Santanera cumbia invaded the living room, urging them to sway their hips and twist their feet. Mami and Eva took the lead, Sebastián wrapped his skinny arms around Mami and buried his face on her thigh, keeping in step with her rhythm.

"Let's go, Jacaranda," Papi said. He held out his hand for her. She took it, uncertain of what to do next.

"You do know how to cumbia, don't you?" Papi asked. He was already moving his feet on the floor.

There was no context for his question. Jacaranda had never seen her father dance or even use the word cumbia until that night.

"Follow my lead, Jacaranda. Do what I do," he said.

Into their second dance the soles of their bare feet made fresh wet prints on the tile. Papi's were long and wide. Jacaranda's were also long but thinner. Each time his feet lifted from the tile the print began to evaporate, but Jacaranda quickly stepped down on the same spot to keep the print alive with sweat, and to soak up the warm ghost of a foot her father had left behind. Papi's calf muscles were strong and chiseled. His biceps and pectorals flexed and extended in synch to the brass sounds of the music. The hair on his skin—from his toes to his neck—pricked up as if in response to the hard-won effort of his skilled grace and tempo. Papi was beauty—a quality not usually embodied by a male, but since she was convinced the term would never be appropriate for her, then it was very much his.

"Let everything that has breath praise the Lord," her father declared when he had tired shortly after the third song on the radio. "Let us praise our Father." He held his right hand up in the air.

"Do we have to stop dancing?" Pretty-faced Eva said in a whiny voice.

"Of course not," Papi said. "But your father needs to have his rest. He's done enough damage celebrating to this sinful music."

Papi had laughed at his own straitlaced ways, proving himself human in a way that both disconcerted and pleased Jacaranda. That dance set in motion the ambiguity that was Papi. Even the innocence of the dark blue boxer shorts seemed to change before her eyes, transformed into the suggestive cloth that concealed his sex. Ashamed, Jacaranda had grown feverish that night, battling headaches and stomach cramps. Papi had sat by her side during the entire ordeal, ceaselessly praying and expressing his pride for her because she had finally become a woman. She had never seen him so enthusiastic. It was as if he had been waiting for that moment all along.

"Hallowed be thy name," Jacaranda whispered.

"Did you say something?" Eva asked. "I think this is all we should pick. Sebastián is making idiot signals for us to stop."

A car honked three times. It was quitting time, but only in the fields. Eva shoved her box toward Jacaranda's side. The weight pushed the soft soil forward, filling up the footprint with dirt and dried grape leaves. Jacaranda lifted the box and walked toward the avenue, her face pushing against a wall of heat. She heard Eva dragging her feet, keeping up on the other side. With everyone moving out at once, trampling over dead leaves and branches, the sound amplified and suddenly Jacaranda thought of the ocean, the surf breaking up at the shore. Papi made many promises in the prayer room. He promised her the marvels of their miraculous God: nature's holier landscapes, the sea, infinite and sacrosanct, the fires of the desert sands, the phenomenon of His invisible hand, all heat and breath. He promised her he would never hurt her. As she spent her last trace of strength delivering the box of grape to her brother, she imagined her father must be grateful somehow that his words hadn't spoken falsehoods entirely. She had her sea, her fires and her heat. He had kept all but one of his promises.

RIGOBERTO
GONZÁLEZ

SISTERS AND SAINTS

Dino   *2:40 p.m.*

Jacobo was leaning against the cargo truck, patiently picking diesel grease out of his nails with the tip of a large splinter from a pallet, when Dino came up to him with the news that the foreman had confirmed the crew's assignment to the warehouse.

"Poor shits," said Jacobo, still focused on his nails. "I hear it's going to be a long night too. Four shipments have already fallen."

"Dirty grape?"

"Low sugar. It's a shitty crop this year." Jacobo wore a baseball cap with a heavy sweat ring across the crown. Above him the truck radio played a tune by Los Tucanes.

"Every year it's worse," Dino said. "Including the hours. Some of the pickers are actually glad they're getting sent to the warehouse all night to make up for the slow work. I know my sister is anxious about it."

No response from Jacobo. Dino let out a whistle through his teeth and jumped up into the driver's seat, his right leg hanging out. He adjusted the sound on the radio. They had to wait for the crew to complete one final cargo before heading to the warehouse themselves, dropping a shipment only to return and load for another crew. From a distance he could tell this crew had already been told to wrap things up by the way the workers suddenly picked up their speed in a spurt of renewed energy, though they were simply changing tasks and not going home. Not any of the men anyway. He imagined his fat brother-in-law groaning and Francisca soothing him with threats of not allowing him to go repack. Valentín loved to play the martyr.

The sun pierced through Dino's skin because he was getting too relaxed, getting caught off guard. Adding to his discomfort was the splinter Jacobo was holding between his fingertips. About five years ago Valentín and Francisca had to drive him to the emergency room after he took in a similarly-shaped splinter under the toenail. Just thinking about it made his foot itch. Valentín had been upset over the hospital bill since Dino had yet to find a steady job and still lived in the living room. But Francisca pulled out her private stash. She kept a wad of bills stuffed under the hollow Virgen de Guadalupe sculpture Dino won playing darts at a carnival in Mexicali. Now every time Dino visited his eye shot straight toward the holy image turned piggy bank.

The hair on his back felt rough against his T-shirt, making him squirm against the seat; the vinyl made a rubbery grating sound beneath him. Another banda tune played on the radio. He wasn't sure who this group was—all of these quebradita versions were the same. He closed his eyes and all he saw was the deep red of the sun filtering through his eyelids. But before he succumbed to the heaviness of that color, Jacobo spoke up.

"Hey, Dino!" he said. "So have you given María Luz any more thought?"

The name made Dino wince. First Francisca tried to fix him up with that Chela woman who could get pregnant with a handshake and now Jacobo was pushing his spinster sister on him. María Luz was so desperate to get married she smiled at anything that could walk itself to the altar. She came out in her tacky swap meet gowns every time Dino came by for Jacobo on his way to the gym. And he couldn't get Jacobo on the phone without first spending five minutes on the line with her giggling. Dino preferred to go after those impossible loves, like Jacaranda—a woman so stiff and unresponsive it was like courting the steel beam of a streetlight. But that was the beauty of her: she would never bend.

"María Luz? Not lately, no," Dino finally said. Just that morning the rosary wrapped around the rearview mirror reminded him of María Luz: she wore too many gaudy necklaces: they became entangled, knotted.

"Well, let me know when you do," Jacobo said. "She asked about you the other day, you know. She was wondering what you were up to and why you haven't dropped in for dinner lately. She makes one hell of a cook, that's for sure. I can't get up from the table without asking for thirds."

Dino shook his head, seeing clearly through Jacobo's ruse. He eased the tension of his eyes once more by shutting them; the redness of the eyelids had darkened.

The problem with these people, Dino thought, was that they didn't grasp the concept of patience. A man couldn't be single past thirty without everyone wondering why the hell he was afraid of growing up or was he a joto. Of course, it didn't help that people talked about him and Jacobo, the two muscle boys. He suspected that's why Jacobo was always hostile and quick to pick a fight, especially with real jotos like that scale boy and Tiki-Tiki. That wasn't the issue for Dino. For him the issue was matrimony. The idea of marriage frightened him because people jumped into it too quickly, like that children's game in which all the players are blindfolded to search for their partners through sound and touch. Groping through empty space is frightening, so when partners finally find each other, their hearts, excited from desperation, calm themselves, comforted and relieved. But what next? Nowadays a courtship was limited to an introduction, a dinner, and a brief engagement. Then the couple signed its life away, writing itself into a two-person cell, a misery that only grew worse with the coming of each child. If that was the case then he had to choose wisely. So far, Marta, Yesenia, and Georgina had failed the test of patience. All three had demanded a commitment long before he really knew who they were and what they were capable of once the ring was in place.

The radio jockey announced a popular Luis Miguel ballad. Dino grimaced. Francisca once said that Mexican music was one hundred percent love poetry; but listening carefully to the lyrics Dino discovered that it was more like one hundred percent heartbreak stories: amor perdido—love hurt. Even the more upbeat Spanish selections played at the gym were songs of sorrow. For a good heart bleed, he preferred Chalino Sánchez. He had even switched nightclubs, moving from El Paraíso Tropical to Los Arcos because it was Los Arcos that heard Chalino's final performance before he was gunned down in México months later.

"Is marriage love, anyway?" Dino thought out loud.

"What about love?" Jacobo asked.

Dino opened his eyes and looked down at Jacobo, at the sunken center of his cap with the button in the middle slanted inward. "Are you going to marry for love?"

Jacobo let out a pensive sigh. "My father used to say that love isn't always something you get from the woman you marry."

"And what did your mother have to say?"

"I guess she agreed since she wasn't the woman my father married."

"How is that?"

"I mean," Jacobo said, "that my mother was my father's mistress. María Luz and I are their bastard children. His legitimate wife and kids live in Colima."

"Oh, one of those arrangements," Dino said, nodding his head. "Well, doesn't that say something about marriage?"

Jacobo looked up at Dino, forehead furrowed. "It says plenty about my father, that hijo de puta," he said in a fiery tone.

"Okay, never mind," Dino said. "I didn't mean to get too personal."

"Well you got personal, baboso," Jacobo snapped, his voice fading down to a mere mumble.

Dino sat back against the seat again, soaking up the sun and listening to the sad music on the radio. He was patient with Jacobo's quick temper. It was hostile but short-lived like Valentín's, not much of a temper at all. Doña Mónica's was an example of a real bile-fed, anger-seething temper.

Doña Mónica was his mother. An object as inoffensive as a teacup infuriated that woman. The handles to every cup and mug had to point to the right side of the cupboard. If even one was set unevenly on the shelf, or at an angle or pointing to the left, he'd hear about it as soon as she got home from her double-shift at Sinaloense, the train station's twenty-four-hour restaurant. Amid slapping and scolding, Francisca was forced to remove every single cup to reorder the shelf. When Francisca finally got to bed, Dino would sometimes crawl over to her side of the room to slide his hand under the covers, Francisca's hand wet with mucous and tears. When he woke up in his own bed the following morning, he would have thought it had all been a bad dream, except that Francisca was in the kitchen whispering apologies to the teacups.

Dino's throat felt that familiar lump whenever he recalled his childhood years in Sinaloa. His father had been absent for most of those years, working as a bracero up north, never to be seen again after Dino and Francisca ran away. Dino wondered if his father thought like Jacobo's father and had sought comfort in creating an alternate home, with an alternate family. Was there a man Dino's age, maybe younger, maybe older, that resembled Dino's father? Could this man have found the woman that should have been holding Dino's hand on those nights doña Mónica clawed her way into his sleep?

Without fail, lonely and angry, doña Mónica came home drunk on her nights off. Sometimes she couldn't make it through the door and Dino and Francisca had to drag her in. Once she bit Francisca on the cheek, scarring her face. The semi-circular trail of teeth marks could pass for pockmarks. They were barely visible on Francisca's light skin.

Dino didn't remember exactly who made the suggestion, but he and his sister packed their bags one day and bought two bus tickets to Baja California, to the international border. He was not yet ten, she was not yet twenty. They traveled overnight. In the pitch dark of the bus, Dino stared wide-eyed, disoriented. Through one dangerous portion of the road the shoulders were lit with torches strewn at short intervals. One after another the fires blurred too quickly to keep count, but they were building up to something big somewhere else not Sinaloa. Francisca and Dino never discussed their destination, or their plans, or their father, who was lost in the north, or their mother, who would come home that same night wanting to take out her anger through the teacups. They didn't even laugh about the surprise that awaited doña Mónica—not the missing children, but the missing teacups. When they stepped off the bus in the station in Tijuana, brother and sister refused to look back. Neither wanted to know the color of the bus, its number, or where it was headed next, because whatever that place was that's where the teacups were scheduled to arrive.

Jesse drove up in his red truck, shaking Dino awake from his daydreaming. Through the trail of dust a number of workers began to slowly materialize.

"You can start picking up the cargo," Jesse said through the window slightly cracked. "We're leaving Scaleboy behind to stamp for three crews in these blocks so make sure you take him around with you."

"Whatever," Jacobo responded. Dino nodded once.

Jesse made a three-point turn back to the opposite end of the block, the speeding truck lifting another layer of dust clouds. The workers made their way through the ghostly air like shadows taking shape with umbrellas over the shoulders and ice boxes in hand. Two large masses rose out of the dust—Valentín and Francisca side by side. Two pink leg warmers glowed, radiant in the sun, and Francisca floated above them. Dino watched her wave from afar, the money she had given him warm in his pocket. Her arm went up peacefully, delicate as an air bubble in a fish tank. Dino could never know how to replace the beautiful woman in his life who now drifted toward him like a stray bottle guided by the current of an invisible sea.

RIGOBERTO
GONZÁLEZ

HER BEST MISTAKE

Reluctantly, Amanda agreed to drive doña Pepa home since her grandsons were headed straight for the warehouse and the old woman lived only a few blocks from the trailer park. She thought she was going to have to drag the old woman into the truck, kicking and screaming, since she strongly objected to not being allowed to repack with all the other grape pickers. Merengue wouldn't hear any of it and simply dismissed her with a wave of his hand. Of course the grandsons got it worse since they had always weaseled their way out of the warehouse using doña Pepa as an excuse. On any other day Amanda would have been reveling at the thought of those two lazy boys getting their backs broken as they unloaded the cargo, but today she was put off by the peck on the cheek Jesse had given her right before he handed over the keys to the truck. He had not shown affection that publicly in years and it was disconcerting. She tapped her nails on the steering wheel as the truck traveled north of Highway 86, the radio turned low because the disc jockey frequently indulged the female callers with airtime. Their stupid giggling annoyed her. Through the rearview mirror she caught a glimpse of the Salton Sea glaring at the panorama of grape fields. She quickly approached Travertine Rock, a small mountain of boulders graffittied with gang tags and declarations of So-and-So loves So-and-So.

"Slow down," doña Pepa said in her squeaky voice. "We're going to miss the Indian head."

Amanda rolled her eyes, but eased up on the gas pedal nonetheless. The Indian head was a large boulder protruding from the north side of the rock pile. Only at an exact angle could the passerby make out the profile of an Indian, headband included. The rippling of shadows against the stone surface gave the effect of hair pulled back.

Amanda had seen the face so many times she only bothered to glance at it through the corner of her eye, almost out of habit.

"That Indian gives me the comfort that I'm going home," doña Pepa said. Amanda kept silent, stoic behind her sunglasses.

Doña Pepa took off her oversized glasses and squinted at them against the light. "Dirty things," she said, blowing into the lenses then wiping them with a blue bandanna.

After another brief period of silence doña Pepa spoke up again. "One time I had a prescription filled across the border," she began. "You know how they accept the company's vision plan now. Much cheaper. Well, they gave me a pair that looked a little strange, but I took them anyway. I didn't even think to wear them home because I was still attached to my old pair. I just put them away and forgot about them until the next day at work. I had to show them off at the date-packing warehouse, you know." Doña Pepa got no reaction from Amanda.

"Well," doña Pepa continued, "my ride took me to work the following morning and I arrived in my new glasses, a little dizzy from the stronger lenses because I wasn't used to them yet, but I don't worry. I walked in like a contestant in a beauty pageant, presumida that I am. I got a few compliments by the time I took my place in front of the conveyor belt. Well as soon as the dates started rolling in I jumped back in shock. I said *Madres! What are they sending down, papayas?* The girls around me gave a giggle, but I'm serious. Pinche fruit looks huge. *What's the matter, comadre?* doña Betita asked me as I pulled off my glasses to take a look at the dates, bald-eyed, and I said to her, *Doña Betita, I went to the optometrist in Mexicali the other day and he must have thought I was an astronomer.* I showed doña Betita my glasses. *Here,* I tell her, *put them on. You can see clear to la chingada moon!*"

Amanda spat out a burst of laughter.

Doña Pepa shook her forefinger at her. "And you thought you were going to sit there behind your fancy dark glasses, acting like you were born without ears."

Amanda's laughter quickly subsided. "I'm going to stop for gas," she said softly, signaling to the crowded gas station with her chin. "Do you want to go in for anything?"

Doña Pepa turned and said, "I'm going to get a Sprite and sunflower seeds." She reached under her bright red sweatshirt to pull out a five-dollar bill stuffed inside her brassiere.

Amanda let the truck idle behind a car with the pump nozzle sticking out of the tank. Jesse's kiss lingered warmly on her cheek, as did Naro's touch. Except Naro had stuck his fingers between her knees when she drove up next to him to say that Jesse was riding with him to the warehouse. She had opened her legs for him, but then doña Pepa walked up and Naro didn't have time to run his large hand along the path to her crotch—a favorite tease of his.

The driver of the car in front of her finally walked out of the minimart with an open bag of chips under his arm and a soda can in each hand. His patience in putting his snacks away angered Amanda, who stuck her head out the window and yelled: "I don't care if you pump the gas with your teeth, but start pumping!"

The man ignored her, chewing slowly. Amanda felt like honking the horn at him to get him moving, but decided not to—not with doña Pepa in the truck. She didn't need the old woman to show up to work the next morning with a confirmation that Amanda the tallier was as big a bitch outside of the grape fields. Before the man climbed into his car he gave Amanda the finger, asserting in a gruff voice: "Pinches viejas!" Unfazed, Amanda pulled up to his spot. Doña Pepa got off. "I'll be right back," she squeaked. She stumbled across the raised service island toward the minimart, the five-dollar bill waving in her hand.

Using her credit card to operate the pump, Amanda dwelled on the man's two hostile words. Not because they had stung her, but because Jesse had made a similar statement once, the time he bought a new fan belt for the truck. The cashier who attended him at Star Auto Parts had been a woman, and she had made a mistake with the size of the belt. Jesse had to get a ride all the way back to exchange it. He returned, fuming. *Pinches viejas! What do they know about auto parts?* The anger had drained him, so he decided on a nap before bothering to open the hood again. When he finally woke up he searched around the trailer living room.

"Where did I leave that fucking belt?" he asked. He sounded agitated again.

Amanda sat on the couch with a file in her hand and two bottles of red nail polish on the small coffee table. Trabalenguas lay curled up against her side, purring. "You mean that auto part?" she said, coyly.

Jesse looked at her strangely. "What's with you? Of course that auto part. Where did you put it?"

Amanda blew into the fresh coat of polish on her thumb. "In the truck," she said. "I replaced the belt myself."

Jesse grabbed the closest thing to him—a plastic tumbler on the kitchen table—and threw it against the trailer floor as if to say *Not again, you bitch!* But even the tumbler betrayed him because when it struck the carpet it made no noise.

Grinning, Amanda finished filling up the tank, took her receipt, and looked around for doña Pepa. There was still a long line inside of the minimart but there was no sign of her bright red sweater. She regretted having given the old woman a chance to go inside. When the car behind her honked for the second time, she quickly spent her patience and parked the truck out of the way. The minimart entrance was visible through the rearview mirror.

"Pinche viejita," Amanda mumbled with annoyance. She rested her elbow across the car window.

The odor of gasoline permeated the air. She imagined the gas station instantaneously combusting in the heat, charred flesh flying out into the street the way burnt pieces of chicken popped off the barbecue when Jesse was in charge of the grill.

Jesse was a sad case of a man, born with only a fistful of guts and a brain no better than his beloved deep red truck's engine—high maintenance and with the constant threat of overheating. Yet she had decided not to leave him at the end of the harvest as she had planned all season. That decision was as whimsical as the determination to divorce him had been. Abandoning Jesse would be like dumping a kitten into an empty lot—a cruel act laced with guilt. Besides, eight years ago it was Jesse who had rescued her from the long dawns at El Gato Negro. It could have been any man. All the men who came into *that* place and at *that* hour were nothing but losers. The liquor was strictly bottom shelf. Most of it came from underground distilleries across the border. The whores were old enough to be grandmothers. In fact, la Tabasqueña *was* a grand-mother helping raise six grandchildren after her son ran off, leaving behind his wife and kids. An attractive-looking woman under the dim lights of a windowless cantina, la Tabasqueña also sold Mary Kay Cosmetics door-to-door and hosted Tupperware demonstrations at bachelorette parties. She was a small woman who wore thin white blouses to all her jobs. The round necklines hung low across the tight skin of her chest, which created a dramatic contrast with the loose wattle of her neck.

"I've got just the right ointment for those bags," la Tabasqueña would say to Amanda as she took a closer look at her face. La Tabasqueña's skin always glistened, thick with face cream.

Amanda was the bartender's assistant. When she wasn't doing the books she helped serve. The customers eyed her but rarely approached her because they believed she was Cecilio's woman. Cecilio was the two-hundred-seventy-pound owner of the cantina. He rode a Harley and shaved his head to highlight the tattoo on his scalp—a skull with a cobra slithering out of each socket. Yes, she slept in the same bed with Cecilio, but Cecilio liked men. They kept up the farce, for the sake of her safety and his business. The men came for the cheap booze, the cheap piece of ass, and even cheaper drugs.

"These goddamn wetbacks don't know the good stuff from shit," Cecilio always complained. El Gato Negro always got the weak stuff because of it. Cecilio had to get his own private supply from somewhere else.

"Are you tired?" Cecilio would ask Amanda at four in the morning. If Amanda nodded, he would snap his fingers and queen out. "Do a line, girl." And if la Tabasqueña walked in on them bent over the flat surface of a mirror, she'd say in her motherly tone, "Just be careful, mis hijos."

Then Jesse came into El Gato Negro days after she had made up her mind to move on. The police were getting suspicious about the goings on at this cantina in the middle of nowhere, so her dawns were numbered. A clumsy skeleton of a man, Jesse had dared to put his hand over hers when she set the beer tray on the edge of his table. She was about to point back to the bar with her chin and say,

That's my man with the tattoo, like she usually did when a man showed interest in her but his eyes left her speechless. They weren't dilated so he wasn't a junkie; they weren't bloodshot and round as a toad's so he wasn't the typical El Gato Negro alcoholic. Jesse's were the eyes staring out of an empty bed, from an empty room, of what was left when she turned off the lights and the walls disappeared—of the sink in the kitchen cradling a solitary saucer. His was the look she had held all these years on her own sad face—the face that her first husband left her with when he found out she was barren. She knew this face and this man. She could breathe like him, swallow like him, move across the floor like him—control his foot as if it were her own.

Amanda pressed the palm of her hand to her cheek. Jesse's kiss was warm under the fingers. This was Jesse: lamb, cotton ball, a handful of la Tabasqueña's almond cream—easy to break down into clarity. Did he think he could hide the fact that he had taken her pistol? Let him make a fool out of himself, which is why she had loaded the cartridge while he was in the shower this morning. He'd shoot himself in the foot. Poor, stupid Jesse. He always learned the hard way.

Suddenly aware that she had distracted herself for too long, Amanda looked back and made a thorough search from a distance for doña Pepa who was nowhere in sight. A man wearing a straw hat walked up to the truck. "Excuse me," he said, "but is the little old woman with the glasses and a red sweater traveling with you?"

Amanda raised her eyebrows behind her sunglasses. "Doña Pepa?"

"I don't know what her name is. All I know is that she sat in my truck and won't get out. She says she's waiting for you." He motioned to the red truck parked at the gas pumps with his head.

Confused, Amanda got out of the truck and walked back with the man. She removed her sunglasses as soon as she stood in front of doña Pepa who was comfortable seated on the passenger side.

Before Amanda had time to speak, doña Pepa scolded her. "Where were you? I've been waiting here almost half an hour."

Amanda let her jaw drop in disbelief; the man shrugged his shoulders. "Doña Pepa," Amanda said, "I'm parked over there."

"What?" doña Pepa asked, her eyes glossed over suddenly.

Amanda pointed to the truck. "I'm *over there,*" she said, and the red truck's color deepened like a drop of blood growing out of a puncture wound. She stared at it as doña Pepa made her way out of the man's truck, stuttering excuses. *Over there. That* was Jesse's truck. Maroon, burgundy—Flame, Ruby, Cardinal, Malaga. A box of red grape with the crooked stems weaving in and out made the fruit look like trapped lightning, electric as a cache of fuses. *That* was Jesse. The man couldn't put a sentence together without setting himself on fire, but the man knew how to *love.* There was no better word for it, Amanda mused as she walked toward the truck. There was no better reason for why she felt she was moving inside him when he moved inside her. If she drifted away from Jesse, she was running away from herself. Jesse had been her best mistake.

Amanda remembered the loaded gun, Jesse's clumsy temper.

"Doña Pepa," Amanda said as she rushed to climb into the truck. "We need to go—" Her body froze with the scene unfolding on the other side of the highway: a parade of people waving picket signs and the familiar red flags of the UFW. Cars passing cheered them on with honking.

"Huelga," doña Pepa muttered.

"There are two other groups walking about," said the man in the straw hat. "They want to shut down the entire grape industry in the Valley in one afternoon."

"Get in the truck," Amanda commanded, "We need to get to the warehouse."

THE ORIENT STAR

Moreno   3:15 p.m.

When Moreno was born he fit inside his father's hand, a premature baby small as a hairy rat, mouth puckered into a yellowish snout-like knot. To his father's relief, the tiny body eventually shed the birth hair, and the snout relaxed, transformed into the fine pretty face of the mother. Moreno considered his reflection on the side-view mirror, turning the mirror toward the car for a better look, for traces of those once-delicate cheekbones and feminine jaw line.

Up ahead the railroad crossing sign flashed its warning. Cirilo sat at the wheel and they were stopped five cars back from the tracks, waiting for the train to pass. Moreno finished folding a small piece of paper into the shape of an elephant and flicked it into the glove compartment with the missing panel door.

In the back seat Ninja smoked a cigarette and Tamayamá dozed in one corner with his baseball cap pulled over his face. "What do these boxcars carry anyway?" Ninja asked.

Moreno glanced up at the freight train, at the cartoon pig face on the sides of the railroad cars.

"Spam, I think," Cirilo offered. "Gringos like that shit."

"I read somewhere about a dozen wetbacks who tried to sneak across the border hidden inside one of those. They suffocated to death," Ninja said through his cigarette.

"A movie was made about that," Moreno said.

"Of course," Cirilo said. "México likes to make movies from its headlines. There was a movie about the earthquake of eighty-five less than a year after it happened. I heard they even shot on location in the Mexico City rubble."

"What about the movies you were in, Tiki-Tiki?" Ninja asked. "Where did those ideas come from?"

Cirilo's voice deepened. "Calm down, Ninja Turtle," he warned.

"It's only talk," said Ninja. "We all know Moreno likes women. Right, Moreno?"

Moreno's mind flashed back to the seventies flicks about drug trafficking. Sixty pounds and twenty years ago he was Tiki-Tiki, the olive-skin geisha. Clad in a gold kimono and an obi lined with Austrian crystals, Tiki-Tiki was a favorite for brothel parties. The pair of ivory chopsticks sticking out of the wig's bun was studded with abalone shell. Tiki-Tiki exploded with sparks each time she bowed.

The railroad guards lifted once the caboose was out of sight. Moreno leaned back into the seat as Cirilo stepped on the gas pedal to move forward. When the wheels struck the tracks, the chassis rattled beneath them. Traffic was heavy since all of Lozano's crews quit for the day. Moreno searched for more scraps of paper in the glove compartment.

Ninja sang a song, blowing smoke out with every high note. Cirilo's Datsun didn't have air-conditioning or a functional stereo, just a large hole in the panel where they stuffed the dirty bandannas and work clippers.

"How long do you guess we'll stay at the warehouse?" Cirilo asked.

Moreno ran his palm along his nape and shook his head. "Until midnight, I hope," he said.

"Aijodesutamayamá," Tamayamá said, weakly.

The Datsun followed Naro's white Bronco most of the way to the warehouse until the highway entered the city limits and a traffic light separated them. When the light turned green, they passed the indoor swap meet, its parking lot deserted. Back in Mexicali his father had once told him that the Chinese lived beneath the city, within a labyrinth of tunnels that only they knew how to enter and exit. As proof of that theory he pointed out the time la Chinesca, the Chinese business district, was ablaze in flames. Out of nowhere hundreds of Chinese materialized. Even the firemen became distracted; the invasion made them stop to look for a minute. "And where do you think they all came from?" Moreno's father asked the ten-year-old Moreno.

Ever since he was a boy Moreno suffered from an Asian fetish. The Chinese abounded along the border, owners of businesses on both sides. Fong's Liquor in Calexico had a counterpart in Mexicali, Baja California, Norte: Licorería Fong. He loved browsing the trinket stores and buying cheap items made in Taiwan, everything from pocket wrenches to Buddha key chains to rice paper fans. But mostly he liked to stare at the people, which none of them seemed to notice. The Chinese were more interesting to watch than the gringo tourists, who were clumsy and loud, imposing in their large, overweight bodies. The Chinese were everything graceful.

Like the childish taunt *Chino-Chino-Japonés*, Moreno didn't learn the difference between Chinese and Japanese until much later in life, so in the beginning he grouped his favorite singer Yoshio and his favorite Japanese-Mexican actor Noé Murayama with the owners of Restaurante Chung Hua. He used to stand in front of the mirror for hours, admiring his new face as he stretched out his eyes to the shape of almonds. Behind him a pair of cane scrolls with hand-painted Chinese calligraphy decorated his bedroom wall. His breath savored the aftertaste of Japanese peanuts. But standing in those long theater lines to see the latest martial arts film did not bring him closer to the Chinese merchants who were polite yet distant in their treatment of him; training to yell at karate class and mimicking the motions of T'ai Chi did nothing to help him understand what the old Asian couple said to each other over a bowl of miso. Whatever secrets to success and happiness these peoples had were not revealed in a fortune cookie, or in the origami books he had mastered. Moreno never dared to ask for fear of appearing as ignorant and invasive as the gringo tourists. Instead he resigned himself to his private indulgence at home with his mother's make-up. Moreno coated his dark skin with powder and rouged his brown lips. During these sessions, the sounds escaping his throat were too light and quick as knuckle knockings to be flat border Spanish—they had to be Chinese-Chinese-Japanese. But not until he discovered the adult film star Lyn May, the Asian beauty rumored to have been a man once, did Moreno's vision burst open like a firecracker to conceive Tiki-Tiki.

"Are you a transsexual or a transvestite?" asked la Malinche, owner of Club El Dólar and director of the weekly drag cabarets.

"I only dress like a woman," the teenage Moreno answered nervously. He had dressed like a woman at la Malinche's request. He wore his mother's blue flowered Sunday skirt, a black T-shirt tucked inside of it. He had thought of borrowing her old brown leather purse as well but changed his mind at the last minute, realizing it didn't match with the black mules. La Malinche had shaken her head in disappointment when he walked in after changing in the bathroom, but she had complimented Moreno's choice of foundation and rouge. "There's some hope," she had declared. The interview took place at the bar with a mural in the background depicting a Greek orgy. La Malinche had ordered piña coladas for them.

"Are you a joto?"

"No," Moreno said defensively. Then he stuttered before adding, "I don't have to get fucked by men to work here, right?"

La Malinche twirled the straw in her glass. She wore a shoddy version of a pre-Columbian tunic and a thick gold headband in the shape of a snake, suggesting an Egyptian queen. Her eyebrows were neatly plucked and the cleft on the large chin betrayed her true sex.

"I need performers, not putos," she finally said. "The cocksuckers work the second floor; you work the stage. Nobody confuses the two. Not me, not you, not the customers. Understood?"

Moreno understood. La Malinche became his mentor and perfected his craft. Tiki-Tiki blossomed into an exotic flower, bright as a lotus in her lamé kimonos designed by la Malinche herself. With practice, Tiki-Tiki flowed across the stage like a petal descending slowly on a stream of moonlight. She bowed delicately as a brush stroke to the Hunan music, and when she waved, her hand stopped the world. Even Moreno's parents attended his performance on one occasion. Their only condition was that he never shame them by wearing those kimonos outside of the club, to which his father added, "Or by becoming one of those castrated freaks with titty implants." Moreno complied: Tiki-Tiki was a costume, a stage personality, a weekend mask that he rubbed off over the washbasin. Just a game and nothing more. Or so he believed until his growing girth began to force the satin sashes outward, and his skin began to sprout the coarse hair as a result of a latent puberty. Moreno waxed, shaved, plucked, dieted, starved, but his body resisted, determined to become stocky and furry like his father. La Malinche was devastated. She fed Moreno pills, restricted him to fluids, and insisted he treat his skin with a compress damp with ethyl and concentrated lemon juice, which only burned his skin, making him darker.

"Chingada madre," Cirilo said, his eyes fixed on the rearview mirror.

Moreno looked over his shoulder. An INS squad car flashed its lights behind them. "Mierda," he said.

"Wake up, Tamayamá," Ninja said as the Datsun pulled over. "La migra."

By the time the INS officer came up to Cirilo's window, the four men had their green cards ready. A number of cars passing by honked their horns or slowed down to yell or whistle at the INS officer. Moreno thought he heard los Caraballos laughing from one of the vehicles.

The INS officer greeted them and took their cards, patiently inspecting them through his dark glasses.

"He's going to make us late," Ninja complained.

"What's the problem, amigo?" the INS officer asked defensively.

"Don't piss him off, pendejo," Cirilo muttered.

Moreno entertained himself with a piece of paper on the dashboard as the INS officer asked Cirilo a series of trite questions that Cirilo answered politely. The INS officer returned to his vehicle with the green cards, and stuck his hand in through the window and pulled out the radio receiver.

"Now what is he doing?" Ninja asked.

"He's reporting us," Tamayamá said, concern in his voice.

The paper crane Moreno had made refused to flap its wings when he pulled on the tail. He flicked it into the glove compartment and took another scrap of paper, an old check stub, and began to size it into a square, creasing on his knee with his thumbnail.

Ten minutes later the INS officer came back, smiling. He handed each man his green card, tipped his head and apologized for the inconvenience. Cirilo turned the ignition key and shifted into drive.

"What a waste," Ninja said. "What time is it? Can we still stop for a quick snack? I need to buy cigarettes."

"Mierda! We're not going to make it anywhere tonight," Cirilo said. "Look behind us."

Another squad car flashed its lights, this time the police.

"They're out to get us, all right," Moreno said, shaking his head. He fingered the piece of paper he had just tightened into a Chinese star. "Well, the only contraband in the car is that box of grape."

"What do you want with a box of grape? Man, I can't even look at it after work," Tamayamá said.

"It's for my sister," said Ninja. "She's been bothering me to send her some. You can ship a box of grape through the Greyhound, you know."

"Quit your yapping!" Cirilo reprimanded the men. He had broken into a sweat and was visibly shaken.

"Aijodesutamayamá, what's his problem?" Tamayamá said as Cirilo pulled over for the second time.

Moreno slid his green card out of his wallet again. He immediately recognized Ninja's laminated photograph: brown lips, dark skin. Anyone could have made the same mistake, he thought, tapping the stiff, unbendable card against the dashboard. The glove compartment was a nest of paper animals.

When the police officer yelled nervously at the men in broken Spanish to vacate the car, Moreno knew they were in for it. What would Tiki-Tiki have to say about all of this unglamorous treatment?

"This is it," said Cirilo. "Let's go."

"I'm not going anywhere," said Ninja.

"I'm not either," Tamayamá added. He rolled himself into a ball and pulled the cap over his face.

"You pair of idiots! This is the police!" Cirilo yelled out.

"Calm down, Cirilo, for shit's sake," Moreno said. "There's no reason to get all nervous. We haven't done anything wrong. They're just trying to scare us."

"He's scared all right," Ninja said. Tamayamá let out a small laugh.

"Do you want us to get arrested? Let's go!" Cirilo slapped the cigarette out of Ninja's mouth. He burnt his hand on the tip and cried out.

Caught off guard, the police officer crouched low and yelled out again, voice shaking, hand positioned over his weapon.

Already out of the car, Moreno turned around and laughed at the young and obviously inexperienced police officer. The Chinese star twirled in his hand. When he saw the frightened boy in the police officer, Moreno decided to poke fun at him by aiming the Chinese star and flicking it toward him.

When the first shot was fired, Moreno slumped down against the side of the car. By the second shot, Cirilo was huddled in the front seat, sobbing.

"Aijodesutamayamá, aijodesutamayamá," Tamayamá said over and over in a whisper, a whisper that reminded the half-conscious Moreno of his private childhood vocabulary of made-up words in Chinese-Chinese-Japanese.

RED

The reds were coming. Los rojos. Tinman could hear them marching down the highway, thickening the air like a swarm of hornets. He lay pressed against the ground and the workers stepped around him, too exhausted to care, their faces hardened into stone. The roofed structure at the entrance to the warehouse offered shade, but the cement floor steamed, fluid as scalding water. Tinman was swimming in it. People were thirsty. Grape juice acidic and sticky turned dust to outlines of mud down the sides of the fingers, into soiled maps on the palm.

Los Caraballos arrived early because Tinman drove. With him behind the wheel the road opened like the Red Sea, los Caraballos said. *Like a two-finger V, like chayote in cuaresma, like a pair of knees when the man takes to the stool, like sugar cane under the fierce machete.*

Earlier arrivals to the warehouse were Pifas and don Nico. Pifas stood on a low stack of empty pallets, making the one on top pivot with his shifting weight. Don Nico massaged his knobby shoulders. Other grape pickers straggled in: Silvania, Eva, and Jacaranda. Sebastián, Valentín, and his group. Doña Pepa's grandsons. Felipe, his family, and don Manuel, who was dropped off by his wife. As more workers arrived, the few women broke off from the men since their tasks were completely different in the warehouse. Men unloaded, women helped inspect the fallen shipments—but everyone moved on their knees until the last shipment passed inspection and was purchased, or until midnight.

"It's going to be a prayer meeting all the way to midnight," Pifas declared. "I can feel it in my bones."

"We can only hope, can't we, Felipe?" don Manuel said.

Felipe stuttered back, "Yes, yes, we can. Hope, yes."

On the opposite side of the warehouse Francisca pulled out a pamphlet to show the women. "I've got the new Tupperware catalog, girls," she said coyly.

"You'd be better off selling negligées in this heat," Silvania said. Eva gave her a reprimanding push on the elbow.

"Cirilo and Ninja?" Valentín asked, looking around.

"And Tiki-Tiki and Tamayamá?" Pifas added.

"La migra took them," el Caraballo Uno said, laughter creeping up on his face.

"That's right!" el Caraballo Dos chimed in. "They got stopped back by Copa Cabana." He shot both thumbs over his shoulder.

"Aijodesutamayamá!" Valentín yelled out. A few others also chanted, *Aijodesutamayamá! Aijodesutamayamá!* followed by laughter.

"I bet Ninja's going through his cigarettes like water," Pifas said, fueling the laughter.

"Goddamn migra," Valentín said. "They're just wasting our time."

"They sure are," el Caraballo Uno said. "Everyone knows only Freeman hires the wetbacks!" More laughter.

"All right, quiet already," Pifas said, waving his hand at the men. "Don Nico's going to finish his story." The laughter quickly subsided.

"Go ahead, don Nico," Pifas said, his voice nervous.

Don Nico sighed. "Well, I was talking earlier about the movie theaters back in the old days," don Nico began. He reached back beneath his hat to scratch the back of his head.

"What about them, Nico?" don Manuel said. He nodded to grant don Nico permission to continue.

"Well, in the old days, back in our parts of Monterrey we only had two: Cine Princesa and doña Meregilda's.

"Doña Meregilda's was actually a living room with the first television in town. She charged a few centavos if you wanted to sit on the floor and watch, and a few more if you wanted a chair and a cup of warm milk."

"That's service!" el Caraballo Uno said. El Caraballo Dos swatted him with his hat for interrupting.

"I was about thirteen years old, but like any chamaco, making a line outside of doña Meregilda's in the afternoons was a matter of curiosity. Besides, the tiny screen in the old woman's living room had better picture quality than Cine Princesa, where you always got to see a trembling hair snake in and out of the projector lens every couple of minutes, followed by the shadow of the manager's finger trying to rub it off.

"And making a line for the matinée was an even bigger hassle. There was no order because you never knew where the ticket booth was going to end up. The manager had this portable booth he rolled out into the sidewalk, sometimes to the left of the entrance, sometimes to the right." Don Nico indicated direction by using both hands. "He liked to watch los chamacos push and shove each other, the big ones trampling all over the smaller ones, the little ones scurrying between the legs of the bigger ones. It was one big riot every Saturday. At least one chamaco went home with a bloody nose, a few others with torn clothing.

"Well, finally we caught on to the manager's perverse game one hot morning. We could see him grinning behind the entrance window as he prepared to roll out the booth. A few of the older chamacos got together and whispered the plan from ear to ear. The scheme spread like a lighted trail of gunpowder. We were ready for him all right. When he threw open the door, booth first, not a single body moved. As instructed, everyone remained perfectly still."

"Chingado!" Valentín rubbed his hands in anticipation.

Don Nico paused a moment. "The manager's grin disappeared quickly. He became nervous and suspicious watching every face watching him. But still no movement on our part, and not a single sound. His face grew serious. *What's the matter with you?* he stammered. No response. He slowly opened the narrow booth door, slowly crept in, and as soon as he shut the door behind him we all rushed toward it, screaming and hollering. Trapped inside, the manager could only look on helplessly as we rolled the ticket booth down the stretch of street, and then we overturned al hijo de la chingada into the muddiest ditch in town."

Los Caraballos were the first to whistle and hoot, throwing their hats into the air. Others quickly followed. Tinman rose from the ground and waved his arms, stomping his feet against the cement. Chela walked away from the group of women on the other side of the warehouse to join him in his dance, taking hold of the ends of her dusty sweatshirt and pretending she was hiking up a skirt. Pifas and el Caraballo Uno had just formed a second couple when a huge cargo truck plowed through their dance floor. The forklift moved in, the steel beams poised to unload the pallets.

"Where are those chingado foremen?" Chela said over the noise of the machines. "I want to make sure they take my name down."

"I hear you," Valentín said.

"And I better see more than two cargoes coming in or I'm leaving like la chingada," Chela added.

A second truck made its way through. Jacobo stuck his head out the large window. "I've got your treats!" he said, maneuvering the wide steering wheel. A few workers jeered. El Caraballo Dos flicked a crumpled piece of toilet paper at the windshield. It caught in the wiper like a dead moth.

As the cargo truck pulled over, Dino opened the passenger door and jumped out. Aníbal was about to take that same leap off the truck when Jacobo yelled out, "Hurry it up, Scaleboy!" and shoved him off with his foot. Aníbal dropped on top of a pallet as the truck inched forward; the sound of wood cracking pierced the air.

"What a cabrón!" Pifas declared.

As Dino helped an infuriated Aníbal out of the broken pallet, Merengue drove up with Jesse. Behind them, Naro. He honked a few times to announce himself. A second forklift crawled out of the shadows. In the back two semis loaded up with grape from the refrigerators for delivery. The warehouse echoed with the clamor of machinery, with overheating engines, squeaky brakes, and the overlap of honking and beeping as more vehicles huddled into the structure, herding the workers into a smaller space.

On one side of the mass of bodies Aníbal and Jacobo were being pried apart by Dino; on the other side, Merengue and Jesse were shouting out commands, but every other pair of eyes and ears was distracted by the line of marching strikers crying out *Huelga! Huelga! Chávez, Sí! Teamsters, No!* as it made its way through the gates of the warehouse parking lot.

"Get those bastards out of here!" Merengue shouted out in English, his words barely audible.

Jesse responded. "This is private property, you're trespassing!" he yelled out at the marchers.

"This isn't private property," don Nico corrected. "This is the warehouse!"

"Walk out, brothers and sisters!" a voice from the crowd shouted to the workers. *Huelga! Huelga!* the others echoed.

The two groups faced each other, a few yards of space separating them. No one made a move as the dusty air settled around them. "Do we still strike in the Valley?" a confused voice asked.

Merengue picked up on the question, "Of course you don't strike. You work!"

"Don't let this gringo talk to you like that," a voice from the group of strikers said.

"Fuck off, you lazy fucks!" Naro barked.

The encounter grew awkward as voices rose without direction, hurled across the way like random stones. A wall of silence kept the groups at bay until from the crowd of newcomers a lonely voiced beckoned, "Join la huelga, comadre!"

"Comadre?" Chela responded, craning her neck in search of a face. "Is that you out there?"

"You walk out and you never come back," Merengue threatened.

"Come back to what, chingado gringo?" Chela snapped back. She went up to him and looked him up and down before making her move. She was the first to cross the line. The strikers cheered. *Huelga! Huelga!*

"Goddammit!" Merengue hollered.

"Yeah, man!" doña Pepa's grandsons began to clap. "Huelga! Huelga!" They jumped up and high-fived each other as they joined the strikers.

"You come back here, you motherfuckers! I'll tell doña Pepa!" Naro's threat came across as childish. The two boys took off their propaganda T-shirts and waved them in front of him. "No more grapes! No more grapes!" they sang. The strikers quickly adopted the slogan into their chorus. *No more grapes! No more grapes!*

A dark man in a business suit stormed out of the office attached to the warehouse. Everyone recognized Lozano and the gingham coat that made its appearance at the end-of-the-season celebration.

Every year the coat looked smaller because Lozano was getting wider. "What the fuck is all this?" he demanded.

"What does it look like? It's a walk-out," the spokesperson for the strikers answered. He was a small dark man with a bulging belly. He wore a sky-blue baseball cap with an image of la Virgen de Guadalupe stitched on the crown.

Lozano went up to the leader of the strikers, disconcerted by the similarities in their skin color and the girth of their bodies. Sweat glistened on both their faces. "Who put you up to this? Why are you disturbing my workers?" he said with a shaky voice. The blue on the man's cap matched the blue of his shirt collar.

"People have a right to organize and mobilize," the man answered.

"Don't you preach to me, wetback," Lozano said. "I've been in the business since Chávez and I have respect for my people."

"Exploiter!" someone in the crowd yelled. "Traitor!" someone else said. "Malinchista!"

It was the third word that angered Lozano the most. "I'm calling the police," he said. "You have no right to come into the warehouse like this. It's ungrateful people like you that give all of us a bad name!"

Malinchista! Malinchista! became the new chant of the moment.

Lozano shot out of sight, yelling back, "You bunch of ungrateful Mexicans, it's the white men that sent you here to ruin me. But you'll get yours. I'm calling la migra to take all you wetbacks home to the sties!" An uneasy silence descended on the warehouse.

"We're not walking," don Manuel said. "Isn't that right, Felipe?" Felipe's face was bug-eyed and shocked. He responded with an uncertain shaking of his head.

"I guess that means no," Mariana, his wife, spoke on Felipe's behalf. Her son pressed his body against hers uneasily.

"We're not walking either. Isn't that right, don Nico?" Pifas said.

"Speak for yourself," don Nico said. "After all I've told you, haven't you learned a thing?"

"Don Nico?" Pifas muttered as don Nico slowly made his way across to the strikers. The strikers cheered some more. Flags waved back and forth; picket signs bounced up and down.

"A la verga!" Los Caraballos said in unison. They took a long step back into their group. Tinman, who towered above the rest, hunched down to hide himself in the crowd.

"Fuck it!" Silvania said.

Eva held her back. "Are you sure?" Silvania pulled Eva with her. More cheers from the strikers. Eva yelled back, "Jacaranda! Sebastián!"

"We're walking, Jacaranda?" Sebastián asked uneasily.

Jacaranda turned to look at him. "We better." Los Caraballos toot-tooted as she strutted across to the other side.

As Jacaranda and Sebastián left the group, Valentín managed to keep Francisca from moving forward as well. He then turned to Dino. "And you better not make a move either," he warned.

A long silence followed as both groups quieted down to wait for the next person to make a move. Jesse took advantage of this opportunity to yell at the strikers. He took one step forward. "You are all a bunch of lazy dogs! You're worse than dogs, you're—you're— cats!" He was answered with a wave of caterwauling that sent him stumbling back. Naro started to laugh derisively. Workers on both sides of the picket line did also. Los Caraballos began to meow. Just then a red truck came speeding madly through the gates. The group of strikers broke apart as people narrowly escaped from getting hit from behind. Jesse recognized the crazed driver, which only got him more agitated, so he reached under the cuff of his pants and pulled out the small pistol from his boot. He aimed it at Naro, then at the strikers, and then at anyone who spoke up.

"Put that goddamn thing away, what the hell—" Merengue froze at the threat of getting shot. People backed away from Merengue and bowed down, staying close to the ground. Tinman was crouched so low, his white face looked like an upturned plastic bucket on the floor.

"Jesse!" Amanda called out. Jesse pointed the pistol at her. "What the devil is wrong with you? Put that down before you hurt yourself!"

"Virgen santísima," doña Pepa said as she crossed herself and ducked into the seat of the truck.

"I said put that down before I beat the shit out of you in front of all these people," Amanda said. The pistol trembled violently in Jesse's hand. "I mean it, Jesse. I'm going to break bones this time."

The reprimand set a contagious ripple of muffled laughs and snickering into motion. This angered Jesse even more. Suddenly everything came back to him—every mocking comment, every joke, every word and gesture that cut away at his manhood like a flock of vultures eating away at carrion. And here was Amanda once more, providing fodder. A nervous twitch made him press the trigger. The report of the pistol sent people running in all directions. Flags and picket signs toppled, bodies collided. The quick pivot of elbows and knees threw a few people down. Hats and baseball caps rolled on the floor like bottle caps. Jacobo seized the opportunity to take Aníbal down with him; Aníbal, though taken by surprise, was able to twist his body around to overpower him. Silvania pounced like a cat and landed on Naro, who carried her on his back until he flung both of them against the side of a cargo truck. Out of nowhere, Lozano reappeared sporting a handgun of his own. His coat was off. The sky-blue shirt was soaked in sweat. The second shot fired only caused more confusion and fear. Then a third shot. Jesse's body was thrust forward to the ground, landing close to Amanda.

"You sonofabitch!" Merengue called out. "You almost shot me."

"Who were you shooting at?" the strike leader asked, anger and fear laced his voice. "Who were you shooting at?"

"Who was shot? Who was shot?" someone else asked.

"Stop the shooting! Stop the shooting!" doña Pepa squeaked as she crawled out of the truck and toward Amanda. "Abuela! Abuela!" her grandsons screamed out in tears. When the police sirens began to grow loud, los Caraballos attempted to get into their truck and leave but the entrance was quickly blocked by the two patrol cars. Bodies were pressed close to the ground even before the bullhorn's commands. The cement floor was covered with bobbing baseball caps, bandannas, and hats. It was impossible to tell if anyone had been shot. Only doña Pepa saw the facts as she felt her way over to Amanda's body, trying to find the source of the leaking blood. She was puzzled by the growing wound on the earth, until she realized that the puddle was being fed by two estuaries of blood: one coming from Amanda, the other from Jesse.

PART THREE

Cruz

TELL ME LIES

Hernán, 5:00 p.m.

The last time Hernán remembered coming to the hospital was after his father found him eating glass at the age of five. It had all started innocently enough. First he had licked off the lemon pulp clinging to the lip of the glass until it squeaked, then he bit into it as if he could squeeze out more lemonade. When the glass broke between his teeth it was almost natural that he taste it, chew it until he felt the fluid in his mouth. He became alarmed when he realized that it was his own blood he tasted. That's when his father had walked in and nearly exploded with panic.

Hernán's father was so melodramatic in these situations it was almost embarrassing. Now he was outside the room pacing back and forth and yelling at the nurses that walked by. Each time he passed the doorway Hernán closed his eyes, afraid his father would dive in screaming for assistance as soon as he saw him blinking. A needle attached to a tube hydrated his body. His mother sat in the corner of the room with a handkerchief against her face. Good, he thought. That will teach her. That will teach all of them. Even Ernesto had to concede that victory was Hernán's. Good-bye, grape. His face couldn't hold back the smile. But then tío Severo walked in with Mamá Patricia on his arm. She carried her handbag over her shoulder. The circus was about to start. Hernán watched through the cage of his eyelashes.

"What happened here to my poor boy?" Mamá Patricia asked.

Hernán's mother got up from her seat. "He'll be all right, mamá," she said. "The doctor said it was the heat. He just needs to rest awhile."

Mamá Patricia swatted tío Severo. "I knew something was going to happen. Didn't I say something was in the air last night?"

Tío Severo mumbled, head bowed, "Yes, you did."

"It's a good thing I came prepared." Mamá Patricia reached into her handbag and pulled out a branch of ruda. "Where did I put the matches?"

"For the love of God." Hernán's father rushed in. "You can't light a fire in the hospital. Gaby!" he pleaded to his wife.

"It's all right, mamá," Hernán's mother interceded, "we'll do that when we get him home. Right now he needs his rest." She whispered to tío Severo, "Take her out for a walk in the rose garden. It's not safe to let the doctors see her like this."

Tío Severo nodded. "Mamá," he said, "let's go outside for a little bit until he wakes up. The doctors won't let us all sit here, it's too small. He needs room to breathe."

"There's a beautiful rosebush outside," she said as tío Severo led her out, "but I noticed the flowers were a little sick. We should offer them a few words of encouragement to make them better."

"For the love of God," Hernán's father said, eyes cast heavenward.

"Oh, stop that, Juanjo," Hernán's mother said. "You make it sound like she's crazy."

"She makes herself sound like she's crazy."

"I said stop!"

Hernán's muscles tightened. The needle in his arm began to sting. His eyes shut themselves, blocking his parents out. Put mother and father in a room all by themselves and they were a pair of territorial magpies trying to chase each other off the same limb of a tree. He felt his eyes welling up with tears. He might as well be lying in his own bed at home, pretending that his parents weren't fighting in the next room. But this was much worse because they thought he was unconscious and they carried on as if he couldn't hear.

"This is all your fault," Hernán's father declared.

"My fault?"

"You baby him too much. You're turning him into a sissy."

"What the hell does that have anything to do with our son getting sick in the fields? It was your idea to send him out into the heat as if this was something he was going to do all of his life."

"Well, he just might if you don't stop making excuses for him and start pushing him to do better in school."

"School? What good is that? Look at Severo," Hernán's mother stumbled over the logic.

"Oh, fine example that is," Hernán's father said sarcastically. "Well, if our son turns out to be a sissy I know it's not coming from my side of the family."

"You leave my brother alone, Juanjo, because he's trying hard to change his ways."

"Right, right. That's why I hate Hernán going to your mother's house. Don't think I don't know about those naked muscle men magazines Ernesto hides in his room."

"And what are you doing in Ernesto's room?" Hernán's mother demanded, her fist on her hip.

"Severo told me about it. The things that poor man has to put up with in that house. Your crazy mother, your joto brother. It's disgusting."

"Just shut up! Shut up!"

Hernán could not believe this banter was unfolding while he lay on a hospital bed recovering from heat stroke. Suddenly he knew too much. Ernesto's magazines flashed before his eyes and it disoriented him. Ernesto's hatred and unhappiness took a different shape and it disturbed him. And here were his parents making disconcerting connections between him and his uncles, the two people farthest from the reach of his personality and temperament. His entire skin burned with mortification.

"If only you had agreed to have another child," his father said, "maybe he wouldn't have turned out so spoiled. This boy only thinks about himself. Do you remember what shit we had to go through with that girl's parents? He's so careless and misguided."

"Well, if only you spent more time with him," his mother retorted, "maybe he would mature into a man much faster. But no, there you are last night going to some funeral of some old woman you don't even know. But you enjoyed the booze all right, didn't you?"

Hernán's muscles began to spasm. This was not how his parents were supposed to work, airing out their shame in public. They were supposed to do what they always did, keep information secret, truths hidden, and realities veiled beneath the polite mask of discretion and decorum. They were supposed to protect him. He became distressed so he let out a slight moan to warn them he was coming to. They didn't hear him the first time so he cleared his throat and shifted on the bed a little. Beneath him, the sheets were damp with his sweat.

"Hernán!" his mother called out excitedly; "Mijito, mijito," said his father. Their demeanor changed completely.

"What happened?" he asked in the drowsiest voice he could muster. The whole scene was theatrical. The hospital bed, the white sheets, the needle in his vein, they were all props necessary to make the act convincing. He had witnessed his parents make this shift dozens of times before. Once he walked in on them arguing with each other across the dinner table. His mother had been peeling potatoes; his father had been slicing the thorns off the skin of nopal with a knife. Had Hernán not walked in they would have started holding their tools like weapons, but he did walk in and their tools remained tools, and they prepared a delicious meal for him, ingesting their pent-up anger with the food.

"Mijito, we're so sorry we sent you out into the fields," his mother said as she pinched his cheeks.

"No more fields for our son," his father declared. "He's not a farm worker, he's a schoolboy."

Hernán's mediocre report card flashed through his mind. He was enrolled in basic math and in basic writing, but so were all the Mexican kids. At least he hadn't flunked his sophomore year, though he had come close.

"My mouth is so dry," he managed to say on the verge of a cough, and his parents nearly collided as they competed to get him a cup of water. Much, much better, he thought as he regressed into the comfortable role of helpless child that excused him from thinking about those things that had given him headaches. This was going to be a promising summer after all. Of course it wasn't right, but it was necessary. How else were any of them supposed to carry on with the charade? The doctor was called in and approved his dismissal, glowing with pride at the handshakes and hugs from the grateful Juanjo and Gaby. Hernán felt as if he had just been born again, delivered into the comforting hands of his parents. He was giving them a second chance to do right by him this time. Perhaps after this they would be more tactful with their bitter battles and more careful to conceal the evidence of their unhappiness. His mother would lower her voice on the phone when she complained to her friends about his father; his father would stay home after work instead of vanishing into the streets with his drinking buddies. And both would direct their attention to his whims and desires: more television, less curfew. For once he wanted to take charge, to demand and protest on his own terms, the terms of the child he had lost inside of him when his parents, his uncles, and even Analí had pushed him into the frightening adult world of the disillusioned and the disappointed.

Moments after his discharge from the hospital, Ernesto arrived with a soccer ball. The exchange of glances was awkward, but Hernán recognized it as the peace offering it was. Ernesto was a sad case and Hernán pitied him, imagining that all this time he hadn't been hating Hernán, he had been hating himself. When Ernesto offered to wheel him out of the hospital he allowed him to, knowing his uncle would do so carefully, almost tenderly. The scales had been tipped in his favor, and Hernán was going to bleed the last drop of juice from his fortune.

When they passed by the nursery Hernán asked Ernesto to stop a moment so that they could look in on the newborns yawning behind the glass window, their mouths so clean of lies and deceit he could see right through to the delicate palates.

"They're so cute," Hernán's mother said.

Hernán's father leaned into her gently. "Now don't get any ideas, Gaby."

Tío Severo and Ernesto laughed softly, Mamá Patricia blessed all the babies faithfully, and Hernán tried to memorize the reflection of his family's faces staring out with false docility on the glass. Suddenly Lalú appeared behind them. Hernán thought he saw Lalú put one hand on Ernesto's shoulder and whisper into his ear. He also thought he saw his father nudge his mother with his elbow, but he ignored that too. He didn't want to know.

"Welcome, Lalú," tío Severo said. He grimaced with disapproval. "Our patient's going home."

"How wonderful," Lalú said. "We were all so worried."

The light was hot when the automatic exit doors opened. It was like stepping through a curtain of fire. And Hernán almost made it to the car safely, feigning a weakness that wouldn't allow him to open the car door all by himself, when his mother resurrected a grim reminder. "Get up now, mijo," she explained when the wheelchair reached the yellow curb of the loading zone. The phrase sent a paralyzing chill up his back that made him want to cry out a glass-shattering shrill of pain. Numb, he moved one leg off the metal support, and then the other. The act was automatic like the one tear he shed and which he selfishly claimed for himself.

RIGOBERTO
GONZÁLEZ

CLEANING THE SLATES

Oralia   5:40 p.m.

Oralia had just emptied the silverware into the sink to rinse each piece separately for the third time today when her children rushed in from work.

"We were almost killed at the warehouse!" Eva explained. "Gun shots everywhere! I need to call Ramiro."

"It was a massacre," Sebastián added and he lunged himself in front of the television. "People bleeding all over the place. The cops asking the same questions over and over."

"Are we still on strike?" Jacaranda asked, deadpan.

There was a system to drying silverware: wiping spoons thoroughly was like cleaning out ears, the thumb rubbing counterclockwise; butter knives sliced through the washcloth on the palm five times on each side; and fork tongs went in and out between the knuckles of the forefinger and middle finger eight times. She had long ago stopped trying to make sense of anything that could not be wiped, washed, dusted, or cleaned into an unambiguous clarity, so when her children came to her with a fragmented report about a shoot-out at the warehouse she simply set it aside and focused on the silverware.

"It's all over the news!" Sebastián reported from the living room.

"Jesus Christ, Ramiro, we're on television!" Eva screamed into the telephone. "What are they saying, Sebastián?"

"Holy Mother of fuck!" Sebastián yelled out.

"Sebastián, watch your mouth!" both Oralia and Jacaranda said at the same time. They looked at each other and then shied away.

"What's going on?" Eva asked. "What station are you watching? I think it's Channel 42 or 36, Ramiro. One of the local ones."

"They're saying Moreno was shot," Sebastián reported.

"Moreno?" Eva said. "But he wasn't even at the warehouse,

right? Moreno is this guy that used to dress up as a Chinese girl," Eva explained to Ramiro over the phone. "No, not to pick grapes, menso, to come out in the movies. No, not pornography—"

"Cielos, this is enough!" Oralia grabbed a handful of forks and threw them into the sink. The clattering of metal put a stop to all the excitement. She stomped into the living room. "You," she pointed at Eva, "get off the phone! And you. Turn that thing off before I kick my foot through it. Don't you have any respect for the dying?" As soon as that word jumped out of her mouth Oralia's face froze. She had never said it aloud before though it had always sat in the back of her mind like an old rug waiting to be beaten on the clothesline. Eva whispered into the telephone and hung up, Sebastián turned off the television and walked away.

"I'll listen to the radio in my room," he mumbled. "Chema Ramos is always on top of these things."

"I'll go with you," Eva said, and followed after him.

Oralia rolled her eyes to the left to catch a glimpse of Jacaranda leaving through the front door. She puckered her lips, imaging how ridiculous she must have seemed to her children at that moment, exerting a power that did not belong to her. The power of life and death was their father's, all caged up in that Bible that snapped open and shut like a tight purse, greedy with meaning.

She walked softly to his room and pushed the door ajar. He snored in his sleep now. He had never snored before the accident. It was as if his injured body had succumbed to every flaw his healthy one had rejected. His breath was always rank. His feet grew claw-like toenails, cloudy and thick as droplets of wax. His back sprouted tendrils of coarse hair as if it were taking root in the mattress.

"Oralia," he used to whisper in her ear from behind when he had the urge to have sex. "You make me feel like I'm swimming in heaven." His love-making was pure poetry as he spread his hands across her bare back like a pair of wings and dug his heels into her ankles as if he was catching up with her in that waltz over the sheets.

"They always begin that way," her sister from Texas had warned her. "But men are not good with passion. As with anything, it's always much stronger than they can ever imagine, and in the end it defeats them."

Oralia pulled the door closed. The scent of sulfur wafted through the air. Her immediate impulse was to demand that Sebastián and Eva shower and change, but she stopped herself right outside Sebastián's bedroom door.

"I don't fucking believe this! There was another shoot-out?" Sebastián's voice pierced the door.

Eva's voice came next. "I can't fucking believe they haven't said anything about Jesse and Amanda. Are they still alive or are they chasing each other around in hell?"

"Quiet! I want to hear what all this is about."

"But it's not even about us!" Eva protested.

Oralia drew back from the door. Children were so careless with death. She knew now that the last time she saw her mother she was dying. Oralia was only ten at the time, the youngest in the family. Her mother was a huge woman with an explosion of premature white hair that flowed back as she relaxed on her recliner. The box fan blowing against her created the illusion that she was traveling in her chair. She couldn't open her eyes and she could only groan answers to questions. Oralia snuck in when the room was empty.

"Mamá, why are you like that?" she asked. Her mother groaned in response.

"Mamá, why can't you talk?" Another groan.

"Don't you love me anymore, mamá?" Groan.

"Mamá, are you going to be dead when I'm grown up?" Groan.

Her mother's skin was already clammy. It was as if she had held on for a few seconds more to entertain her youngest daughter. When she stopped groaning Oralia simply concluded she had fallen asleep, defeated by the parade of questions. At the funeral later that week she skipped around the coffin a few times and went outside to play because life went on without Mamá. And the next thing she knew, there she was in her own kitchen, awkward as a ten-year-old in that same pair of clunky shoes. Adults were just as careless with death.

A stream of smoke rising outside the window betrayed Jacaranda. Oralia walked outside to scold her for taking up cigarettes, but again she changed her mind about the reprimand once she saw her daughter relaxing with one knee against her chest and the cigarette burning slowly at the end of her long, bony fingers.

"So there was plenty of excitement at work," Oralia said as she closed the door behind her. "That must have been odd for the grape pickers. Farm labor is usually so dull."

"It will give people plenty to talk about for years to come," Jacaranda said. She took short drags when she smoked.

"Stories are important," Oralia said, though at the moment she couldn't think of any that were. Partly because she never told them, except for the Biblical ones and even those only at church. Stories about herself or about her family weren't really worth repeating. Who would care?

The back of Oralia's blouse began to dampen with sweat. In the afternoon light the rows of palm trees looked like burnt matches. Oralia complimented herself on this observation. She was about to share this with her daughter when Jacaranda suddenly spoke up.

"Eva and Ramiro decided that if their firstborn is a boy they will name him Cruz, like father."

"Cruz is a beautiful name," Oralia said. "Will there be a middle name?"

Jacaranda pressed the cigarette to her lips. "I hope so," she said through an exhaled stream of smoke. "A name like Cruz is too heavy a burden for a child."

"And what if they have a girl?" Oralia asked.

"I think they're confident it's a boy," Jacaranda said. "Didn't you know what you carried in your belly the times you were pregnant?"

Oralia tried to remember, but it was so long ago in places so far away. What did it matter anymore that she once thought she knew what the future held for her when the future was always too near and so capriciously independent of her wishful thinking. Years ago she longed for the days she could sit with her daughters as comfortably as three friends. They would fantasize together and share secrets and plan weddings and baptisms and first communions— in short, she would become the mother she was cheated out of having herself. That's why she took such extreme care of her health. She was terrified of growing obese and sickly and weak like her mother—a phobia aggravated by her husband's transgressions, by the thought that she would not be around to protect her daughters. Oralia had become as strong as an ox, a beast of burden sentenced to pull the weight of her family's misfortunes behind her.

Jacaranda extended a comforting hand toward her; Oralia took the knobby fingers into her hand. She was overwhelmed with the desire to offer her daughter some useful words of advice. *You should eat more. Use some of that lotion I made with olive oil. Rub a lemon on your knuckles to soften your skin.* But again her motherly impulses failed her. It was as if she had given up on being a mother because this family had given up on being a family. Besides, she thought, as she looked into Jacaranda's deep brown eyes beneath the shadow of her bulging conductor's cap, who knew what surprises she would find as a recently widowed woman in Texas? Who knew what her daughter would discover in México? Nothing they could say or do at that exact moment would prepare them for the days and nights to come. Oralia simply let her words remain unspoken because they already existed in the air and in their breath and in their bones. They didn't have to say what they already knew—life went on without Cruz—clean slates and fresh beginnings and another chance to open an entirely different book upon the world. Jacaranda, more than Eva, more than Sebastián, had her blessing because of what she had to endure. Cruz was a weak man, his mouth so used to letting go of words he couldn't even swallow his own confessions. How different this family would have been had he known how to hold back the truth. And just this morning, when she kneeled beside him to spoon the broth into his lips, he mistook her for Jacaranda and asked her to come closer. Oralia's suspicions grew. Was he still tempted after all these years and after all that penance? "I'm here, father," Oralia had whispered, and her husband told her that he had loosened the security belt on purpose, he had done it just for her, so couldn't she forgive him now, her broken old man on his deathbed? Oralia looked at her grown daughter, her beautiful Jacaranda. Oralia knew, she wanted to tell her daughter that. She knew everything about the past and that was more important than prophesying the future. That is why she felt obligated, no, entitled to answer her husband's pathetic plea on her daughter's behalf. "Never," she had told him. And she said it again, the second time using the anger in her own voice so that her husband knew that his careless life concluded with yet another of his careless acts. "Never."

SHOTS

Lozano   6:10 p.m.

The Caliente Valley police precinct's waiting room was sterile and stuffy. The air conditioning was broken, but the unit was prepared for such emergencies because the large box fans crept out of the closets and were propped up strategically in pre-assigned locations. A large noisy fan next to an artificial tree in a planter thinned out the hot air coming in through the front door. Lozano used a red paisley bandanna to wipe the sweat dripping down his nose and chin. Merengue fanned himself with his hat; the damp blond curls stuck to his head reminded Lozano of those dolls with plastic brown hair he bought for his daughters. Naro slept against the wall. His sunglasses were crooked and his mouth slightly opened. He looked dead. Nothing could look alive in this heat. When they arrived with the police squads their entrance into the precinct was anticlimactic because people looked up lazily and without much interest. At first Lozano was confused because the building was right across from the hospital and for a minute he thought they had been escorted into the waiting room at JFK Memorial. He was led into a conference room and interrogated by a Chicano officer who appeared annoyed throughout the questioning. It was the heat, he explained apologetically.

The heat drove men to sickness, to do crazy things. Is that what the officers would write in their reports? It was the heat that did it, the heat set the whole Valley on edge, the heat pulled triggers. Tamayamá, Ninja, and Cirilo had been sitting in those chairs they now occupied—Lozano, Naro, and Merengue had come to replace them.

"You goddamn grape pickers went loco today," the officer behind the counter pronounced as he shuffled through a stack of crisp paper. Three men out and three men in. "The pesticides doing this to you?"

There had been too much confusion to exchange stories, so Lozano stared at Cirilo as if they could communicate telepathically, one wide brown eye looking askance at another wide brown eye, like frightened cows in a burning barn. In the air the stink of sulfur, making one of the woman officers sneeze repeatedly.

His right hand felt warm, as if it were still wrapped around the gun that shot at Jesse in the leg. He knew his aim was good and that there was no chance in hell he could have missed and hit someone else in the head. But that's not what that sonofabitch from the UFW was claiming. He was using this act as leverage against him, to saw him off at the knees. Of course, he would use the connections the company lawyer had at the precinct, but that's exactly what that wetback had declared in front of the camera. When the company lawyer finally showed up he kept winking from a distance as he spoke to the officer in charge, both bantering without much conviction, bored really, which could work to his advantage. The heat had a way of sucking up the excitement out of a crisis. He would bank on that. In the end, only the ringleader and a few of his minions were still in custody on the charge of trespassing.

"I need a damn drink," Merengue said.

"Here, here," Naro mumbled. He pulled out a flask from his pocket and passed it around.

"Goddamn, you're always prepared," declared Merengue.

Lozano let out a heavy sigh. He imagined his breath dropping like a dusty rug on the white floor. He coughed.

"What the fuck's taking so long, anyway?" Naro said. "That goddamn Jesse."

Lozano coughed again. He shuffled over to the small water cooler in one corner of the room and helped himself to a few cups of water. The tank was sweaty and blue. When it bubbled he became nauseous. As soon as Jesse and Amanda cleared things up at the hospital he would be free to go. Of course, this was going to damage an already delicate relationship with the grower's association. That's what pissed him off the most, that all the ground he had gained could be so easily lost by a bunch of troublemakers with red flags and a few disgruntled employees, all of them peons that didn't know the first shit about what it meant to have a brown skin in high places. He wouldn't be surprised to find out that someone from the organization had set the whole thing up. He was becoming a force to be reckoned with, popular among the buyers, and that was enough to make him dangerous.

"Sit your ass down, Lozano, you're making me nervous," said Merengue.

Lozano took a few steps back to the chair with his gingham coat. "They're taking too long."

"That Jesse's probably a mess and they can't get anything out of him through all his sobbing," said Naro. He and Merengue passed the flask back and forth between them.

Merengue shook his head. "Amanda's going to pull his balls off for sure this time."

"Well, I'll tell you one thing that's for sure," Lozano interjected, "if either of them comes near me I'll aim for the spot between the eyes."

"They won't be back for awhile," Merengue said. He played with his hat, twirling it around on his fist a few times before losing interest quickly.

"They won't be back at all," said Naro. "The first chance they get they'll run out of town. Especially after Jesse's father finds out."

Lozano raised his eyebrows, curious but unwilling to invest time in more questions.

After a brief silence Naro added, "And don't worry, Lozano, they won't do you much harm. They're like that—a pair of rattlers that will only fuck with each other."

"Or anything smaller than them," Merengue added as an afterthought.

"Hey, what the fuck are you trying to say, gringo?" Naro snapped.

Merengue and Lozano looked at each other in surprise. Naro turned his head away and let out a faint whistle as if in shame.

"You know what this room reminds me of?" said Lozano, without waiting for an answer. "Of my first job as nighttime janitor at the Boys Club."

174

RIGOBERTO
GONZÁLEZ

"No shit, you worked as a janitor?" Merengue asked.

"Just briefly, while I was going to junior college. It was my father's idea. He said it would keep me humble, which it did, I guess."

On Tuesday nights at the Boys Club Lozano fixed up the basketball court for Bingo. During the games he sat in the corner studying for his junior college exams, getting up once in a while to collect discarded Bingo sheets and dried-up markers. The players were so focused on their numbers he floated freely without notice. He became bitter at his invisibility, wanting to shout at the old people that he was more than a janitor, that he would surpass them in education and ambition. On the night he knew would be his last at the facility it was a Bingo night. He stuck to his routine as usual, unfolding tables and chairs, dragging the trash bins to different points on the court. The floors were waxed and clean, the table legs squeaked when they rubbed against its surface. He wheeled in the oversized Bingo grid with flashing digits and the electric panel that operated the random number selection. The number spheres lay at the bottom of a glass case beneath the panel like a pile of discarded mothballs. Everything normal. But when the players were in place and the caller began to shout the numbers into the microphone, Lozano grabbed the mop and began to waltz at the center of the gym. He twirled it around and around and around, expecting the caller to freeze and to force each face staring down in concentration to look up at him, to acknowledge him, to admit that he was better than any stupid parlor game. But the caller simply continued without distraction and no player blinked away from the cards while Lozano, the fat brown man, spun in the room. Throughout his dance it was only him watching them not watching him.

After Lozano had zoned out for a while, Merengue brought him back to the present. "He was afraid you were going to have it too sweet, stepping into his big chair at the office?"

A grave expression flushed out of Lozano's face. "Oh, yeah, I've got it real good, all right. I mean look at this glorious life of mine: one hundred degree heat and above all summer in the middle of fucking nowhere, and a membership to a goddamn golf club where I get mistaken for a groundskeeper even if I show up in this godforsaken suit. And if that weren't enough, I also inherited my father's predisposition to hemorrhoids that makes me feel like I'm fucking cultivating a crop of thorn bushes in my ass. And the one day that I wake up feeling really good because I was finally able to fuck my wife into an orgasm, I get to be the goddamn welcome wagon for the strikers and my foreman goes nuts and shoots his wife in the tit right on my property!"

"So, you're saying it's not all as glamorous as it looks?" Naro said.

The three men burst out laughing, making the few heads in the precinct turn to stare. "You goddamn grape pickers got your brains fried," declared an officer behind a small fan on his desk.

Lozano cleared up his tears with the red bandanna. "Fried, broiled, sautéed: grape picker brain is a delicacy, amigo." Lozano reached down to Naro's lap and took the flask out of his hand. He sniffed at the metallic mouth.

The men's laughter quickly died down when the company lawyer returned to the precinct with the two policemen not far behind. He rushed over to Lozano. "A cinch," he said to Lozano with his voice low. "Don't worry about a thing."

"What the fuck do you mean, what's going on?" Lozano asked in alarm.

The lawyer patted Lozano on the shoulder. "Calm down, you're getting too excited. Everything's been cleared up. Jesse's not pressing charges and we'll grease some wheels to control things with the media and with the higher ups, and in return we'll be working closely with the district attorney to smooth things over with this whole Moreno thing."

"Moreno?" asked Naro. "What does Moreno have to do with this?"

"Keep your voices down," the lawyer said. He tapped the mouth of the flask in Lozano's hand. "Just relax. We'll talk about it in the car. Let me just sign a few papers and we'll be out of here in minutes. Simple as that."

"What the fuck is all this about, Lozano? Is that why Cirilo and them were here earlier?" Merengue said.

Naro added, "Yeah, I thought they were getting questioned about the warehouse. But they weren't even there now that I remember."

"Something's fucked up," Lozano agreed. Another game was being played, he suspected, at his expense. He took a swig from the flask. The charanda burned going down his dry throat, making him choke unexpectedly. Naro patted him on the back but it didn't help, his throat had constricted and he couldn't breathe. And yet in the midst of his panic he didn't think about life or death but about a habit he had acquired from his father: visiting the grape fields at the various stages of development, a way of paying his respects. The fields blurred before his mind. He envisioned them coming into focus next season when the crew returned to the old grape trunks still fastened to the thick wooden stakes. It would or would not be the same crew. During the pruning season the trunks stood bald. It was a field of crosses filled with whispers to be repeated the following month by different mouths. Who says it is not as important as what is said. What is said is not as important as what is heard. What happened happened to some other crew in some other valley. And the news of some conspiracy will have come and gone like a brief and unexpected breeze.

"Are you all right? Are you all right?" someone asked, and Lozano, hunched down in his recovery, nodded to no one in particular.

WHAT FEARFUL HEARTS

Eloisa   6:15 p.m.

Chicken was moody. If it was dipped into the frying pan at home the skin thickened into a crispy dark brown that exploded between the teeth like wood crackling in the fire. But if it found its way into those sterile fast food kitchens the skin was removed and the meat emerged with nothing more than a thin layer of café con leche colored paper that broke apart at the touch. The taste was just as brittle, the breast offering no more juice than the leg. Don Nico and Pifas did not complain, except to protest the expense Eloisa must have incurred with this purchase of restaurant food. She waved away their concern, explaining that there was a two-for-one special and that at the moment Tenorio was hopefully choking on a bone just like the one she was sucking on now.

The comment did not faze the men. They ate automatically, slowly, shell-shocked. Eloisa scooped the mashed potatoes out of the small container with a white plastic spoon. The gravy sticking to the plastic made the spoon look soiled. In the center of the table sat three sweaty beers.

"The macaroni salad looks good," she said. Don Nico nodded.

"How about some cole slaw, brother?" she asked Pifas. Pifas shrugged his shoulders indifferently.

"Well, if cole slaw doesn't excite you maybe you'll throw a party if I offer you corn on the cob," she added, chuckling at her own sarcasm.

"What's the matter with you, Eloisa?" Pifas asked. "Did that husband of yours whack the brain right out of your head finally?"

"The only brain that's getting whacked around here is yours if you don't settle down and stuff that big mouth with the fried chicken I bought," Eloisa snapped back, taking a bite of her food and chewing loudly. Pifas dropped the drumstick on the plate, left the table, and stepped out the door. He suddenly took a step back and yelled through the screen before disappearing again: "And don't forget to take your box of grape when you leave. It's in the trunk."

"What's the matter with him?" Eloisa asked.

Don Nico spoke up slowly. "We had an adventure at work today, that's all," he said. "To tell you the truth I'm not very hungry, either."

"Well, that's gratitude for you," she said. She flung her piece of chicken on her plate. She rested her elbows on the table. Her neck hurt when she faced away from don Nico.

"Don't be offended, Eloisa," don Nico said. She saw from the corner of her eye how he had attempted to reach out with a comforting hand, only to change his mind after a mere twitch. Typical of a man, she thought.

"I get no respect from you men," she burst out. "I break my back at home and at work, and I take pity on you old bachelors because you can't get yourself a woman to clean your chingados dishes and this is how you thank me. I might as well stop expecting any kind treatment by the way you all carry on like I'm no different than la chingada chair you sit on. Next thing I know you'll start complaining about my charity, then you'll spit it back on my face."

"You don't understand, Eloisa—" don Nico began to explain, but gave up mid-sentence.

"Understand what?" Eloisa asked. She looked at don Nico and realized he was following a tear running down her cheek. She surprised herself crying.

"I'm exhausted, don Nico," she said, wiping the tears.

Don Nico did not cast his eyes down for a change, which pleased her. She was tired of men who could not meet sorrow face to face, of men like her husband who beat the light out of it because they were afraid. Yet even now she sensed her anger thawing.

"What is it about you men that makes me love the misery of your selfish ways?" Eloisa said. She watched don Nico's eyes widened, puzzled. "It's a line from a song, don Nico. My mother used to say it often." Eloisa picked at the skin on the piece of chicken. Her nails were short and scratched. She couldn't remember the last time she had used nail polish. She blushed at the fact that there was none in her home.

"I don't think I've ever heard that song before," don Nico finally said.

"She wrote it herself," said Eloisa, more comfortable now with the way she was tearing apart the piece of meat. "Our parents were performers, didn't Pifas ever tell you?"

"No, he never mentioned it. It doesn't sound like something he wouldn't tell me."

"Well, it's one of those brief stories. There's not much to tell." Eloisa sucked the juice off one of her fingers. She relaxed, watched the old man's face soften with curiosity.

"Our father was a guitar player in a trio. Trío Los Arcángeles. Their singer Angelina, our mother, came later. They met when Los Arcángeles were playing at her cousin's wedding. Our mother was not young by that time. Some might say she was a spinster. In any case it gave her permission to drink with the older women to the point of drunken giddiness. That's when she noticed the guitar player, a nervous bachelor with a marble-sized mole on his fore-head."

Eloisa envisioned the courtship in her mind the way she had romanticized it so often, passionate and theatrical—heavy with the melodrama reserved for the black and white Mexican cinema: the beautiful señorita reaches down to lace her boot with the grace of a river flowing, the gentleman slides his fingers across the guitar strings—every gesture a seductive suggestion.

"When Pifas and I were children, we attended many of their shows. Our father played, our mother sang. She wrote the songs, inspired by her love for that man. They loved each other with such intensity there was no room in their music for anyone else, not even their own children. They were an older couple; we grew up being constantly mistaken for their grandchildren. Such was the distance between us." Eloisa took a sip of her beer.

"You must have learned to love music through them," don Nico offered.

Eloisa's face stiffened. "Mexican music is too sad to love. I don't remember much of their songs except for the verse I just told you, and even then I sometimes think I made that up in my head."

Eloisa looked directly into don Nico's eyes. The old man stared back nervously. "There's a tragic part to this story. Don't you want to hear it, don Nico? Don't you want to hear about how Angelina died from a brain hemorrhage and her husband, rather than face life without her, joined her in the dark hereafter just a few days later? It was so don Roméo y doña Julieta. Maybe only the old are capable of such fire anymore; the young nowadays are stupid and passionless as snapping turtles. And why do the old even waste their time on the foolishness of love? Who do they love? Who loves them back?" Don Nico did not respond. This frustrated Eloisa.

"How can you just sit there, don Nico? Why is it that you men either hold everything in or don't hold anything back?"

Eloisa felt dizzy, her head spinning with emotion. The small room shrunk around her, pressing its stale green walls against her face—an event she endured in the cramped bed at home, in the dark, with her husband's heavy weight sinking low on the mattress. She doubted seriously that if she died first her husband would have the guts to follow. He was a coward. There were only three hard things about that man: his heart, his cock, and his fist. He could exercise his three simple pleasures with his one arm: hold the bottle, fondle her into sexual excitement, and then beat her into tears—in that order. And yet, she didn't leave him out of guilt, each night turning over in her mind that afternoon she shifted into neutral and nearly killed him, sealing both their fates. But she had killed him, hadn't she? The man she was sleeping with was a dead man. And she was the widow murderess suffering her lengthy penance. When he slapped her, she was slapping herself. When he kicked her, she was kicking herself. Oh how much this dead man hated her because she hated herself for the coward she was. If only there were a savior, a salvation, a flesh and blood mortal—a real man—who would step forward and forgive her, take her by the hand and love her, kiss her, be kind to her, and heal her wounds. Where in this godforsaken hell of a Valley could she come across a man like that?

Just as she was about to collapse into the despair of her own hands don Nico reached across the wobbly table and placed his two fingers on her forearm. His face looked strained, as if he had concentrated the last traces of his strength into the fingertips.

"What a dirty old man you are, don Nico," she said, suddenly hostile and out of breath. "Do you think you can do anything for me?"

"Maybe not," don Nico said, refusing to lift the weight of his fingers from her flesh. "But maybe I can. If I'm allowed to try."

Eloisa laughed and stood up. Don Nico's hand fell on the table. "What a dirty old man you are! Pifas! Pifas, are you hearing this?"

Don Nico blushed. Eloisa saw him shrivel down, hiding his hand on his lap. She laughed some more, disconcerted at her lack of control. She felt suffocated so she burst out the front door where Pifas sat in the folding chair on the elevated deck, looking confused. She stammered, babbling incoherently. She wanted to turn back and apologize to don Nico, but she also wanted to humiliate him again by telling Pifas that he had just expressed romantic interest in her, a married woman half his age. Her brain couldn't decide on either. She simply babbled, laughing and crying at the same time. And as she stumbled off the deck, she managed to turn around to catch a glimpse of the tender old man fading away behind the tiny window's glass. She knew then that no matter how short or how long of a life she had left she still had a few more stupid mistakes to make.

MISSED

Aníbal   6:20 p.m.

The orange Celica did not make it out of the warehouse. Everyone had left with such urgency that no one had noticed Aníbal having engine trouble. But neither had he sought help at the first signs of his predicament. He watched the ambulance rush out with Amanda and Jesse; the police cars sped out right after it with Lozano and company. After that every other vehicle fled out of the parking lot gates and vanished into the road and across the railroad tracks. The group of strikers divided itself among cars with room for one more passenger, the sentiments that had kept them apart from the pickers just moments before quickly forgotten in the midst of the crisis. The Celica, he decided, would be safe inside the warehouse lot, and with the clearing not too far away he headed out to the road on foot.

The sun would be setting soon but that wouldn't do much to abate the heat that had been growing all afternoon. The desert held on to the blaze through the crackling fields of dried brush, and walking next to them was like swimming through a fire—the air turning fluid as with the fumes of petroleum. Down the road a trailer park appeared to melt away from the ground. It looked more like an oasis slowly consumed into the air as he got closer. He had only seen one fire in all his life, at a small housing complex behind a project of Industria Pérez. The circumstances of that fire were suspicious and the landlord had even threatened Aníbal's father with a lawsuit. His father, an influential contractor and a man not easily intimidated had to admit the company stood to gain by this tragedy—now that the old building in the back was demolished the new hotel had a better view of the international border's wire and steel barrier. México's Great Wall—a perfect tourist draw for the new hotel, and a discreet bonus for his father's company.

"Would you look at *that*," Jorge said the night they visited the site with a bottle of wine and a blanket. They were sitting on the floor of the unfinished second level, kicking at the gravel with their heels every now and then. The stars glared back from the black sky.

Aníbal wrapped his arm around Jorge from behind and rested his chin on Jorge's shoulder. "It's so beautiful."

"That?" Jorge exclaimed, pointing down with his finger. "It's atrocious!"

Aníbal grinned. "I meant the night."

"If you look closely you can see the wetbacks crawling through the shadows like rats. I wish they'd learn not to wear white when they cross."

"Maybe they're thinking ahead for the long walk through the desert," Aníbal said. "They need to fight off the sun somehow."

"If these people could actually think ahead they wouldn't be sneaking into the United States to compensate for their lack of education and money, not to mention common sense."

Aníbal drew his head back. "You sound like a true Mexican aristocrat, Jorge. Should we also establish a second border in the middle of México to keep back the Mixtec-Zapotec peons and Central Americans?"

"Sometimes I wonder if we wouldn't be doing them a favor by doing so."

Jorge took a sip of his wine and turned his head to kiss Aníbal on the cheek. Aníbal leaned his head back to avoid the kiss; he breathed out the faint odor of alcohol.

"What's the matter?" Jorge asked.

"Of course you'd think you'd be doing them a favor, otherwise you wouldn't believe in what you just said."

Jorge laughed. "My poor socialist. You didn't actually believe all that shit we said at la prepa rallies did you? That was college politics. Please, baby, be real. We're different from them, like it or not. I mean, what kind of people are they, these migrant farm workers? They might as well be from another planet. What could they possibly have to offer us?"

Aníbal kicked a stone on the road and watched it crumble against the edge of the asphalt. He had to smile at the irony. Had he taken

Talina up there with him that night, the conversation wouldn't have been much different. He shamed himself with the knowledge that he had become the complete opposite of who Jorge and Talina would be searching for in a lover—a man without privileges, Scaleboy. Aníbal blushed at the illusion of his martyrdom, at the farce of his poverty, because there was a plump bank account in Brawley steadily accruing interest and it would pull him out of this life as quickly as he had plunged himself into it. But he was not yet ready to quit this game, which made him wonder all of a sudden where he had learned that to hurt others he had to hurt himself first.

"You suffer because you like it," his father had yelled out as Aníbal left his parents' house for the last time. "Always making yourself more miserable than you are meant to be. There's a name for your sickness!"

His father never got to name that sickness, though Aníbal suspected it might have been something like masochism or immolation. He couldn't imagine either word becoming airborne from his father's mouth.

As he approached the trailer park he took in the familiar smells of Mexican cooking: oregano, cumin, cilantro, onion, basil. The earth surrounding the trailers was damp, recently watered to keep the dust settled and away from the kitchens and the clean sheets on the lines. An old dog looked in his direction with disinterest, panting erratically with the side of its belly against the cool ground. Aníbal heard the faint receptions of radios and televisions. Somewhere in the clutter of metals he could make out a small satellite dish.

"Amigo!" a man yelled out from a makeshift porch. He waved Aníbal over.

Aníbal hesitated, unsure that it was he who was being hailed.

The man waved again. This time Aníbal waved back and moved in closer, feeling awkward and suddenly invasive as he entered the trailer park grounds.

"Are you coming from the warehouse, amigo?"

The man sat with his shirt opened and his large beer belly exposed.

"I was left behind," Aníbal began to explain, "my car—"

"There was so much commotion earlier," the man interrupted.

"We thought maybe there was an accident or something, right, mama?"

"That's right," a voice from behind a window screen responded. No face was visible. "I thought for sure one of those cargo trucks had overturned a shipment on top of you poor people. Would you like something to drink? A beer or a glass of water?"

"A glass of water, if it's not too much trouble, please," Aníbal responded.

"I was telling Lety it had to have been those Chavistas that marched through here earlier. They probably got themselves in trouble or something. Growers don't like them coming around getting people excited."

The woman came out of the trailer with a glass of water in her hand. She had short dark hair and was as large as the man. "Here you go," she said as she handed Aníbal the plastic tumbler filled with cold water.

"Thank you," Aníbal said.

"Did that sonofabitch Lozano call the cops on them?" the man asked, anxious for information.

Aníbal took a drink before answering. "No. It wasn't like that at all. There was a shooting."

"I told you I heard gun shots, Pepe, but you didn't believe me," the woman said, swatting at the man. The man hushed her.

"Well, what happened?" the man urged Aníbal.

Aníbal gave a brief summary of what had happened, but the man kept interrupting, pressing for more details. Aníbal provided them, frequently glancing over at the road as a hint to the man that he wanted to get going soon. The road seemed farther away now though he didn't remember having walked much to join the man at his trailer. Aníbal heard chickens. As he looked around to find them Carmelo's car went speeding by.

"Carmelo!" Aníbal dropped the tumbler and ran toward the road but the car was already closing in on the warehouse by the time he reached it.

"Someone you know?" the man asked as he joined Aníbal at the side of the road.

"Yes, but I'll just wait here for when he passes by again," Aníbal responded impatiently. He craned his neck for a better look. His temples had been pounding violently the last few minutes.

"Did he also see what happened?" the man asked.

This angered Aníbal. He realized now that the man's courtesy was motivated by his need to become informed and afterwards be able to brag about what he knew. Aníbal pictured him sitting on his porch, a beer sweating in his hand as he retold the events at the warehouse with all the authority of an eyewitness account. He had a good story to tell and that made him important, almost necessary to this small middle-of-nowhere community of trailer park residents.

"You people—" Aníbal's frustration escalated but he left his sentence unfinished as he watched the man look up at him with knitted eyebrows.

"Hey, amigo," the man said. "I'd offer you a ride but the truck isn't working. It's at Padilla's. Do you know Padilla? He'll do good by you if you take him your car."

Aníbal turned away from the man and headed back to the warehouse, expecting to meet up with Carmelo soon enough. Again he miscalculated distance—the walk toward the warehouse looked longer than the walk he had taken moving away from it. Behind him he heard the man yell out, "Take care, amigo! Let me know how it all turns out!"

After a few minutes of walking, his head throbbing with the heat of an intense ache, Aníbal spotted Carmelo's car turning out of the warehouse lot. Carmelo had spotted him, too, because the car honked and picked up speed. Aníbal forced a weak smile. He looked forward to Carmelo's eyes, his mouth, the rough hands, and knobby knuckles on the steering wheel. What would he say to Carmelo? Well, there was no need to say anything. The silence in their sharing that small space of the vehicle together would say it all. They would hear each other's breathing, smell each other's musk of sweat and sulfur, catch glimpses of each other through the corners of their eyes and through the rearview mirror.

The anticipation of this meeting made Aníbal nervous as the car began to slow down and move toward the curb. Perhaps he would not be able to contain himself and he would burst out with emotion, teary-eyed with relief and gratitude. Maybe he would even dare reach out and place his hand on Carmelo's shoulder, or on the exposed skin of his nape. Poor Carmelo, he was probably sick with worry.

But when Carmelo's car finally pulled up, Aníbal was dismayed to find out Carmelo was not alone, nor was he sitting behind the wheel—he was fast asleep in the back seat with his body pressed against another sleeping man.

"Hey," the driver said. Aníbal recognized Trujillo.

Salomón rode the front passenger seat. "We knew we'd find you here. Hop in and we'll see if we can jump-start your car."

"Carmelo," Trujillo said, reaching back to wake the sleeping Carmelo. "Carmelo we found him."

"Hey," Carmelo said drowsily. Aníbal watched with disappointment as Carmelo's return to consciousness was slow and uninspired. He rubbed his fists against his eyes and yawned once more before asking, "So what happened out here, man?"

"We heard people talk all kinds of crazy shit when they arrived at the clearing," Salomón added. "And we all knew that if anybody saw what really happened it would be you."

"Get in, get in," Trujillo said.

Salomón opened the door and pulled the seat forward for Aníbal. The man next to Carmelo pressed himself even closer to Carmelo to make more room. When the door closed Aníbal felt cramped, paralyzed, and unable to breathe. And as the car re-entered the gates of the warehouse parking lot he noticed that his little bright orange Celica was smooth and beautiful and lonely, and that it would work perfectly again in a matter of minutes, and that if Carmelo decided to ride with him back to the clearing he would either sleep all the way there or he would keep interrupting Aníbal, pressing for more details as Aníbal summarized the incident at the warehouse. He grew angry that the knowledge he possessed had become more important than him. And the sadder truth was that what he knew did not rightly belong to him, an impostor.

"There's your car," Trujillo declared.

The warehouse was so quiet, frozen in time. Perhaps, thought Aníbal, he had imagined the whole afternoon. There were no traces of activity or any evidence of the events he had been coaxed into retelling by the man at the trailer park. Perhaps he had made it all up. He was so good at making things up, at inventing identities, creating romances and projecting a sentimentality on the unsuspecting victim of his desire. Carmelo's eyes were closed. In the self-deceptive screen of Aníbal's mind, Carmelo could see right through his eyelids and was at this moment looking at him, memorizing the shape of him, this Scaleboy, this lover, this liar, this masochist, this fraud.

NEEDLE AND THREAD

Jesse   7:00 p.m.

A Chicano nurse wheeled Jesse toward Amanda's room. At the entrance Jesse signaled to him to stop, and the young man understood the patient wanted to finish the journey on his own. Ten minutes, the nurse warned using all fingers before he moved back politely and disappeared into the hall. There was no reason to push him around in a wheelchair through the hospital halls to begin with because it was his left arm in the sling, not his legs. But Jesse didn't argue. His mind was on Amanda, whom he had shot clean through at the right shoulder. The nurse said Amanda had lost more blood than he had, and despite her size she had weakened more than he, her condition delicate but stable. The police were confused about the sequence of events and about where to demand accountability. Knowing Lozano, Jesse guessed the blame would be placed on the striking farm workers and their unlawful entry into the warehouse parking lot.

Jesse moved through the door, pushing the wheel with his good hand, and began to crane his neck in search of Amanda. Like him she was not given a private unit but checked into a bullpen of a room, three beds on each side. An old white woman with cottony hair stared at him intently, her head twitching. Her eyes appeared dilated, dazed. Jesse pictured himself an apparition wandering awkwardly across the old woman's line of vision. Perhaps she, too, was puzzled about the need for a wheelchair. In his mind he explained to the old woman that this was simply a prop to incite pity in case Amanda was furious with him.

Amanda was lying in the bed nearest the window. Peaceful was not a word to describe her, no matter what the circumstance, but that was the glow emanating from her body. She looked tame. And it took a bullet to stop her, finally. In that instance, Jesse felt a surge of anger. It was Amanda who had loaded the gun behind his back. She wanted him to make a fool of himself, maybe get himself into trouble by shooting Naro. She could be rid of both of them at once and pursue other men or live on her own as she had been wanting to do for the last few years. Manless. Headacheless. Perhaps it was the new blood from the transfusion making the rest of him boil at the extremity of the relationship—a passion so hostile it was almost fatal. He looked up and surveyed the other occupied beds. Visiting hours were over and the orderly had already removed the dinner trays. Sated, the patients in the room rested soundly, some sleeping and others imitating the dead. Even the old woman near the entrance had lost interest in him and shut her eyes to the four-walled world of her final days. He might as well be alone in the room, with Amanda unconscious by his side, vulnerable as she would never allow herself to be. A disturbing possibility opened up like a dark red rose in the back of Jesse's brain. If he willed himself to end Amanda's life, he could rise from the chair, grab the spare pillow and push it against her face with his one healthy hand. Amanda would be too weak to fight him off. If she struggled at all he imagined hers would be more of a delayed reaction, an afterthought of a spasm or a soft cry, either one a gesture buried so deeply into the pillow that even he would scarcely notice it. Yes. If he wanted to he could halt her breathing in seconds. Acting quickly, he followed his plan up to the moment the pillow descended on her face. She was so serene, beautiful again, like the Amanda he used to love years ago in the beginning, before she sprouted claws.

During their first year together, they enjoyed staying at home on weekend nights, both of them long-since tired of the late ventures to El Gato Negro. Amanda had been encouraging Jesse to complete his high school GED through a correspondence course. They had developed a ceremony around his study hours after the opening of the monthly envelopes. She would busy herself with a quiet activity while he labored over the reading material. On one occasion as he stretched his body across the bed while leaning on both elbows, the booklet spread open in front of him, Amanda sat next to him mending the sleeve to one of his shirts. Jesse was concentrating on the page when his eye caught their shadows against the wall: it looked as if Amanda was mending his back. The needle went into his spine and she pulled until the thread stretched out completely, leaving a tight stitch behind. Amanda was always keeping him together.

Jesse looked at the faint shadow on the hospital wall. The pillow resembled a stone and he looked like the strong man with the power to keep it steadily balanced above the fragile body of Amanda for a long period of time. His mind split in two. In one scene, Amanda suddenly came to consciousness and was slightly startled to see him standing over her with a pillow. Her long hair came alive beneath her as she dug her head to the sides of the bed trying to wake herself up completely. Jesse let the pillow drop to the floor before the drowsy Amanda had time to make conclusions with a clearer mind. "Jesse," Amanda whispered. "Amanda," Jesse responded. And that would suffice for a verbal exchange because the space between the utterances of their names was pregnant with forgiveness and affection—with the unspoken understanding that they would stand by each other come arrest, come trial, come jail sentence. She was his woman and he was her man. They would mend each other's wounds, taking turns with the needle and sharing the thread. Together they had two good hands. One would hold the needle still while the other inserted the end of the thread through the eye. Each would be from this moment on, the other's perfect compensation.

But in the heavier side of his mind where the brain pulsated with pain an entirely different scene unfolded: Amanda didn't stir at all. She remained passive, receiving the fury of his weight over the pillow. When a cry shot into the air, he shocked himself with the discovery that it had been he who had birthed it. The shriek fluttered like a bird of prey let loose in the room—an eagle or a hawk, confused and out of place among the stillness of the bedsheets and curtains. The other patients woke with a start. The old woman with cottony hair let out a terrified screech of her own, a downy chick of a sound that alarmed the hospital staff no less than if she had jumped out of bed and into the halls, her crooked fingers tangled in the knots of her white hair. When the staff arrived they came upon a nightmare of a ward: patients gathering their limbs close to their chests, the sheets twisted at their feet as if they were hopelessly uprooting themselves from the beds. The woman with the cottony hair had been possessed by seizures. Foaming at the mouth, her eyes blank as porcelain basins, she had dug her fingernails into her thighs and the deep wrinkles were quickly filling up with blood. But more horrifying of all was the sight of a man in a sling, smothering a patient with a plump pillow. His arm trembled and his hand seemed to bounce like a jackhammer over the woman's face. He bared his teeth like a dog, hackles arched. The only sign of humanity was the constant flow of tears that sprung from his eyes, full of sorrow and remorse for the uncontrollable frenzy of his body.

Jesse's muscles relaxed and he let the pillow drop. He sat back down on the wheelchair, rolling back a few inches from the bed. Amanda hadn't moved the entire time his mind wandered through the two emotional journeys. His disappointment grew when he saw the nurse poke his head into the room to signal with his hand that it was time to go. His ten minutes were up. He spun the chair around and pressed on the metal wheel, but before he completed one rotation, a faint moan escaped from Amanda's lips. Jesse froze, but didn't dare look, afraid that stress was playing tricks on him. Then the second moan. He turned in time to watch Amanda's head tilt toward him.

"Jesse?" she whispered.

Jesse's eyes began to water. Before Jesse had time to respond the nurse reacted and rushed in to check on Amanda. He took her chin into his hand and bent down to take a closer look.

"It looks like Sleeping Beauty is waking up," the nurse said. "I think she'll be fine, but I better alert her doctor." The nurse left the room.

Jesse moved in closer, reaching out to her from the wheelchair because he was too nervous to lift himself up. "Amanda," he said, excitement in his voice. "Amanda I'm here, mami."

Amanda turned her head to face him, her eyes opened slightly, reddened around the lids. Jesse picked up her hand and pressed it against his mouth to kiss repeatedly.

"Did I have a boy or a girl?" Amanda uttered.

Jesse brought his eyes up, knitted his brows with concern. A slim string of spittle began to drop from the corner of Amanda's mouth. But before he could even decide about a response, whether he was going to play along with her dream-induced confusion by telling her they had had a son, or whether he was going to snap her out of her drowsy state by telling her she had been shot with her own gun, Amanda, exhausted after only a few words, fell right back to sleep. And suddenly Jesse felt like the fool pulled along by the gravitational force of his wife. Even without trying she jerked him around because theirs was pure inertia. She acted and he reacted. They were the Adam and Eve of the word and the worry, the action and the consequence. And goddammit, how he loved her for it, so there he sat by her side, waiting, just waiting for his wife to move or mutter or twitch or moan so that he'd know what to do next.

ADIÓS

Chela   7:25 p.m.

Each of the men held a child in his arms for comfort: Little Mickey slept on the floor with Tamayamá, Pablito sat on Ninja's lap, and Cirilo held Lucita close to his side on the couch, his hand toying with her smooth fingers. The heat had broken and the children were in their underwear, so the air conditioner was turned down, the persistent hum low. Chela stood in front of the stove, emptying packets of Top Ramen into a pot boiling with water. She set a few eggs aside to crack and add into the mix later. She had learned this trick from Moreno, who had seen the Chinos do this in a restaurant once. No one was particularly hungry. The children had been fed ham and mustard sandwiches by the babysitter. Still, there was nothing more sobering in a home than the smell of cooking. She stirred the pot vigorously with a wooden spoon. Once the noodles softened she released the spoon and let it spin inside the soup on its own.

"I could use some company to the hospital tomorrow," she said, flatly.

"I'll go," Cirilo said. "Unless you need someone to look after the children."

"We should all go," said Ninja. Tamayamá and Cirilo nodded in agreement.

"I'm sure Merengue will understand if we don't show up for work tomorrow," said Cirilo.

The sight of Cirilo with their firstborn pained Chela, but she tried not to become too sentimental. Her emotional defenses were weak at the moment, grieving for Moreno. She had been puzzled by the Datsun's unexpected arrival, remembering suddenly that the men had not been at the warehouse. And she was just about to tell them about all the commotion they had missed—the strikers, the shots, the police, the ambulance, the television cameras—when Cirilo stopped her breath with the news that Moreno was dead. Since she was the next of kin, she had to report to the hospital tomorrow and make arrangements. Arrangements, she thought with contempt. Everything had to be so neat and clean, all traces of unpleasant matter eliminated. It was like plucking out the rotten grapes to make the bunch look agreeable—make it look as if it picked itself off the vine and not betray the pair of overworked hands that planted it, watered it, pruned it, cut it, packed it. Here they came again, those chingados gringos, eager to hide the unsightly grape picker's body.

"I still think we should demand a criminal investigation," she said, taking a place on the couch. "Maybe get the Chavistas involved. They've got funds and those college-educated Chicano lawyers working for them."

"I've already told you, Chela," Cirilo said. "It was an accident. There's nothing they can do for us. Besides, they told us Lozano was going to take care of everything. We can trust him. He's raza."

"Lozano?" Chela spat back with disdain. "You go ask Jesse how much Lozano can be trusted."

"Why Jesse?" Cirilo asked.

"Never mind," Chela answered, too tired to explain.

"I think Chela's right," said Tamayamá. "We should tell somebody."

"And who are we going to tell, huh?" asked Cirilo. He put out one hand as if waiting for someone to place the answer on the center of his palm.

"He's right," said Ninja. "All of those people in Primer Impacto are in Florida."

"What's the use in raising hell?" Cirilo added. "Even if we manage to get some fancy lawyer to consider the case, he might change his mind after he finds out Moreno was a transvestite. I've seen this type of information used on television to humiliate the dead. Moreno deserves his peace, doesn't he?"

"I hadn't thought of that," Tamayamá said. "I guess maybe you're right."

The men all sighed the breath of resignation in unison.

Chela shook her head and let out a scornful laugh. "If you could only see what I see," she said. "Three beer guts talking themselves stupid."

Chela walked over to the stove and lowered the flame beneath the pot. She cracked the eggs and dropped them in, discarding the shells in the sink.

"You three losers couldn't roll down the hill without somebody kicking your nalgas all the way down," Chela added. "This is the reason the gringos get away with all this mierda they throw at us. We have to fight back, throw some chingada mierda their way. It's not so hard. You just pick up the stinky brown stuff and aim. Come on, Lucita, help me take your brothers to bed."

Lucita led Pablito by the hand. Chela picked up Little Mickey off the floor and carried him into their room. All three children slept in one bed. Because of the humid nights there was only a sheet and no cover. Only Lucita liked sleeping under the sheet, so Chela lifted it for her when she was ready to crawl into bed. And then she surprised herself when she leaned down to kiss them good night— a gesture she had always condemned as too gringo. Lucita's sleep was slightly shaken.

"That's from your tío Tiki-Tiki," she whispered to Lucita.

"Is he in heaven?" Lucita asked.

"If he is he's not liking it," Chela answered. "Your tío Tiki-Tiki always looked better in red."

When she returned to the living room, Tamayamá and Ninja were already heading out the door.

"Where are you going?" she asked. "I've got a whole pot of noodles on the stove."

"We need to get our rest, too," said Ninja.

"Actually we're going to El Gato Negro," said Tamayamá. "You want to come? Get someone to look after the kids."

"No, thank you. I can do without the cheap booze," said Chela. "It gives me a headache."

"I'll be there in a minute," Cirilo said to the men. They walked out and closed the door behind them.

"Are you going to be all right?" Cirilo asked her.

Chela could feel her heartbeat picking up speed.

"No," she said. "I've been very angry all week."

"I know," Cirilo said.

Chela could smell him, even from a few feet away. He hadn't showered and neither had she. The scent of sweat and sulfur was heavy in the air. Being this close to him had made her senses grow keener.

"I just want to run away, but that's not me," she said. "And Moreno knew this. That's why he came to talk to me this afternoon. He wanted me to tell him I wouldn't run away."

"You don't have to run away," Cirilo said.

"No, I won't," Chela said. "I'm going to stay here and fight!"

"Fight?" Cirilo said. "Who? The cops? Are you crazy?"

"I'm not keeping quiet, Cirilo. I'm going to kick chingadas nalgas," Chela said, her voice raised in a spurt of energy. She walked toward the phone.

"Chela, who are you calling?" Cirilo asked.

"Los Chavistas," Chela said. "They'll know what to do."

She moved across the room, determined to grab the telephone. Cirilo stepped in front of her and placed his hand on her shoulder.

"Let it go, Chela," Cirilo said. "At least wait until tomorrow. There's nothing anyone can do tonight." He said these last few words softly, almost in a whisper.

Chela didn't struggle against the weight of Cirilo's hand. She tilted her head slightly and breathed in the scent of his fingers spread open on her shoulder. She shut her eyes, feeling them well up with tears. She didn't know if it was she who had leaned toward him first, or whether Cirilo had sensed her need for his entire body and taken that small step to meet her. It didn't matter now. This wasn't a compromise or surrender. She dug into his shirt with her chipped nails and thrust her grief upon him with her mouth open, sobbing against his chest. And then the strangest memory came to her like a silent pause in the back of her crowded mind. She and Cirilo had been married no more than a month when they rented an old cockroach-infested trailer—their first home in the United States. By moonlight she could see the shadows of the roaches scurrying up and down the walls. Drowsy after an evening of strenuous lovemaking, Cirilo held her tightly from behind, his head against her neck. He breathed softly, and the tickling startled her, so she raised her hand to swat at the cockroach she thought was crawling on her shoulder. But she stopped in time, reprimanding herself for not recognizing the difference. She nearly turned her hand on her own face. This was the man who loved her. This was the man who would sleep with her for the rest of her life. This was the man who would father her children. With or without the sun or the rain, the flowers of her happiness would grow fertile within the arms of this man, her lover, her husband, her man. This was her man. She would never ever be alone again.

"Cirilo," she said, moving away from his shoulder, her tears spent.

"Yes, my love," Cirilo said. His eyes were dreamy with hope.

"It's time for you to go," she said. She pushed him away and he seemed to float back with the look of concern on his face. He moved farther and farther back, just as he had been doing over the years, sending himself into the selfish safety of his untouchable, unreachable space.

"Good-bye," she said. The phrase escaped her like a helium balloon.

CORO

Leonardo   8:05 p.m.

"¿Está prendido, comadrita?" the first voice said.

"Está prendido, está prendido. Alguien hable," doña Ramona replied.

"O cante," a third voice chimed in.

"Bueno, pero no me culpen si el chingado aparato se quebra cuando le eche ópera." The women laughed. Leonardo pressed the tape player's stop key.

Leonardo recognized his mother's laughter among the gathering of women, which was odd because he couldn't remember the last time he had heard his mother laugh. This was the only entry in which his mother had allowed others to speak into the recorder. He had listened to the recording enough times to figure out whose voice belonged to a Gertrudis, a Chela, and a Mariana, friends of his mother's he had never met. He placed a star next to the line in his logbook. TAPE 6/SIDE B/ ENTRY 7. Initially he had considered discarding the recording altogether but given the nature of his sociocultural studies this was actually a gem of a keeper: the subject interacting candidly in her social environment. He opened up his notebook and wrote down the exact wording; professors welcomed such precise and stilted phrasing in academic writing.

He flipped through the local news stations but any mention of the shootings involving the grape pickers was thin with detail, reduced to a brief paraphrase stripped of urgency and import. He would have to get his mother to conduct a few interviews at work tomorrow since his father, who had seen the whole thing, still refused to talk to him after last night's disagreement at dinner. When puckered, Leonardo's mouth still stung around the area his father's knuckles had struck. It was like having kissed a battering ram head-on. Leonardo's father had never been violent toward him nor had he believed him capable of such a loss of control. It was a good thing he was studying his parents because he realized how little he knew about them.

The television provided some background noise as he sifted through the material he had collected so far. For people who were hardly literate his parents had so much paperwork lying around, everything from church records to personal correspondence written in semi-legible scrawls. So much for oral history. Hence the tape recordings.

He snapped open the laptop and typed in some notes into a file once the screen was on. He smiled at the awe the computer had caused when he pulled it out at one of the family gatherings. One of his nephews had run up to his mother. "My uncle's watching television in that little thing!" he shrieked. Leonardo realized what a mistake that had been. In an attempt to impress his older brothers with his new resources Leonardo had managed to alienate them further. They already resented that he was the youngest and the better looking of the lot. Now he was also the most educated. Whenever he came around to visit his parents nowadays neither of his brothers bothered to show up to say hello.

Of course he didn't blame them much. His transition into higher education had been a painful one even for him. When he filled out his college applications and financial aid forms he had been disheartened by the many times he had to write down his father's occupation. Embarrassed to fill in the line with the words "farm worker" he searched for alternatives. "Farmer" was misleading although his father did in fact work on farms; "laborer" was just a heartbeat away from "serf" or "peon." Finally he found the perfect word: "agrarian." It was vague and ambiguous enough for the occasion.

In college he learned fast and adapted swiftly to the tenets of the culture. Books were knowledge. History was subjective. The past informed the future. Identity was political. Anything was susceptible to challenge, analysis, or deconstruction. He now searched for deeper meanings and more difficult truths in that vocation of his father's that had once caused him such anxiety. Farm worker. The title was a task, like butcher or fortuneteller—a noun a few letters away from a verb. Farm worker. Dull and nondescript, the concept sounded so simple to explain, and yet here he was concentrating his thesis on the bigger questions: Who are these farm workers? What keeps them going? And perhaps, more implicitly, how was he like them? They had no formal education, few opportunities, and no hopes except for some misguided faith in religion and in the California Lotto. Well, there was more than that, but that it was easy for him to be cynical only showed how precarious a position they inhabited on the sociopolitical stratification ladder. What made them tick? He could hear the flurry of activity outside his room. It was well past quitting time. Men laughed and drank beer in groups of three and four; cars cruised by with the stereos pumped up to obnoxious levels.

Leonardo wiped the sweat from his brow. The neighbors' chatter made him wish he could shut the window, but that would keep the air from circulating. The apartment had a swamp cooler in the living room but he kept the door closed because he was wearing only his boxer shorts. The small rotating fan at full speed and directed at his body made it just comfortable enough for him in the humid bedroom. He reached for the phone and dialed. He turned the television off before the first ring.

"Hello," a sleepy voice answered.

"Sandra. It's Leo. Did I wake you?"

"Nah, I just took my siesta. You know how it is. Where you calling from? I thought you were back home."

"I am," Leonardo said in a dejected tone. "I'm bored as fuck. There is absolutely nothing to do here and it's hot as hell."

"Well, if anything that's a good reminder of why you left. It gives you something to think about the next time you get homesick."

"Yeah," Leonardo agreed.

After a pause Sandra asked, "Is that the only reason you called? Because you were bored?"

"Don't take it like that, esa. I'm going through a crisis here."

"A family crisis?" Sandra asked.

"It's too complicated. I'll tell you when I drive back to LA. Let's just say that the gap between my family and me has widened.

I swear to God I don't know who these people are anymore. And I doubt that I'm all that familiar to them either."

"Hey, ese, it happens to all of us," Sandra said.

"It sucks, big time. Here I am thinking I'm going to change things around here and my father still behaves like it's pre-Columbian Mexico."

"Well, it's hard for them. And sometimes when they do try to adapt it still backfires."

"I don't get you," Leonardo said.

"Well," Sandra explained. "After my mother learned how to use the oven she wanted to bake everything, including the flan and the tamales."

"Get out!" Leonardo said.

"No lie," said Sandra.

"Shit," Leonardo said. A lengthy silence followed.

"Well," Leonardo said, "I can't wait to see you again. We gotta make the next Ozomatli concert."

"Yeah," answered Sandra. "Sure thing."

"Well, I'm just procrastinating here and running up my family's phone bill. I need to get back to work on that Chicano Studies paper."

"*Chale* with that, ese. That turned out to be a huge headache for me. My jefa was telling me all kinds of made-up shit to make our family sound less Indian than we really are."

"Get the fuck out?" Leonardo rolled over on the bed.

"Yeah, ese. She was all telling me we're descendants of those Spanish bluebloods from Albuquerque. I mean you've seen my mom. She's like part Navajo from my grandfather's side of the family."

"And your grandmother?" Leonardo asked.

"*Chale*, she's a peroxide blonde Chicana from Fowler."

"We gotta teach our gente to be down with the brown, esa."

"No kidding, ese. It's all internal colonialism and shit. Bueno, pues I'll let you go. Call me when you get back into town from wherever the fuck you're coming from."

"The Caliente Valley. I'll talk to you later, esa. Take it easy."

"Laters," she said.

"Laters," he said.

Leonardo smirked as he hung up the phone. The Valley was tired. As soon as he collected his notes he was heading back to LA. How ridiculous he felt at the moment, thinking that immersing himself in the world he had left behind would fuel his inspiration. The heat and humidity were tightening around him just like on those nights of the past when all he wanted to do was bust his way out. His mother had found an escape by learning the wizardry of technology, rejecting the old hand labor ways at least in the kitchen. But his father was stubborn and old-fashioned—and easily threatened by change.

"What happened to the answering machine I brought you, Ma?" Leonardo had asked as soon as he arrived from Los Angeles. "I couldn't leave a message to tell you I was coming in this afternoon."

His mother looked back at him with an expression of defeat, and he knew right then that his father had yanked it out of existence.

"Why did he get rid of it?" Leonardo asked.

"Oh, well, you know your father. He got frustrated with the machine because it sometimes picked up the call before he could."

"Goddamn contraption," his father interjected. "Why should I have to race with it in my own house?"

"But there was plenty of time for you to answer the phone before the machine picked up," Leonardo tried to argue, but his mother warned him with hand signals, pointing at her ear with one hand and at his father with the other.

"Maybe it's time to get you a hearing aide," Leonardo suggested to his father.

"And get ear cancer?" his father said, waving away the suggestion. "No, sir!"

Leonardo rolled his eyes and shook his head. Why hadn't he stayed enrolled in that fiction writing class? He would have learned to invent his family history. Too late, he concluded as he shuffled the papers strewn across the bed. At least all of his mother's Cleotilde stories would serve well as footnoted and cross-referenced material in the folklore/oral culture section of the project. *Crossing Vines: A Field Study of the Culture of Work (Grape Pickers Are People Too!)*.

He still needed to scan the photographs and organize the index. Yet somehow, no matter how neatly he categorized there was something missing. Something was lacking in his methodology and he hoped to identify it before he submitted the final product to his Chicano Studies professor for review.

Leonardo's eye caught the mustard yellow spine of a book shoved into a cubbyhole in the closet. He pulled it out and remembered the inscription in red ink even before he opened the cover. *Dedicado a mijo Leo. Tu pa te quere.* The handwriting was long and compressed, a deliberate attempt by his father to confuse his spelling errors. Leonardo never understood what this gift was all about. Firstly, it was in English; secondly, it was a book of illustrated Bible stories. The Bojórquez family had never even been to church. Sure they believed in God and all, but they weren't into baptisms or first communions or any of that. In fact his father had been the one to put up that silly sign on the front door to keep the Jehovah's Witnesses from coming around every other day: *bienvenido buda* the sign read in all crooked lower-case letters.

Leonardo rubbed the sweat off his forehead. This was the problem with the whole project. There were no beginnings or endings, exactly—only exhausting returns to the middles. Leonardo opened a file on the computer folder marked TRANSCRIPTS to double check the translation to TAPE 6/SIDE B/ ENTRY 7.

GERTRUDIS: Is this thing on, comadrita?

RAMONA: It's on, it's on. Someone say something.

MARIANA: Or sing.

CHELA: Okay, but I'm not to blame if the damn machine breaks down when I bust out with some opera. (Laughter)

GERTRUDIS: Then recite a poem.

CHELA: I only know those mother-in-law ones.

RAMONA: Which ones are those?

CHELA: I wish my mother-in-law
would turn into a lizard
so I could stone her to death
and keep her daughters.
(NOTE: wit suffers gravely in translation.)

GERTRUDIS: Well, I just want to make an official statement

narrative

that I believe Mario Bezares did not assassinate Paco Stanley and that Gloria Trevi should be left alone in Brazil.

CHELA: Hey! Keep politics out of this.

MARIANA: Down with the Teamsters!

RAMONA: Viva César Chávez!

ALL: Strike! Strike!

RAMONA: All right, all right. Seriously now. This is for my son's college project. He wants to know about us.

CHELA: (affecting a Spanish accent) Rocío Dúrcal at your service.

MARIANA: (giggling) In that case I'm Thalía.

GERTRUDIS: All right, all right. Here I go. My name is Gertrudis Marrón. I am forty-five years old—

CHELA: In her dreams! She's eighty-five years old.

GERTRUDIS: That's not true, that's not true. Tell them, Ramona.

RAMONA: No, not true. Gertrudis is more like twenty-five.

GERTRUDIS: Now why did you have to say that?

MARIANA: My turn, my turn. (Pause) My name is Mariana Arceo de Robles.

CHELA: De Felipe, you mean.

RAMONA: Ignore her, Mariana.

MARIANA: (whispers) Well at least I have a husband.

CHELA: What? What did she say?

RAMONA: Nothing, nothing, Chela. Let her say something.

MARIANA: My name is simply Mariana. I am… (Lengthy pause)

CHELA: A strained silence?

GERTRUDIS: Holy heavens! You see how she is? She can't take anything seriously.

CHELA: Goddamn! I'm just having a little fun. We don't want those professors thinking we're all tragic like the damn Mexican soap operas.

GERTRUDIS: Well we're not all Cantinflas either.

RAMONA: Let's start all over. Mariana, stand over here. Chela, you stand over there and keep your voice down. Gertrudis, over here. Now everyone gets a turn. I'll be like—what's her name, that newswoman who speaks really fast?

MARIANA: María Elena Salinas.

RAMONA: All right, I'm María Elena Salinas. You, woman in the orange helmet.

GERTRUDIS: Why did you have to tell them that? Holy heavens.

CHELA: I'm the woman with the beautiful long legs.

GERTRUDIS: Frog legs, maybe.

CHELA: You started it this time, Gertrudis, the woman who looks like a bottle of Tres Flores brilliantine.

RAMONA: We're losing control again.

MARIANA: And I'm the woman who looks like Lupita D'Alessio.

CHELA: How come she gets to be Lupita D'Alessio and I can't be Rocío Dúrcal?

GERTRUDIS: How about you both get to be those transvestite celebrity impersonators.

RAMONA: That's Tiki-Tiki.

CHELA: Hey, watch it. That's a relative of mine.

MARIANA: Let's start all over then.

RAMONA: I think I'm running out of tape.

CHELA: Well flip the damn thing over. I've got plenty to say.

GERTRUDIS: Too much to say.

MARIANA: Flip it over, flip it over.

RAMONA: That side is full already.

GERTRUDIS: Then don't waste any more on this side. Stop the tape.

CHELA: Stop the damn tape! Stop it!

RAMONA: Give it back to me. I'm going to rewind it and we can record all over again.

CHELA: What for? We're going to end up saying the same things again.

MARIANA: That's true.

GERTRUDIS: Take it to him like that, comadre. Something's something, said the monkey.

RAMONA: What? We even stuck a monkey in here? Goddamn! (End of tape)

Something's something all right, Leonardo mused. He closed the file and shut down the computer. His restlessness was a clear sign he needed to leave all of this behind again. The room he had occupied as a child and as an adolescent appeared smaller and cramped because he had outgrown it. The bed still wore the same old sheets and the spider webs clinging to the ceiling's corners might well be the same ones he saw the day he moved out. And to disconcert him even more, Leonardo realized he had pushed his body against the coolness of the wall, his bare leg stretched up and pressed against the wall as well, unconsciously repeating an old habit.

Just then he heard his parents muttering in the living room. Usually they sat in front of the TV with the volume turned up so he could never really hear when or if they spoke. But today, what with all the excitement at work, his father had barged in demanding silence. His mother had complied without objection, stunned by his father's ramblings about a strike and a shooting. He would have continued offering a confusion of details, but then Leonardo stepped out of the room to arm himself with a pencil and notepad and that angered his father into cutting short his account. Leonardo turned off the bedroom lights and opened the door to take a peek, hoping to eavesdrop on the conversation. The swamp–cooler air rushed into his face. He could just make out the image of his father lying down on the couch with his head on his mother's lap. His mother stroked his father's balding hair lovingly, in a tender gesture he had not witnessed in a long time. The memory shamed him enough to make him withdraw from the door and shut it.

Leonardo closed his eyes and let his body drop down to a sitting position, the weight of his back against the door. There they were, the three of them. His older brothers had already moved out of the house and Leonardo was going into his second year of high school soon. Although this was only six years ago, Leonardo remembered his parents much younger, with less gray hair and certainly with more strength in their backs. His father had brought in an application to work as a groundskeeper at the high school, and Leonardo humored him, filling out each line in clear, legible script. His mother was already excited about the prospect: father and son carpooling to the same site. *Maybe you could even have lunch together?* she had mused. The thought had sent shivers down Leonardo's spine. A bead of sweat grew out of the base of his nape and then plunged down between his shoulder blades. His father on the other hand wasn't looking forward to leaving the fields. The fields were all he knew and he took pride in his work. Leonardo didn't want to be responsible for removing him from his element, so he perceived it as a favor to his father when he took that completed application and filed it away in the bottom shelf of his personal library, right between the two old dictionaries.

Upon opening his eyes, Leonardo rushed forward to seek out that application. Sure enough it was still archived in the same place after all these years. The pages were stiff and dusty. He recognized his awkward adolescent writing, the *t*s and the *l*s were short and stubby, nothing like the ostentatious spears he now drew when he wrote longhand. But before he let shame get the best of him, he concluded yet again that he had done right in hiding that application. Who was he to interfere in the life of his father? He was happy just as he was. A little more aged, a little more deaf, but content nonetheless. Satisfied with his conclusion, Leonardo tore the application into smaller pieces and discarded it into the wastebasket his mother was sure to empty by the following afternoon.

Hearing Talk

As soon as her husband closed the door to his room, her son opened the door to his and came swiftly at her with questions.

"So what happened, Ma? What did my father say?" he asked. Doña Ramona took a step back towards the recliner. "Who got shot? Anyone die? What are the police saying? Has the UFW been contacted? Are the farm workers organizing? Do you think I can go to the field tomorrow and conduct some interviews? What's the boss like? Here, speak into this."

"Enough, Leonardo!" doña Ramona yelled and accidentally slapped the beloved little black box out of Leonardo's hand. The tape recorder bounced off the carpet and struck the wall.

Leonardo, taken aback, stared at her with surprise as he knelt down to pick the recorder up. "What?" he said. "I'm just asking."

Doña Ramona placed her hand on Leonardo's rounded back. "I'm sorry, Leonardo, I'm sorry. But I don't want to talk now," she said. Once Leonardo stood up, she lowered herself slowly on the chair. One of the smaller picture frames on the wall behind Leonardo was missing a photograph. She hadn't noticed it missing until that moment. Leonardo must have removed it recently. The white square stared out like a blown-out eye.

"But Ma," Leonardo insisted. "Don't you understand the importance of this incident? At least give me a first impression?"

"Please, son, leave me alone tonight. I'm sorry." She turned away from him and it pained her.

After a brief moment of suspended animation, Leonardo's shoulders slumped in defeat. Lips pursed, he set the recorder on the television set before walking off. "In case you think of something later, Ma," he mumbled. "Good night."

The bedroom door closed. Doña Ramona shook her head in shame. In her left ear a constant high-pitch humming like the telephone line continued to annoy her. All afternoon it had been drilling into her brain. Usually it was water in the ear that caused it, but that was not the case today. Her mother once told her that if an unexplained drone flew into her right ear, someone far away was praising her, but if the drone came to the left ear, ill words were being said about her. Except for her jealous women neighbors, doña Ramona couldn't imagine who would be slandering her at the moment. She dismissed this childish idea as she walked into the kitchen to prepare her tea. The cupboard exhaled the aroma of cinnamon, cumin, and turmeric when she opened it to pull out the box decorated with chamomile flowers. She set the microwave humming for two minutes next and watched the cup make its circular journey until it reached the steaming point.

Dipping the teabag into the hot cup of water soothed her. Fidgeting soothed her, she realized, because deliberate twitching kept her body in motion even at rest. Manuel had been so upset about the incident at the warehouse that he had asked her for the first time in years not to take too long in coming to bed. She promised him she wouldn't. She imagined he wanted to wrap his arm around her belly and to push one of his knees between her legs, as if he were trying to weave himself into her. She imagined that Jesse, despite having shot his wife, liked to do the same with Amanda. Poor Jesse. Men were most certainly the weaker lot.

"I once heard talk about a woman," doña Ramona said in a low voice, the cup of hot tea in her hands. To subdue the mood she switched off the living room lights. The kitchen light would suffice. The row of kitchen appliances glared on the counter like a cartoonish set of polished buckteeth. She exchanged the cup of tea with the tape recorder and sat down on the reclining chair. The gesture had been automatic, almost a reflex for comfort. She pressed play, repeated her phrase and then rewound the tape.

She frowned. Tonight she would not work with the little black box. In his mad rush, Leonardo had forgotten to insert a tape. She left the recorder lying at her feet, speechless as a tiny black coffin. She wouldn't have been able to concentrate anyway since her mind was as noisy with thought as bubbling oil on the skillet. What had happened at the warehouse? Was Jesse dead? Was Amanda dead as well? Even Gertrudis had neglected to call, which only meant she didn't have any answers either. During the last few weeks, that snake of her daughter-in-law had been switching off the ringer so that Gertrudis never knew when someone called. Doña Ramona felt lucky that her daughters-in-law stayed away, avoiding don Manuel and his temper. Her older sons had been staying away recently as well, refusing to cross paths with Leonardo, her vain and arrogant baby boy.

In some other neighborhood the dogs were howling. Dogs no longer howled in the projects because of the ordinance passed last year banning all breeds of canines. The destructive cats, however, had been given free range to multiply. Manuel fumed with anger each time he dug up cat shit as he tilled the small plot of soil. When the cats used the garden, they disturbed the seeds and chewed on the young plants to purge.

I once heard talk about a woman . . . The phrase continued to haunt her as she focused on the missing photograph again. She was sure Leonardo had selected that one in particular because it was the only one she owned in sepia, cracked and faded with age. Its removal bothered her because it was the only picture she had left of her mother, Cleotilde. The white backing of the pictureless picture frame appeared to glow almost obscenely, as if her mother's dress had been removed, leaving her to hide behind the embarrassed undergarments. At best the pristine pillow of her mother's casket came to mind. In either case the missing body of her mother hinted at a sacrilegious act. She didn't fault Leonardo, but perhaps this small theft was taking his college project a little too far. She would have to ask for the photograph back. Better yet, she would steal it back. Leonardo had so many papers stacked about in his room that he would never notice one tiny photograph gone. This private plot amused doña Ramona enough to make her tense face relax.

Suddenly the lights went out and blackness descended like a tarp over what remained of the dim light. The cooler and the fans went dead. This brought out immediately both her husband and her son. Doña Ramona observed their shadows cross paths in the dark.

"Sonofabitch," don Manuel said. "Open the living room window, Leonardo, or else we're going to suffocate."

"How long do these blackouts last?" Leonardo said.

"An hour or so, don't you remember?" don Manuel said. "Ramona, where are you?"

"I'm sitting down on the big chair," doña Ramona answered. The living room window slid open, but no breeze came in, only the sounds of voices from the nearby apartments.

"I'm going to open the doors as well," Leonardo said. "Get some air circulating at least."

"Grab me a cold beer on your way back from the kitchen, will you?" don Manuel said.

Doña Ramona grinned as she heard the refrigerator door, followed by the sound of the beer tab opening on the can.

"Where are you, Pa?" Leonardo asked.

"Over here," don Manuel responded. "Thank you, son."

"Do you want anything, Ma?"

"No, thank you, Leonardo."

"Looks like the neighbors across the way have their candles ready," don Manuel said.

Doña Ramona saw the small flames lighting up hands and faces as the murmur of their talk and laughter took over.

"We're okay without candles, aren't we?" asked Leonardo. Once the sentence was finished the stillness flattened Leonardo's body into invisibility against the blackness of the wall. Except for the occasional sound of his gulping, don Manuel also became undetectable. Doña Ramona's eyes were not as quick to adjust to the dark, so before she could feel any more disoriented she clapped her hands twice.

"What is it?" don Manuel said.

"I've got a story," doña Ramona said.

"A story?" don Manuel said.

"Where's the tape recorder?" Leonardo asked.

Doña Ramona felt at her feet and pushed the little black box blindly toward Leonardo, who took it and fumbled with the keys until he pressed play.

"But Leonardo—" she started to say.

"It's all right, Ma," Leonardo said. "I've got it all under control."

Doña Ramona sighed, but was grateful her husband didn't raise any objections. So before don Manuel had any more time to react she jumped into her story.

"I once heard talk about a woman," doña Ramona began, "whose name was Cleotilde."

"Cleotilde?" don Manuel said softly. "My mother-in-law?"

Leonardo shushed his father.

"Cleotilde lived in a modest home in the outskirts of town. The shack was mostly wood insulated with cardboard. She could have lived better, but chose not to. Such was her pride in her own humility. When she went into town she always stopped at church to pay her respects to her saints and to intercede for the souls of others, a devotion she believed essential during these dark and dangerous times. At work in the packinghouse she only spoke to the women who were members of her church, and looked down on those whose behavior and speech she found offensive. When she heard them cursing or saw them acting out, she prayed for them, congratulating herself for being the righteous one, for calling upon God at the right moment.

"At home, Cleotilde's faith did not waver. Half of her small shack was an altar bursting with plaster saints, rosaries, prayer cards, crucifixes, and a choir of votive candles that flickered into song as dusk came down. She prayed for the women, for the men, for the children, for the souls south of the border, and for the souls to the north. There were souls to the west and souls to the east that also merited salvation so she prayed for them as well. There were countless souls in purgatory, the sinners of the past, that also needed to be prayed for, and weren't they lucky that Cleotilde was there, kneeling before her holy niche, sweating and losing sleep in her humble attempt to remember them all?

"But one evening, lost in her own fervor as she saved the souls of many, Cleotilde let her body drop against the altar like an offering, her limp cluster of muscles just one more blessed relic. A few of the candles tipped over and went out and she imagined the essence of her body blending into the smoky cloud rising toward the heavens. Cleotilde's skin burned with the passion of the dripping wax, and the heat intensified as she twisted her body around in the white cloth covering of the table until the altar collapsed, joining her on the floor.

"Cleotilde continued murmuring her litanies despite the fever that had seized her when suddenly she realized that she *was* ablaze. The spilled wax melted and bubbled as the cloth quickly succumbed to the flames. She put out the small fire on the hem of her dress, but the second fire was already raging out of control. She watched with horror as the altar burned, as the cards and crucifixes were consumed, and as the plaster snapped and the saints caved into themselves.

"Soon Cleotilde had to watch her entire home blacken and crumble, leaving no trace of her dedication to the world. A neighbor came up to her and placed a comforting hand on her shoulder, but she shook it off, angry and confused. *Why? Why?* she screamed out, expecting the stars to widen like mouths and shout back an answer. Even the moon, a harmless witness until then, seemed to mock her. *Why? Why?* she demanded again. She dropped to the ground on her knees and no sooner did she land than she received her reply as the embers of wood kept crackling before her. There was no God, not here and not in this undoing. The only hand responsible for Cleotilde's sad fate was her own. She had sent God and His army of saints to everyone else and to every place, including the farthest corners of the globe, all the while neglecting to keep a single prayer, a single word of safety, for herself."

Doña Ramona savored the silence of the moment with a long and deep sigh.

"Can you get me another beer, Leonardo?" don Manuel said just before he burped. Leonardo yawned as he fumbled with the little black box until it clicked. Doña Ramona could hear him shifting on the couch as he stretched in preparation for his trip to the refrigerator so she stopped him by raising her voice with an air of immediacy.

"I have another story if you want to hear it," she said, stomping her feet and she stood upright. "I can tell you a dozen stories and then a dozen more. My head is filled with them. What good am I if not to entertain you with these senseless little tales? How else will you know I once lived? And what will you remember of me when the last word has been spoken, Leonardo? Even now I'm simply a ghost of a voice to you, aren't I? Well, you know what? Forget about the next chingada story, you ingrate. Forget about me entirely. I have nothing more to say. Chingado."

As suddenly as the lights went out, they came back on again, illuminating part of the room. Doña Ramona felt herself blush as the awkward moment paralyzed her and the two men who sat across from her, their faces locked to hers in shock.

Seconds passed and no one moved. Doña Ramona, don Manuel, and Leonardo looked at each other through eyes that began to soften as they considered the unintentional architecture in the living room of the Bojórquez home: theirs was a triangle of bodies, each considering the other two, all three joined together through the rhythm of their breathing and the inescapable telepathy of the unspoken affection for one another. Don Manuel smiled first, and the gesture was contagious, drawing them closer as they depended not on stories or meals or even the embrace of light to achieve the intimacy that the simple fact of their familial bond allowed them to have. Of course, they realized that in the minutes that followed they would continue their journeys in separate directions, but the knowledge and memory of their common points of crossing would keep them connected and somehow comforted until the sweet or bitter end.